# THE LAND BEYOND

BILL GULICK

# the land Beyond

HOUGHTON MIFFLIN COMPANY BOSTON
The Riverside Press Cambridge
1958

For

NORMAN A. FOX

with whom I have ridden many trails
these past two years — *sans* horses

ONCE UPON A TIME I thought it would be fun to write what is known in the trade as a "historical novel." This was before I wrote one. This was also before I realized that the terms "historical" and "novel" are incompatible.

History leaves many loose ends; a novel should leave none. History poses many riddles and asks many questions which it is under no compulsion to answer. A good novel, if it poses a riddle or asks a question, should also supply answers.

The history of the Pacific Northwest is filled with riddles and questions. What was Captain Bonneville's real motive? Why did the Oregon country become American rather than British property? What part did the missionaries play in settling the Oregon question? What part did the mountain men play?

In *The Land Beyond* I have attempted to write a novel that gives a reasonably accurate picture of the forces at work — humanitarian, geographical, commercial and historical — in that particular place and time. I have had to oversimplify, of course, for which I expect little forgiveness from the historians. This alone I ask of the historical-minded: that you assume, as I did for purposes of dramatic unity, that events which actually covered a span of three years took place in one. Grant me that knoll to stand on and I'll defend myself as best I can.

Of the reader who opens this book for its story alone, I ask only that you turn the page and begin to read. No apology is needed for a good novel; no forgiveness deserved for a bad one.

BILL GULICK

*Walla . Walla*
*Washington*

# CONTENTS

PART ONE

# RENDEZVOUS

# 1

IT WAS a scarecrow band of men that paused on the high, sage-covered ridge as evening fell. A wolf-pack band of men, whose only outward resemblance to human beings was that they still walked on two legs and still retained will enough to direct their steps toward a known goal. Their buckskin shirts and leggings were in tatters; their hide moccasins in ribbons. What few horses remained to the party were little more than skin and bones, stumbling badly under their light packs, not one of them capable of supporting a rider. The condition of both animals and men mutely testified that the trail behind had been a long and desperate one.

Gentle as this last slope had been, it had sapped the strength of the horses. While animals and men rested on the windswept crest, Clint Davidson hunkered down on his lean shanks and studied the smokes of the distant rendezvous grounds with mixed feelings, weary to the bone but cheered by sight of the harsh journey's end. Two fellow trappers, Judd Smith and Zack Parkins, squatted beside him, their sun-punished faces and crow's-footed eyes haggard with fatigue but their wit still alive enough for the dry humor their kind loved so well.

"Why, Zack, 'pears we've come full circle!"

"Blamed if we ain't, Judd."

"Mountains yonder don't look wore off much."

"River still runs downhill, seems like."

"A few Injuns left alive, I do believe, if them hoss herds an' lodges I make out down thar ain't mirages er optical delusions."

"Now that does beat all! Thought we killed the last 'un an' et him fer supper last night."

"That was his shirt we et last night, Zack. We et *him* day 'fore yesterday."

It was good to hear their chatter, for there had been little such of late, but Clint took no part save for the faint, appreciative smile on his parched lips as his eyes moved slowly across the distant valley. Yonder lay the meeting place appointed twelve months before. The lush green grass carpeting the valley floor, the tracework of willow and cottonwood marking the river's course, the yellow skin tepees of the Indians and the dust-gray tents of the whites, the snowcapped mountains rising sharply in the blue distance on the far side of the valley — all looked just as they had when he and the forty other mountain men in this sorry band had set out for California a year ago. Now the year was spent — badly, to his way of thinking — the circle closed, the time of reckoning near at hand.

A rangy, well-set-up man with direct gray eyes, he took a stubby pipe out of his pocket, absently put it into his mouth and chewed broodingly on it. The stem had a taste to it: a taste of leather and sweat and salt and alkali grit, but nothing at all of the taste he craved. Taking the pipe out of his mouth, he scowled at it, then looked at his two companions.

"Which one of you is best fixed for tobacco?"

Judd Smith looked mournfully thoughtful. He was an extremely tall man with a long face, long legs and arms, and a long body which now had thinned down to the point where he appeared to be no more than a walking skeleton. His belly, he claimed, had had so little food in it these past few weeks that it had shriveled up to the size of a musket ball and climbed his gut to his throat, where it had choked him one day and he'd had to spit it out. Which pleased him fine, because now he was saved the nuisance of having to feed it two or three times a day.

"Tobacco? I've heerd that word afore, seems like, but I was a mighty small boy then. Seem to of forgot what it means. You know, Zack?"

"Can't say as I do. It's somethin' you eat, I think. Er wear. Er rub on sores."

Burn Rapp and Oswald Fram straggled up and stood considering the valley, Fram chuckling at something Rapp had just said. It had been a brag, likely — Burn Rapp was a great one for that kind of talk — an obscene boast of the favors he'd do the Indian gals at rendezvous soon as he'd got a bellyful of food and whisky. Though gaunted down some now, both men were big and powerful and filled with animal vitality, Rapp dark of hair and eye, Fram of a fairer make. Burn Rapp grinned down at Clint.

"Big doin's tonight, Clint. I'm figgerin' to jack up hell an' put chocks under it. You with me?"

"A couple of drinks, a square meal and a pipe of tobacco will do for me."

"I got livelier plans."

"You usually have. But count me out."

Rapp's laugh boomed and he came over and dropped a big paw on Clint's shoulder. "We got things to celebrate, you an' me. Why, if I hadn't pulled you out of the river the time you come nigh onto drownin' out Humbolt way, you'd have gone under fer sure. An' if you hadn't saved my skin when that Spaniard tried to knife me out in Californy, I'd of been rubbed out, no two ways about it. We're goin' to git roarin' drunk tonight, both of us. Last man on his feet's the best man. You want to lay a bet on which it'll be?"

Too weary to argue, Clint smiled and shook his head. Giving him a slap on the back that near toppled him over, Rapp moved off to laugh and brag with the other trappers. But he was careful, Clint noticed, to walk wide and soft around the party's leader, Joe Walker, who was squatting apart from the rest of the mountain men, brooding upon the valley. Walker had the look of a man with things on his mind. And no wonder. He'd have to answer some sharp questions shortly, Clint guessed. Joe Walker had bossed the party. But Captain Bonneville had paid for it. When the two men met at rendezvous, Bonneville would want to know what return he'd got for the supplies, trade goods, traps, and wages for forty men for a solid year which he had invested in the expedition. Maybe Joe Walker had answers that would satisfy Bonny. But right now he had the look of a man in no mood to be pestered, and Burn Rapp wisely gave him a wide berth.

Zack Parkins, a squat, thick-limbed man with a quiet habit of seeing a good deal more than he appeared to see, lazily watched Rapp swagger away, then dropped his eyes to his own feet and considered them ruefully. For the past week he had been practically barefoot, for the moccasins he had made out of the hide of his last horse, which had dropped dead back in the desert west of the Great Salt Lake, were now in shreds. Tearing off a piece of the crumbling horse-hide, he stroked it fondly.

"Poor Horace. You was the best hoss I ever owned. First I rode you, then I ate steaks off'n you, then I walked six hundred miles on you. If we'd been on the trail one more day I'd likely of boiled an' et what was left of yore hide." He sighed. "Can't ask a hoss to wear no better'n that." Tossing the piece away, he glanced at Clint. "Burn Rapp gives you trouble, whistle. You hear?"

"I don't look for any trouble from him."

"He'll bring it to you, jest the same — a bucketful in each hand."

"Because I won't get drunk with him?"

"He'll use most any excuse that's handy. Burn drinks, the mean in him comes out."

"Then I'll just have to cram it in again."

Zack shook his head. "Not jest brawlin' mean. Killin' mean."

Clint smiled. "I never learned how to whistle. But thanks, just the same." Squinting off into the distance, where the valley now lay completely in shadow, he muttered, "Wonder if the Nez Perces are in yet?"

Judd and Zack exchanged winks. Both trappers studied the indistinct cones of tepees for a moment, then Judd solemnly nodded. "Yes sir, they shore are. Matter of fact, I kin see Flower-That-Grows-In-High-Places sittin' in front of her tepee braidin' her hair. She's puttin' a red ribbon in it — "

"Pink, I'd say," Zack cut in.

"The meat's in the pot, she's got new clothes an' moccasins laid out fer ye, the bed's all made an' she's sent yore an' her cub off to visit his grandpa an' grandma fer a week er two. She's a-waitin', no doubt about it, jest a-quiverin' an' a-tremblin' in every pore."

Zack's grin broadened. "She shore is, Clint. I kin see her plain. Only it ain't you she's waitin fer. She's found herself a new man, which, if my eyes ain't gone back on me, is walkin' up to say howdy to her right now. Biggest Injun you ever did see — seven feet tall, coupla ax handles broad, an' the meanest lookin' jigger — "

"You can both go to the devil! I was just wondering — "

"We know what you was wonderin'!"

" — just wondering if the Nez Perces were in yet because Captain Bonneville will likely be with them. He planned to winter out Salmon River way."

"Hope he caught more beaver than we did."

"Likely he did all right. He's been in the mountains long enough by now to know his way around."

Judd rubbed his chin, gave Walker's lone-wolf figure a sidelong glance, then said in a low voice, "What do you figger Ol' Bonny's goin' to say when he finds out the only skins we brought back from Californy are our own worthless hides? What's he goin' to say?"

Clint shook his head. "Plenty, I imagine."

Joe Walker suddenly got to his feet, picked up his rifle and with no word to anybody swung down the slope at a long walk. The rest of the men stirred, gathering up the horses, moving down the hill in a straggling, weary line. As Clint, Judd and Zack followed, Zack muttered, "You know, it's kind of like comin' home, this pullin' into rendezvous. Kind of wish I had me a woman an' family waitin' fer me like Clint's got. Kind of take the edge off a man's lonesome."

"I had a woman once," Judd said. "A Shoshone, she was."

"Purty?"

"Purtiest little thing you ever saw. Kept me a real fine lodge, too, fer the two years I lived with her. But she had one bad fault."

"What was that?" Zack asked curiously.

"She was just hell fer fofarraw. Beads, hawk's-bells an' sech useless glitter, why, she jest couldn't get enough of the stuff. Kept me broke dressin' her. Still, I kind of miss her at times."

"What happened to her?"

"Oh, I mislaid her someplace. Let's see, was it the year we had rendezvous over Pierre's Hole way? Er was it on Bear River? No, it seems to me it was the year we . . ."

They moved on down the slope toward the wide valley where the river ran and the horse herds grazed and the campfires twinkled in the gathering darkness.

## 2

A MAN picked up pieces of news at every friendly campfire. Soon as he got in he dumped his personal gear on a vacant chunk of ground someplace and headed for the clerk's tent aiming to buy a jug of whisky to quench a smidgen of his year-long thirst. Before he'd walked half a dozen steps, he'd come to a fire where other mountain men were drinking, eating and jabbering, and they'd hop up and howl at him.

"Clint, ol' hoss, thought you'd gone under fer shore!"

"Heerd the Diggers scalped an' et you, boy!"

"Didn't them Spaniards do you in?"

They'd swarm on a man and be cussing him and laughing at him and digging elbows into him all at the same time, till the thought would hit somebody he might be thirsty. Down they'd pull him. He'd get a tin cup of whisky in his hand, then it'd be drink and talk, joke and talk, laugh and talk.

"Crows're here. Madder'n hornets, too, that Big Horn bunch is. Didja hear how Bridger foxed 'em when they tried to make off with his hosses? Wal, what Gabe done was . . ."

"Old Bill Williams? Naw, he ain't dead. Not even a leetle. How he come out'n that scrap up Yellowstone way shore beats me, 'cause there he was cornered up a box canyon like a coon in a tree, with a hundred Blackfoot honin' fer his hair, but the fust thing them Blackfoot knowed . . ."

"Nez Perces? No, they ain't here yet, but they're comin'. Forty, fifty lodges, I heerd tell. Due in a coupla days. Ol' Bonny, he done fair, they say. Jest fair. Got him a few pelts but not near as many as he figgered to git. Up agin a tough thing out thar, what with the holt them Britishers runnin' the Hudson's Bay Company got on the Injuns . . ."

"H'yar, yore cup's empty. Now tell me, Clint, boy, jest 'tween you an' me an' the tree yonder — air them Spanish gals as downright purty an' friendly an' willin' as the boys make 'em out to be . . . ?"

"A white woman. Hit's Gospel, I tell ye! Bill Sublette is bringin' a white woman out with him . . . "

"Big medicine, that's what the Injuns figger. Why, you won't believe this, but Bill Sublette was tellin' me jest last summer how these hyar four Injuns showed up one day in St. Looie big as life an' asks Genr'l Clark how's about lettin' 'em have this magic book he's got so's they can hold their own when it comes to fightin' the Blackfoot. You know what he finally figgered out they wanted? The Bible, that's what! They'd heerd about it some blame place an' got the notion it'd make 'em the grizzliest bars ever grizzled, could they git aholt of it. Flatheads, they was, er Nez Perces — Bill wa'n't sure which . . . "

Taken in disjointed snatches there was little sense to any of it, but after a man listened a while the picture began to clear. The tents Clint had seen from the ridge were those of Michael Silvestre Cerré, Bonneville's able young partner, who had lately come out from St. Louis with a sizable stock of trade goods and enough grain alcohol to keep the Indians and trappers properly drunk for the three weeks or so that rendezvous would last. Captain Bonneville and his detachment of trappers, accompanied by several hundred of the Salmon River Nez Perces, would be coming in from the west in a day or two. William Sublette, with more trade goods and whisky, would be arriving from the east shortly, accompanied, some said, by a white woman.

The valley was already full of Indians. The tepees of Crows, Shoshones, Bannocks, Flatheads and half a dozen other lesser tribes were scattered for miles up and down the river, turning the valley into a veritable Babylon of peoples and tongues. White trappers were drifting in from every direction of the compass, bringing their beaver plews and their thirsts and their pent-up appetites for drinking, gambling, talking, fighting, horse-racing, squaw-chasing or whatever other brand of fun might offer itself.

Of one thing there was no doubt: the men most envied were those who had been in Joe Walker's California party. They had been to a fabled land, crossing country few white men had ever seen, and their tales lost no luster in the telling and retelling as whisky flowed and long-parched tongues were lubricated. But their bragging yarns of Indian fights, bear- and bull-baiting and amorous pursuits of dark-eyed damsels who grew lovelier and ran slower with each new story neither amused nor entertained Michael Cerré, Clint noticed. A blond, slim man with a keen eye and a practical mind, he was no greenhorn in the fur trade despite his youth, and the one thing that might have impressed him was conspicious for its absence. Quietly he questioned Clint about it.

"You found no beaver in California?"

"Found some but didn't bring any back."

"What did you bring back?"

"Ourselves."

"An achievement, no doubt," Cerré said dryly. "But it will not satisfy Captain Bonneville."

Clint sat before his own fire now, smoking one last pipe before turning in. The hour was late and his eyelids were growing heavy. Judd and Zack, somewhat the worse for drink, lay stretched out on the bare ground, sleeping soundly. Cerré sat on the far side of the fire staring thoughtfully into the glowing embers. Clint knocked the dottle out of his pipe.

"Bedtime, I'd say."

"So it is."

Judd Smith, rolling fitfully in his sleep, moved one of his long legs and put a bare foot into the fire. Jerking it out with a grunt, he slept on. Voices sounded out in the darkness, laughing and boisterous, and as Clint turned his head half a dozen mountain men lurched into the circle of light. They were led by Burn Rapp, who was carrying a stone jug of whisky. He grinned as he spotted Clint.

"There you are! I been lookin' all over fer you!"

"How are you, Burn?"

"Look, I got a fine little game figgered out. See this here jug? It's plumb full of whisky. Now what you're goin' to do is git up on yore feet an' trade drinks with me. Last man to fall flat of his face is the best man. Git up, now."

"I'm comfortable sitting."

Rapp scowled. "You think you're too good to drink with me?"

"No. Just too sleepy."

"Well, sleepy or not, you're goin' to drink. Fact, I got half a notion to throw you down, sit on you an' pour a drink down yore throat."

"So long as it's just half a notion, it'll get you into no trouble."

"Supposin' it got to be a whole notion?"

Clint smiled and shook his head. "I'm just too tired to celebrate with you, Burn. Now take your playmates and move on."

Rapp started for him. "Not till I've set on you an' poured this whisky down yore — "

Clint took his pistol out of his belt, raised it and fired. The jug flew into a thousand pieces, leaving Rapp staring blankly at the remnant of handle between thumb and forefinger. He let out a roar of anguish.

"You busted it! Jest fer that, I'm goin' to — "

A diversion from an unexpected quarter cut him off. Sound asleep and drink-stupefied though they were, Judd Smith and Zack Parkins reacted to the sound of the shot by seizing their rifles and leaping to their feet, blind as owls at noonday.

"Whar are they?" Judd demanded.

This struck the watching trappers as real comical. Bear-tracks Weaver, who'd do most anything for a good laugh, threw back his head and cut loose with a bloodcurdling Blackfoot yell. Which came nigh onto being the last bit of funning he ever did.

Neither Judd nor Zack could see too well right then but there wasn't a thing wrong with their hearing. Both trappers whirled around and aimed their long rifles in the general direction from whence the yell had come. The onlookers scattered like quail. Burn Rapp, seeing a muzzle center on his chest, squawled and dove for the ground, lit on all fours and went scuttling off like a beetle. Clint jumped for Zack, Cerré leaped for Judd. Both managed to reach their men just in time to knock the gun barrels up a fraction of a second before the hammers fell.

Clint twisted the rifle out of Zack's hands, thrust a foot behind him, tripped him and dumped him to the ground. Cerré managed to disarm Judd, who went staggering blindly around the fire, swearing mighty oaths and making mightier passes with his hunting knife at a whole passel of imaginary foes until he stumbled over Zack and fell headlong. Zack jerked out his knife, whooped and jumped astride Judd's back.

"Got one, by God! Squeal, you rascal, squeal, fer all the good it'll do ye! Yore a dead Injun fer shore!"

Clint and Cerré grabbed hold of the knife arm and twisted the weapon out of Zack's hand. All that remained to be done then was to defang Judd, who thought he had *him* an Injun, pull the two men apart before they clawed and kicked each other to death, toss blankets over them and sit on them till they subsided. The drunken state they were in, this did not take long, and within a minute or two both Judd and Zack were sleeping like the innocents they were.

Wearily Clint stood up and looked around. All was quiet.

Burn Rapp was not in sight nor were his friends. Cerré, looking ruffled both in spirit and person, smoothed his clothes, retrieved his hat and bowed stiffly.

"As you were saying a moment ago, it is bedtime. I bid you good night."

"Good night."

Smiling, Clint watched Cerré stalk off into the darkness, then he unrolled his blankets and went to bed. Somewhere up the valley a shot sounded. From across the river came the high singsong of Indians chanting as they gambled away the night. Closer by the drunken yell of a white man, followed by jeering laughter, sent its puny challenge up to the wide, star-sprinkled sky. He closed his eyes.

Rendezvous, he reflected as he drifted off into sleep, was getting off to its usual quiet beginning.

# 3

IT WAS a perfect spot for a big encampment. Ten miles wide and thirty long, the valley was centered by a swift, snow-fed river whose waters teemed with trout. Willow and cotton-wood fringed the river's course on either bank; clumps of pine dotted the lower foothills, the final petering out of the great evergreen forests which covered the mountain slopes to the northwest, north and northeast. Now in late June the valley grass was at its best, the weather perfect, the air a wine to cure all ills. In the nearby mountains were deer, elk, bear and sheep. Roaming the face of the high plains to the southeast, south and southwest were immense herds of buffalo and antelope. Wood for the campfire, grass for the horses, game to fill hungry bellies, water to quench the thirst of animals and men — all were here. The spot was perfect.

And all trails led to it.

Two evenings after the California party made rendezvous, Captain Bonneville rode in from the west. Energetic and impatient as always, he had left the slow-moving Nez Perces a day's journey behind and ridden on alone, anxious to find out how the projects he had set into motion a year ago had fared. Clint got but a brief glimpse of him as he came splashing across the river ford in the quiet dusk, a compact, muscular man who rode as if born to the saddle, genial and pleasant enough when he had time to be but in too much of a hurry now for anything more than the casual greeting of a lifted hand and a cheery jest congratulating Clint on still being attached to his hair.

There was talk that night, Clint knew, much talk between Bonneville and Joe Walker. But what questions were asked and how they were answered, he could only guess at.

Midmorning, next day, another rider came galloping into camp from the east, bringing word that William Sublette and his party were less than a day's travel away. A dour, knobby mountain man named MacCampbell, the express rider had lived in the mountains so long he had developed the exasperating Injun trait of telling you everything except what you most wanted to know. The curiosity-filled trappers who at once surrounded him and peppered him with questions got only partial satisfaction.

"Is it true, Mac, this hyar rumor we been hearin' that ol' Bill's got a white woman with him?"

" 'Feerd it is."

"Young 'un?"

"Tol'able young."

"Purty?"

"Purtier'n you are, you ol' goat."

"Wal, what in tarnation is she comin' out hyar fer, you tell me that? What's she come fer?"

The express rider raked the trappers with fierce eyes. "What does any woman come slinkin' around menfolks fer? To make trouble, that's what! Why, I tole Bill fust thing when her and her fool brother wanted to jine up with us at Independence — "

"She's got a brother, you say? Wal, what's he come fer?"

"To milk the cows, I reckon. But what I tole Bill was — "

"You mean to say they're a bringin' cows out hyar? What're they goin' to do with 'em?"

"Milk 'em, you blame fool! What would you exect 'em to do, use 'em to pull their wagons?"

"They got wagons too?"

It appeared they did have. But why they had come was something no man could pry out of Mac, beyond his gloomy mutterings that they'd come just to make trouble. So there was nothing to do but wait and wonder.

In the middle of the afternoon the Nez Perces arrived, three hundred strong, making their camp on the west side of the river where there was yet plenty of grass for their horses and plenty of wood for their cooking fires. While the horses were unloaded, the baggage dumped, the tepee poles raised, the skin lodge coverings stretched and the camp generally was brought into a semblance of order, Clint lounged in the shade of a cottonwood tree on his own side of the river, watching the distant bustle of activity with idle interest.

He knew better than to cross the river now. At camp-making time, the squaws wanted no men around. This was their work and they'd accept neither advice nor help from any mere male, even if one should be so foolish as to offer it.

To the inexperienced eye, the scene was bedlam compounded. Children and dogs were everywhere. Household belongings were scattered about in what appeared to be hopeless confusion. Horses, relieved of their tepee poles, travois and packs, snorted and ran, rolled on the ground like dogs, massaging their itching backs on the grass with high-pitched squeals of delight.

Boys whose duty it was to herd the loose animals to the grazing grounds outside of camp made a game of it, driving the horses right through the middle of baggage, squaws and small children, scuffling with one another, tumbling on and off the horses with a reckless abandon that should have cost them bruises, broken limbs or worse, but somehow never did.

The women scolded the boys, shouted commands to the small children and argued shrilly with one another over whose lodge was to go where, but always at the end of each scolding and each argument there was good-humored laughter. The river was full of naked bodies, gleaming like dull copper in the sunlight, as the water-loving Nez Perces bathed and splashed and swam. Horses carrying warriors and chiefs painted and dressed in their finest forded the river at a reckless gait and went galloping through the camp of the whites, while cheerful voices called out greetings in English, French, Nez Perce or Chinook Jargon, and high-lifted guns banged salutes toward the sky.

But there was an order to it all and it was evidenced presently. One by one the bare skeletons of tepee poles formed their conelike frameworks; skins were stretched and skewered together; wind flaps were adjusted to catch or exclude the prevailing breezes; household goods were carried into the lodges; cooking fires were built outside; and the Nez Perce section of camp began to take on the appearance of the other Indian sections, with the tepees set in long curving lines and the horse herd grazing over its appointed expanse of valley floor and the small groups of working women readying food for their families over their frugal, faint-smoking fires.

Watching it all, Clint chewed on his pipestem and was at peace. To him it was a familiar and pleasant scene. Somewhere in the village yonder, he knew, there was a woman who would be expecting him to come to her presently. Flower-That-Grows-In-High-Places. A pleasant custom, the Nez Perce way of naming girl children after Nature's gentler things. Flowers. Running water. The moon, the stars, the spring winds, the harmless animals such as deer.

A good woman, his was, good as any he'd ever known, with a shyness to her that had made her a stranger to him for a while, but an instinct for understanding what was in a man's mind and heart that soon bridged all gaps. He knew that she was proud to be a white man's woman, but she had a dignity to her that kept her from becoming the kind of wife Judd Smith had complained about. No whining for fofarraw from her. Sure, she loved pretty things just as well as the next one did — a mirror, a string of blue beads, a piece of bright-colored cloth, things like that would make her eyes light up bright enough. But give her a present and likely as not she'd just put it away someplace, treasuring it because he'd given it to her, but not showing it off in his sight, and never using it to decorate her person until she had thought for a long while on how she'd work the gift into a dress or a pair of leggings or moccasins she was making. The best he recalled, she had never asked him to buy her a thing.

He wondered how the year had passed with her and the boy. He counted back. In May, it was, that Daniel had been born. May of the year Clint had come so close to losing his hair to the Gros Ventres up near the Three Forks. Which would make Daniel four years old now. And maybe there would be another cub to replace the girl child they had lost to the fever two years ago. Seemed to him that Flower-That-Grows-In-High-Places had had that look, just before he'd left her last year, though of course she hadn't said a thing. But new cub or not, a woman's first duty was to her man, and likely she had spent a good spell of the past winter tanning and cutting and sewing, making new clothes for him as she always did. New moccasins, shirts, leggings. Damned welcome they'd be, too, the shape the rags he was wearing were in.

The sun was well down toward the western horizon now, and he knew it was time. He rose, pocketed his pipe and strolled up the slope to the spot where he had slept these past few nights. Zack and Judd were there. Now that their first big spree was done, they were coasting for a spell, drinking steady but slow, and though there was a jug of whisky on the ground between them and each had a cup handy in case of frost or snakebite, they were just pleasantly mellow as they lay propped up on one elbow watching him pack his things.

"Goin' somewheres?" Judd asked lazily.

"Across the river."

"Now why would ol' Clint want to cross the river?" Zack muttered to no one in particular, "when he's got such fine company here?"

Judd yawned. "Same reason the chicken wanted to cross the road, I reckon."

Zack considered that thoughtfully, not quite sure it was worth pursuing any further. Finally he decided it was. "An' why did the chicken want t' cross the road?"

Judd dropped flat of his back and closed his eyes. "He was a rooster chicken."

"What's that got to do with it?"

"He was a rooster chicken roostin' with roosters, an' he got blame sick an' tired of it. But acrost the road, they was a hen chicken. So he crossed it."

Clint kept packing. Zack indicated the jug with one foot — a foot still encased in what was left of his favorite horse, for he'd been too busy drinking these past few days to do any shopping for footwear. "Want a drink?"

"No thanks."

"You ain't much of a drinkin' man, I've noticed. How come? You got religion or a bad stomach?"

Clint laughed. "Neither. But there are other things that interest me more than whisky at the moment."

Zack nodded. "Such as the hen chicken acrost the river. Well, every man to his own brand of pizen. Me, I think I'll have a drink."

Suddenly Judd sat up, his long face taking on a stricken look. "My God, Clint, I clean forgot! Bonny's been lookin' fer you. Said did I see you, send you to his tent on the double."

"You're a liar," Clint said placidly.

"No, I ain't, Clint! I'm tellin' you the pure, undiluted truth!"

"What does Bonny want to see me about?"

"Didn't say. But he's madder'n a bear with a boil under its tail, I'll tell you that. An' he wants to talk to you."

Clint picked up his blanket roll and rifle. "He wants to talk to me bad enough, he can cross the river. Look after my saddle, will you? I'll come back for it as soon as I can find something decent to put under it."

Grinning a farewell to them, Clint swung the blanket roll over his shoulder and strode swiftly through the camp and down to the river. As he started to enter the water he saw a group of a dozen or so Nez Perce bucks putting their horses into the stream on the far side, and prudently he stepped back against a tree and waited until they had crossed. They rode through the ford at a trot, the water splashing high, not seeing him until they were directly abreast and on dry land, where their horses immediately broke into a run. He raised his hand in greeting, for he knew them, and several of the Indians turned and waved to him. One of them said something to the others, checked his horse as if to turn back, then as his companions called sharply to him, changed his mind, turned and followed after them.

Holding rifle and bundle high, he waded into the river.

The water was waist-deep in midstream, swift-running and cold as ice, and the rounded rocks on its bottom were treacherously slick and cruel to his poorly shod feet. But he managed to stay right side up all the way across, climbed the low, hoof-churned bank on the far side, and with his ragged leggings flapping cold and wet against his calves walked into the village.

He was no stranger here, yet as he walked along the lane between two rows of tepees toward the center of camp, no one spoke to him. The women, working over their cooking fires, glanced up, stared at him briefly, then dropped their eyes to their spits and pots with no sign of recognition. The older men sat huddled in their blankets, gazing vacantly off into space, while the young men, many of whom he knew well, suddenly grew intent on studying some distant spot far off down valley or else became so absorbed in watching the fire that they seemed unaware of his passing.

It was queer. Queer, too, were the silences that fell as he approached each lodge, the faces that froze, the low murmurings that immediately began behind him after he had passed each family group. Uneasiness came to him, then as he neared one of the central tepees, which he recognized as that of Two Bears, his woman's father, and saw the chief and his clan lounging there in the evening quiet, his spirits lifted with the pleasure of homecoming and he smiled and raised a hand in greeting.

"It is good to see you again," he said in the Nez Perce tongue.

Two Bears appeared not to hear. A stocky, medium-statured Indian with the typical muscular build, deep-set eyes and broad face of the Nez Perce race, he sat straight and motionless, his eyes focused on something apparently miles away. There were two women at the fire, one old, one young; they ceased working, put their hands to their temples and began rocking back and forth, moaning to themselves. Spotted Wolf, Two Bears' oldest son, stared expressionlessly down at his moccasins. Clint squatted on his haunches, waiting. At last Two Bears' hands moved, making sign talk at the same time he spoke aloud.

"The-Flower-That-Blooms-In-High-Places has gone to the Spirit Land. It happened in the moon when the snows melt and the grass begins to grow. An evil spirit crept into her and gave her a fever. The spirit was too strong for the *tewats*. They could not drive it away. The White Chief with the Bald Head who lived with us while snow lay on our land was gone on a hunt. We sent for him but he came to late. She was dead."

The women were keening now, not crying as white women cry but mourning aloud with rising and falling moans that were as much expressions of sympathy for him as they were grievings for she who had gone. From the lodges around him Clint heard other women pick it up, heard it spread over the entire village. Grief for the lost one; sympathy for him who had suffered the loss.

It was not fitting that he should speak just yet, he knew, so he remained silent, staring at the ground. He had never given much thought to the relationship that had existed between himself and the woman. It had happened. That was all. In the white man's world which he had left years ago, there always had to be a why to things. Out here, things simply were. Rain fell, grass grew, spring followed winter. Man and woman felt a need for each other, lived together and children were born. It was as simple as that. And death was a simple thing, too. It came, the women mourned aloud and the men were silent.

And presently life went on.

He raised his head. "I would see my son."

Two Bears made a sign to the women, the older of whom shuffled into the tepee, returning after a few moments leading a child by the hand. Daniel had been sleeping, apparently, for he was rubbing his eyes with his fists, and as his grandmother pushed him toward Clint he seemed dazed and uncertain of his surroundings. He was a sturdy child now, Clint saw, and had grown remarkably during the past year, his roly-poly look now beginning to be replaced by a muscular solidity. At first glance he appeared to be all Indian, yet as Clint studied him more closely he felt a sudden sense of shock. The boy's eyes were his mother's, brown and soft and shy, and the bone structure of his face closely resembled that of his grandfather. But there was something more — something about his mouth and the length of his legs and the way he carried himself that was not Indian at all, and for the first time since the child had been born Clint knew the wonder of gazing at a human being who carried his own blood in his veins.

He felt strangely shaken. Then he smiled and held out his hand. "Come here, Daniel. Come and sit beside me."

The child did not move. Wide awake now, he was not frightened, for white men were no novelty to him, merely puzzled. His grandmother made a small urging sound and patted him encouragingly on the back, but still he would not budge. Two Bears said, "Go, child, he will not eat you. He is your father."

Still reluctant and puzzled, the boy obeyed, stopping just out of reach of Clint's hand. Clint motioned for him to sit. The boy squatted. For a time, then, Clint ignored him, turning his attention to Two Bears and Spotted Wolf, talking to them of the past year's happenings as the women went ahead with their preparations for the evening meal. But he could feel the child's eyes upon him, watching his every expression with a curious intentness. Presently he looked down and caught Daniel staring at him. The child blinked but did not look away. Clint gave him a smile. The round, bright-eyed face remained expressionless for several long seconds. Then the mouth muscles crinkled, white teeth showed, and Daniel smiled in return.

# 4

A FEW HOURS after dark Clint learned that Judd had not been funning him about Captain Bonneville's wanting to talk to him, for a messenger from the captain came to the village and sought him out. Borrowing a horse from Spotted Wolf, Clint recrossed the river to the white section of camp, dropping his blanket roll off at the spot he had been sharing with Judd and Zack with no word of explanation.

Captain Bonneville, sitting on a camp stool in his tent writing letters by candlelight, jumped up, greeted him with a hearty handshake, then gestured at the fire burning outside the tent. "Let's sit out here where we can be comfortable. It's been so long since I've sat on anything but the ground that damn camp stool has nearly broken my back."

They sat cross-legged before the fire, which Bonneville replenished while Clint waited for him to reveal what was on his mind. Six years of trapping in the mountains of the West had taught Clint to trust first judgments and to make those judgments quick. Three years ago he had met this dark, sharp-eyed, energetic little man who called himself Captain Bonneville, had judged him and liked him. Nothing he had seen or heard of him since had caused him to alter his original opinion. Three years ago Bonneville had been a greenhorn to the land and its way; he'd been a greenhorn to the fur trade, too, so naïve and trusting in his dealings with such cutthroat competitors as the Rocky Mountain Fur Company, the American Fur Company and the all-powerful Hudson's Bay Company that many a campfire joke had been made about him behind his back.

But the green had soon worn off and the men in charge of the competing companies were so busy now trying to keep track of his rapid movements and ambitious schemes that they had no time for joke-making. In the space of three years he had covered the trapping grounds from the Wind River Mountains to the Columbia, from the Bear River country to the Yellowstone, traveling winter and summer, in company and alone, and had not once lost a man or had serious Indian trouble. True, his luck had been bad with beaver, so far, but he knew all the tricks now, and appeared to be as optimistic as ever.

His dark, intent eyes flashed in the fire's glow as he looked searchingly at Clint. "What went wrong with the California party?"

Clint shook his head. "Joe Walker was head man. You'd best talk to him."

"Damn it, I have talked to him — talked till I was blue in the face! I've milked him dry. Now I want the story from you."

Clint filled his pipe, picked a live coal out of the fire and set it going. When you took wages from a man, he was entitled to something for his money, even if it was only a bare account of how you had spent your time. "Well, we went out there. We tried to circle Salt Lake and map it like you asked us to do but it just wasn't possible. We trapped a few beaver near the mouth of Bear River, then we went west following the shore of the lake. The going got worse and worse. No fresh water, no game, no grass. We came to where the shoreline turned south and we went south for a ways, hoping the country would get better. It didn't. So finally we did the only thing we could do — left the lake and struck out northwest for a range of mountains we saw there, hoping we'd find water. Hit a river, followed it till it disappeared in a sink, crossed more desert, then some mountains, then California. Fooled away the winter there, then came back here."

"Walker's told me all that. But go on."

"There isn't much more. We did some Indian fighting going out and coming back. Diggers, they were. We saw quite a bit of California — "

"How were you treated there?" Bonneville interrupted.

"Fine. Gave us the best of everything they had, those Spaniards did."

"Any trouble with the military authorities?"

"An officer in Monterey asked us some questions. Joe told him a cock-and-bull story about us getting lost in the desert and having to cross the mountains or starve. Seemed to satisfy him." Clint smiled. "To tell the truth, Captain, those Spaniards were scared to death of us. The whole time we were in Monterey I didn't see more than a dozen soldiers and they didn't have a decent rifle among them. Why, if we'd had a mind to, we could have taken over the whole town."

Bonneville stared into the fire for a moment, then murmured softly to himself, "Or the whole country. Go on."

"After a while we headed back. Got a bit hungry, lost most of our horses, did some more fighting. That's all."

"All that happened or merely all you're willing to tell me?"

"We were gone a year. It's hard to remember everything."

"Particularly when it might reflect on the man in charge — isn't that what you're trying to say?"

Clint shrugged. "When the mirror's busted, there's no sense counting the pieces."

Bonneville's eyes smoldered with dissatisfaction. He had heard the boastings of the trappers who had been in the party, Clint knew, and liked none of it. Which was small wonder, considering how much of his substance and hopes had been invested in the expedition.

"What's the truth of this disgraceful Digger affair?"

"We had some trouble. I told you that."

"What started it?"

"It's poor country west of Salt Lake, Captain. Hungry country. And those Diggers are hardly human."

"They attacked you?"

"Gave us pestering trouble mostly. Got on the men's nerves after a while and they lost their heads."

Captain Bonneville's jaw tightened. As a military man he might understand how such a thing could happen but he would never for an instant excuse it. "I've heard the men brag that at least thirty Diggers were killed in that first fight — if it may be dignified by calling it a fight. Afterwards, shooting Diggers became something of a sport, I gather, with the men competing to see which could run up the highest score. Is that true?"

"It wasn't a pretty thing, that I will agree."

Bonneville exploded. "Pretty? Good God, Clint, for men bound on as important a mission as yours it was the sorriest spectacle imaginable! How any man calling himself a leader could tolerate it is simply beyond my comprehension!"

Shaking his head, Clint relighted his pipe, which had gone out. He had no great love for Joe Walker but he knew what the man had been up against and there were a lot of things to be said in his favor. "A man sits here months later with his belly full and no worries about his hair, it's easy to judge the right and wrong of it. But it wasn't so easy then. Joe took us out there and back. Which was no small chore."

"I'm afraid it won't satisfy the men who are backing me," Bonneville said grimly. "They've never been hungry or worried about their scalps. Results are all that count with them. They'll hear about this. They'll judge. And my reputation will suffer accordingly." He was silent a moment, his eyes deeply disturbed as he sat listening to the sounds of the camp: the mutter of voices at adjoining fires, the gleeful howling of trappers encouraging some drunken pair of brawlers; the distant thrum of Indian drums and the thin wailings of savages singing while the dancers performed. Whatever bitter disappointment he had suffered he now seemed to thrust impatiently into the past while with the same impatience his mind considered the future.

"Last summer I sent Cerré east with a request to the War Department that my leave of absence from the army be extended two more years. He tells me that the request was favorably received. Which gives me one more year to accomplish what I came west to do. I've laid out my plans, Clint. You're to play an important part in them. Can I count on you?"

"What have you got in mind for me to do?"

"You're highly thought of by the Nez Perces. You know their country and ways. You've also had considerable contact with the Blackfeet, I understand." Bonneville paused and gave him a sharp, questioning look. "What would you say the chances would be for persuading the Nez Perces and Blackfeet to make peace with each other?"

"They've fought like cats and dogs for years."

"I know. Still, what would you say?"

"That the chances were damned slim. That any man who tried to get them to make peace stood a good show to lose his hair."

Bonneville smiled. "Granted. But will you try it?"

"What's to be gained by it?"

Captain Bonneville picked up a stick and began drawing a map on the ground. "Joe Walker failed me. I'm sending him back to St. Louis with Cerré and the furs I've gathered the past year. When rendezvous breaks up, I plan to outfit one trapping party for the Big Horn Country and a second for the headwaters of Bear River. How much luck they'll have in competition with the trapping parties of the other companies is questionable — but at least they'll put up a fight. I intend to take a third party and head for the lower Columbia."

"Where the Hudson's Bay Company will starve you out,"
Clint said, shaking his head, "just like they did before."

Bonneville's eyes snapped. If he had faults, a lack of confidence in himself was not one of them. "The Company
whipped me before, but they won't whip me this time. I
intend to establish a permanent post on the lower river,
Clint, a post that they'll never dislodge."

"Where does my chore fit into the picture?"

Bonneville placed his stick on the spot where the Snake
River swung northward to slash its way through the rugged
mountain country of the Nez Perces and drew a line extending into Canada. "You're going to drive a wedge for me
right here — a wedge that will split the British off from all
Oregon east of this line forever. You're going to swing the
Nez Perces, the Flatheads, the Kootenays, the Blackfeet —
every tribe east of this line — over to the American side of
the fence so solidly that no damned Englishman will dare
go into their country again."

One thing a man could always count on from Bonny,
Clint mused, was that he'd never think small. Give him
forty men, he'd take California from the Spaniards. Give
him twenty, he'd run the Britishers out of the Columbia River
country. Give him ten, and he'd take on some smaller job
— such as whipping the whole Blackfoot Nation into line.
Clint smiled wryly.

"You had me worried for a minute. I was afraid you had
some big chore laid out for me."

The sarcasm did not seem to disturb the captain. "Don't
you think it can be done?"

"I'll give it a try — that's all I can promise."

"Fine. Now here's what I have in mind — "

They talked for two hours, making their plans. When
rendezvous broke up, Clint was to return to the Nez Perce
country with the Salmon River band, gather the head men
of the entire Nez Perce nation and hold a council. The
Nez Perces would be heading east for the Bitter Root Valley

shortly thereafter to hunt buffalo, and if this summer's hunt followed the pattern of hunts of other years there would be plently of Blackfeet in the valley. Usually the two hostile tribes divided their time in equal parts, hunting for their winter's meat supply half the time, fighting each other the other half. The trick would be to get them to talk rather than fight.

Clint was to take ten white men with him. No undisciplined rabble, such as had made up the California party, but level-headed, dependable men who would obey orders and behave themselves. During his stay with the Salmon River Nez Perces this past winter, Bonneville had seen some indications that that branch of the tribe, at least, might be willing to strike a truce with the Blackfeet, for on several occasions horse-stealing bands of Blackfeet had tangled with the Nez Perces, having all the best of it on their first few raids, then being trapped and forced into a battle whose casualties had been heavy on both sides. Many a Nez Perce woman had been widowed; many had lost a son. It was the men who sat in council and went to war. But when the women wailed in the lodges, the men had no choice but to listen. There had been wailing aplenty, Bonneville said, and the Nez Perce men were weary of it. So weary that they might even give up fighting for a spell.

The fire was almost out. Bonneville replenished it, stood up and stretched to relieve his cramped muscles, and as the flames caught the wood Clint saw him cock his head to one side, smiling quizzically as he listened to the sounds of carousal around him.

"What wild men these trappers are! All year long they risk their lives for a few beaver pelts, come to rendezvous and splurge their whole year's profit in one glorious spree." He smiled down at Clint. "How is it that you're sober tonight?"

"The mood to drink didn't happen to come on me."

A sudden flash of sympathy softened Bonneville's eyes. "That was a stupid thing for me to say. You just today

found out about Flower-That-Blooms-In-High-Places, didn't
you? I'm sorry I couldn't help her, Clint. They sent for
me but I got there too late."

"I know."

There was nothing more to say on the subject, and
Bonneville, sensing that, cocked his ear again to the sounds
of camp and chuckled. "Listen to the men howl! Now
what do you suppose our Eastern gentlefolk think of such
carryings-on?"

"Who?"

"Haven't you heard? We have a lady in camp — a white
lady. She and her brother came in with Sublette's brigade
this afternoon."

"I heard they were coming. What in the hell are they
doing out here?"

Bonneville's eyes were half serious, half amused. "Their
motives tend upward, Clint, not downward. They're missionaries."

"Headed for where?"

Bonneville studied him for a moment in silence, his face
deadly serious now. "For the Nez Perce country. They plan
to establish a mission there. If you've no great objection,
I'll appreciate it if you'll escort them."

# 5

CLINT chewed on his pipe. Earlier in the evening he had
heard some jabber in the Nez Perce village about the big
medicine that was coming to them from the East but he

had paid it little mind, figuring that likely some of the curious Indians had ridden over for a look at such novelties as cows, wagons, plows, a real live white woman and the like, and were pulling the long bow. But white missionaries in the flesh here in this very valley were things deserving of a long, hard look. Mentally he took his look — and liked nothing of what he saw.

"Guess it was bound to happen, sooner or later. But I'd as soon it hadn't."

"I'm glad it happened."

"Why?"

"Because it's exactly what Oregon needs. And it will certainly work to our advantage."

"How?"

"Look at it this way. These are the first white missionaries to come west. They plan to settle among the Nez Perces. That's big medicine so far as the Indians are concerned — the biggest medicine imaginable."

"It's trouble, if you want my opinion."

"Nonsense! Every Indian tribe in the West will be watching the Nez Perces and will be jealous of them. Even the Blackfeet will be impressed." Bonneville squatted on his heels, his eyes snapping with enthusiasm. "Don't you see it, Clint? Knowing that the Nez Perces are under the care of white missionaries, the Blackfeet will think long and hard before they make trouble. Why, for all they know, the medicine of the missionaries might be powerful enough to wipe them off the face of the earth!"

"It's the Nez Perces I'm worried about," Clint said. "Not the Blackfeet."

"Don't you feel the missionaries can help them?"

"Help them?" Clint said curtly. "What good will preaching do the Nez Perces? They're honest, aren't they? They're friendly to white people, good to their kids and old folks. Is preaching going to make them any better? No, I say! All the missionaries will see is that some of them have lice and they let their kids run around without any clothes on."

"You seem to have strong opinions on the subject of missionaries."

"I know the preaching breed," Clint grunted.

"Well, they're here. We must make the best of it."

"What breed of varmints are they?"

"They both seem to be quite capable people. He's a doctor as well as a minister, I'm told. A young fellow, strong-looking and serious-minded. A very sincere sort of person, I would say."

"What's she like — skinny, ugly and near-sighted?"

Bonneville laughed. "Hardly. A brunette, brown eyes, very good-humored. Seems to be enjoying herself immensely. I was quite impressed with her." His eyes twinkled. "I took one look at her and wondered why I had ever left civilization. She'll affect you the same way, I'll wager. Why, I wouldn't be at all surprised but what you become her first convert."

"I was converted once," Clint said shortly. "But it wore off."

Bonneville looked at him curiously. "Why?"

Clint stared into the fire. "Because I went to church once too often."

"That's an odd reason."

"Well, it was a small town I lived in and the people there had some odd notions. One was that when a fellow came to church, he'd ought to come sober. Another was that he'd ought to come afoot. That particular morning I was neither."

"You rode a horse into church drunk?"

"Seems like I did just that."

Bonneville chuckled appreciatively. "What did they do to you?"

"I didn't hang around long enough for them to do anything. Once I got that horse into the street, I headed out of town on the run and never looked back." He shook his head. "I've never been particularly proud of that stunt.

But it happened — and I haven't been near a church or a preacher since." Knocking the dottle out of his pipe, he rose. "I can have ten men, you say?"

"Yes."

"Fine. I'll circulate around and start lining them up. You want it kept quiet, I suppose."

"That would be best for the time being, I think."

The sound of someone approaching interrupted any further discussion of plans. Burn Rapp and Oswald Fram lumbered into the circle of light cast by the fire, both men appearing to be just drunk enough to be amiable and sure of themselves. Fram nodded respectfully to Captain Bonneville, but Rapp grinned and said bluntly, "Cap'n, I've had the damndest run of luck."

"Indeed?"

"Won everything I had, them damn Shoshones did — cleaned me plumb down to the bone. I'd be obliged fer a couple of hundred advance on next year's wages."

"I thought I made it clear to you that you were discharged."

"Oh, hell, you got to have men to bring in yore beaver. Where'll you find better ones than me an' Oswald?"

"I'll look around," the captain said dryly.

Rapp let out a roar of confident laughter. "Shore, look all you please! But when you're done lookin' you'll take me an' Oswald, er I miss my guess." He rubbed a big hand over his chin, which was bristling with beard stubble. "A hundred'll do, Cap'n, but I want it quick."

Clint saw Bonneville's lips tighten. He was not a man it paid to push too far and his patience with Rapp's kind had long since been stretched to its limit. "Your wants are a matter of complete indifference to me, Rapp. You and your partner are discharged. Now get out of here."

Rapp's smile faded. A sullen, sulking look came into his eyes. He stared at Clint. "Ain't you goin' to put in a good word fer me?"

"The captain is able to speak for himself," Clint said.

"But, hell, you know me an' Oswald are good men. All you got to do is say one little word — "

Clint remained silent. Uneasily, Fram tugged at Rapp's arm. "C'mon, Burn, let's go talk to Bill Sublette. He'll stake us."

Angrily Rapp shook off the hand, still staring at Clint. "You been spreadin' lies about me, ain't you? You been tellin' Ol' Bonny all sorts of lies about what I done out in Californy. By God, I got half a notion to — "

Captain Bonneville had had enough. As Rapp lurched forward, the captain seized him by the shirt front with his left hand, put his right hand on the butt of his pistol and snapped, "I've had all your drunken mouthings I care to hear! Now move on — before I lose my temper completely and give you a knot on your head with a pistol barrel that will be worse than any hangover you ever had! Move on, I say!"

Muttering to himself, Rapp staggered away, with Fram tagging after him. Try as he would, Clint could not keep from grinning at Bonneville as the captain let out his breath in a sharp snort of exasperation. Bonneville saw the grin and snapped, "That amuses you?"

"Sorry, Captain, but seeing you grab hold of Burn that way sort of reminded me of a bobcat tackling a grizzly bear. He could have broken you in two if he'd had a mind to."

"I shouldn't have lost my temper, I know. But I've no use for his kind. And it isn't the first time I've tangled with him today. Why, do you know when I was over visiting with the missionaries this afternoon, he and his partner staggered up drunk as lords, swearing and joking and telling the whole world how they'd come for a look at the female missionary lady and what a privilege it was going to be for her to try to convert them." Bonneville snorted again. "I put an end to that in a hurry, believe me."

Clint's grin broadened at the thought of how shocked the missionary must have been at her first sight of trappers on a spree. "How did she take it?"

"Calmly enough. As a matter of fact, I think she was rather amused. She's a very well-balanced, sensible person, Miss Metcalf is. Not at all as you usually picture missionaries."

Clint's smile faded. It was coincidence, no more. Metcalf was a common name. And yet . . .

"Her name is Metcalf, you say?"

Bonneville looked at him curiously. "Yes. Why?"

"Where's she from?"

"A village in upper New York State. She told me its name but it eludes me for the moment."

"Do you know her first name?"

"Ellen."

Clint stared out into the darkness. "And her brother's name — would it by any chance be Stanley?"

"It is."

A long silence followed, broken only by the sounds of high carnival as savages, trappers, traders, clerks, packers — men drawn to this remote valley in the shadow of the continent's backbone by the prospect of financial gain — made brave noises in the night to convince themselves of their importance in the scheme of things, while the dark peaks mocked them. Captain Bonneville's voice interrupted the swift tumbling of Clint's thoughts.

"Good Heavens! You know them, then?"

"It was their father's church I rode my horse into that Sunday morning."

The captain shook his head in disbelief. "It's a small world!"

"Yes," Clint said shortly. "And it seems to be shrinking every day."

# 6

DURING the long overland journey west from Independence Stanley Metcalf had been called upon from time to time to doctor minor ailments, remove splinters, dress cuts and otherwise exercise his talents as a physician in a small way. But the afternoon following his arrival at rendezvous he was called upon to perform an operation that fully challenged his skills.

The patient was a trapper, a gaunt, leather-faced man who confronted Metcalf as he was strolling curiously through the camp, doffed his hat respectfully and said, "Beg yore pardon, sir, but I hear tell yore a doctor."

"I am."

"Wal, I got a leetle cuttin' job fer ye."

"Cutting job?"

"Got a Injun arrerhead in my back, seems like. Shore be obliged if you'd git the blame thing out."

"An arrowhead? When did this happen?"

The trapper scratched his head, looked uncertainly at the half dozen or so other mountain men who had drifted up, then muttered, "Lemme see. It was the doin's we had with the Sioux up Powder River way three years ago, wa'n't it, Luke? Er was it the time we tangled with the Rees over on the Missoury? Nope, seems t' me it was the Blackfoot planted the thing in me four years ago when we sashayed through the Bitter Root country." He grinned apologetically. "Sorry, Doc, I cain't recollect jest how long I have been totin' it around. But it's been a good spell. It's still thar, that I will guarantee."

"Turn around and let's have a look. Now, just where is it?"

"Under the shoulder blade, like."

"There?"

"No, the left 'un. Now you got 'er!"

"An arrowhead!" Metcalf exclaimed. "Why, from the feel of it it's three or four inches long!"

"Huntin' arrer, likely. Er maybe 'twas a spearhead. Fightin' was purty thick then an' time it was over somebody'd pulled the shaft out an' I didn't rightly notice what it was."

"An inch deeper and it would have killed you."

"Wal, it did make me a leetle sick. Couldn't hardly eat supper that night, I recall."

"Take off your shirt and let's see just what we've got here."

The crowd of onlookers was growing. Most were mountain men, pungent with the smell of tobacco, alcohol and the strong "medicine" they used to bait their traps. A few were Indians, who had their smells too. All were intensely curious, but Metcalf had long since learned that a doctor in these parts must accept the necessity of practicing his trade in public. When the trapper had removed his buckskin shirt, Metcalf's fingers probed carefully. The arrowhead would be barbed, no doubt, with the barbs well set in the cartilage and scar tissue.

"Does it give you much pain?"

"Bothers me some of cold rainy days. But it ain't the pain I mind, Doc. It's the gratin' noise the fool thing makes ever time I go to lift my arm." He lifted his arm. "Hear that? Kind of gits on a man's nerves after a while."

"I should think it would."

"Kin you hack 'er out?"

"It's apt to be painful."

"Wal, let's git at it. You want me standin', sittin' er layin' flat of my belly?"

"My instruments are in my tent. We'd better go there."

"Fine. Jest you lead the way."

With the trapper strolling amiably along beside him, they made their way through the camp toward the knoll where the Metcalf tents were pitched. The crowd followed, growing rapidly. Metcalf could hear the mountain men joking amongst themselves, calling out greetings to friends as they passed and inviting them to come along and see the fun. Though not at all pleased by the prospect of having such an audience, he made no protest until he had gotten his patient stretched out on his stomach in the shade beside the tent, rolled up his sleeves and laid his instruments out on a clean cloth. His lips compressed as he heard hoarse voices whispering in the crowd.

"He'll howl like a sick Injun! Betcha a new red blanket he does."

"I won't pay fer plain, ordinary howlin'. What I said was he wouldn't do no cussin'. Won't dare to with the preacher listenin'."

"Beartracks'd die if he couldn't cuss!"

"Wal, I still say he won't."

"I say he will!"

"New red blanket?"

"You got a bet."

Metcalf looked up with a frown. "This is no joking matter. I would prefer to have no spectators, but if you must watch I insist that you keep quiet."

"Shore, Parson."

"Yore goin' to need some help, Doc, Beartracks starts kickin' an' squirmin'. You want four of us t' hold him down fer ye?"

Beartracks raised himself up on one elbow and roared, "Won't be no squirmin' an' ain't nobody goin' to have to hold me down! Now shut up, you fool jackasses, an' let the doc git t' cuttin'!"

A respectful silence fell as Metcalf picked up a scalpel. Bowing his head for a moment, he closed his eyes. When he opened them he found Beartracks staring up at him with a puzzled expression on his face.

"Was you prayin'?"

"Yes."

"Fer me?"

"For the Lord to steady my hand. It's a habit of mine."

"Wal, I shore couldn't ask fer better odds than that. Hop to it, Doc."

Mountain men and Indians watched intently as the sharp blade poised an instant above the bare skin before making the first incision. In the expectant silence a sudden hoarse whisper somewhere in the crowd carried like a shout.

"Jest like butcherin' a buffalo, ain't it? You want a slice off the hump ribs, Kit?"

"Off a tough ol' bull like that? Ruther eat an Injun's saddle!"

Metcalf's hand shook. He was not by nature a high-strung man but there were limits to all things. Gazing sharply around at the circle of watching eyes, he was on the verge of giving them all the tongue-lashing they deserved when he heard a rustle of skirts behind him. He turned to see his sister, Ellen, smiling down at him. "Can I be of any help?"

"No," he said shortly.

"Really I'd be glad to help if you — "

"No! Go to your tent!"

She flushed and hurried away. Taking a deep breath, Metcalf went to work.

# 7

ELLEN METCALF had enjoyed the trip west far more than she dared show. When she and Stanley had joined Captain Sublette's fur brigade in Independence she saw at once that the packers, the mule tenders, the men who drove the party's wagons, the scouts who guarded the train and supplied wild meat for the messes, were a different breed of men from any she had ever met. They had a quiet, watchful look to them, and their eyes seemed always to be reaching out across the wide distances, searching, searching.

One evening after Stanley had left their fire to doctor an ailing packer, Captain Sublette paused and chatted with her for a few minutes. He was a self-contained, alert-eyed man with a ready smile, a decisive mind and a speech that was one moment as polished as that of any St. Louis gentleman and the next as vividly colorful as that of the buckskin-clad mountain men themselves. Presently her curiosity made her ask the question that had long been on her mind.

"I suppose, Captain, that you're acquainted with quite a few of the trappers in the West?"

"I've cut sign on most of 'em, from time to time."

"Did you ever meet a man named Clint Davidson?"

"Sure. Know him well."

A tightness came into her throat. She had had no direct word from him since he had left the village six years ago but on two occasions bits of news had filtered back to her: first, that he was in St. Louis; later, that he had become a trapper in the western mountains.

"When — when did you see him last?"

Sublette thoughtfully fingered his pipe. "Now let's see. Clint was at rendezvous last year. Out Green River way, it was. Hired on with Bonneville, best I recall, and headed for California with the Walker party."

"Oh. Then he won't be at the meeting place this year?"

"If he's kept his hair, he will." Seeing the alarm on her face, he smiled. "Likely Clint's still attached to his scalp. He's that kind. Is he a friend of yours?"

"I — we come from the same village."

"You don't say! Bet he'll be surprised to see you."

"Yes," she murmured. "I suppose he will."

There were other questions she wanted to ask Captain Sublette about Clint. What was he like now? Did he dress in buckskin as these hunters did and carry a long-barreled rifle and wear a wicked-looking knife in his belt? Did he have their distance-seeking look in his eyes? Had the wild, rebellious streak in him been curbed or had it grown worse? But these were not questions a lady could ask of a comparative stranger, so she lamely settled for a trite one which asked nothing, and, at the same time, everything.

"How is he?"

Sublette's glance was scrupulously polite, though a good deal more knowing that she might have wished it to be. "Fine, last time I saw him."

That had pleased her. But now, standing in front of her tent in the valley which marked the midpoint in their overland journey to the Nez Perce country, she felt a strange sense of unreality as she recalled the miles behind, mused on those ahead and listened to the unaccustomed sounds around her. He was here. She would see him. What then? Nothing. There could be nothing now; logic told her that. Yet she found herself trembling with a strange excitement.

The candle in Stanley's tent, which was pitched next to hers, was extinguished and her brother came out to stand beside her. He was two years older than she, square-set of face and as protective of her as their father had been. His voice was gently reproving.

"Ellen, you shouldn't be out in the night air. It's bad for one."

"Listen, Stanley."

He scowled. "Listen to what?"

"The drums. The chanting. The shouting and laughing and all the odd sounds of camp. Aren't they exciting?"

"Only if one ignores the brutalities that cause them," he said sternly.

"Brutalities?"

"Drunkenness, greed, lust, debauchery. The Indians aren't the only savages in camp, I've discovered. Nor the worst."

"Surely you're exaggerating. The trappers are only having a little fun. Men like Captain Sublette and Captain Bonneville wouldn't let their employees do anything really bad. Why, they're both gentlemen."

"Are they? Then why did Sublette insist on traveling on the Sabbath, in spite of my protests? Why do both he and Bonneville bring whisky into camp and let the Indians and the trappers drink themselves into a frenzy every night? Such conduct is hardly that of gentlemen. I intend to have as little as possible to do with them."

She had no answer for that, but recalling the operation he had performed that afternoon she could not keep from teasing him about it. "Would you call Beartracks Weaver a gentleman?"

"Heavens no!"

"Yet you took the arrowhead out of his back."

"I would have done that for any blackguard. It was my duty as a doctor and a Christian."

"I overheard some of the language he used while you were operating. You didn't scold him for it. I also heard you ask someone for whisky. Did you drink it or did he?"

"It was an extremly painful operation," Stanley said stubbornly. "Under the circumstances it would have been cruel to deny him some solace."

"Do you refer to the profanity or the whisky?"

"Ellen," he said sharply, "such frivolity does not become you. But the truth is, as a minister I deplored and condemned both his language and his need for whisky. As a doctor, I sympathized and understood. Whatever turned your thoughts into this vein?"

"The strangeness of it all, I suppose. Our being so far from home, the Indians, this camp — " Suddenly she turned to him and said bluntly, "Clint Davidson is here."

His voice was quiet. "So I've heard."

"You haven't seen him?"

"No, and I have no intention of seeking him out. No doubt he's as bad as the rest of his kind." He turned away. "You'd better go into your tent, there's a chill in the air."

"Good night, Stanley."

Before retiring, she took one last deep breath of the keen mountain air, which in this high valley grew glacier-cold as soon as the sun went down. The drums, the chanting, the cries of the white men seemed to have risen in intensity and the faint odor of wood smoke from hundreds of fires pleasantly seasoned the faintly stirring night breezes. In a land such as this, she mused, there would be no small virtues and no small vices, for here there was neither organized law to check the worst in man's nature nor the pressure of stabilized society to encourage the best.

Not quite sure what had fathered that vagrant thought, she went into her tent, blew out the candle and undressed for bed.

# 8

WORD that Clint Davidson was hiring men for a good cash wage soon got out.

"Seen Hugh Marlow's new Hawken? Shore a beauty. But how come he's dead busted one night an' moanin' like a sick owl 'cause Bill Sublette won't give him a dime's worth of credit less'n he signs on as a company man, then next night shows up with a new rifle, fine fixin's an' a grin as big as a bear's on his fool face, tell me that? Somethin' queer in the wind — mighty queer . . . "

"Figgered to partner up, me'n Luke Young did, an' try the Yellowstone next season, but all of a sudden Luke's gone cold on it — colder'n last winter's freezeup. What's he been jawin' with Clint about . . . ?"

"Makin' up a party fer the Nez Perce country, that's what it is. An' good pay, beaver er no. Ol' Bonny's got some cunnin' scheme to chop the Blackfoot off from the Britishers . . . "

"Burn Rapp? Shore he's sore. He'd give his eyeteeth to hire on but Clint jest won't have him. Bad blood thar . . . "

No, there was no concealing it, and Clint soon found himself beseiged by men wanting to go along. But he made his pick carefully, selecting only men he knew he could depend upon. Judd Smith, Zack Parkins, Beartracks Weaver, Hugh Marlow, Luke Young . . .

He enjoyed taking Daniel with him as he made the rounds of camp. The child's initial shyness had long since worn off and he accepted Clint now just as naturally as he did his Nez Perce grandparents and his numerous Indian aunts and uncles. But now and then Clint would look at the boy for a moment, then raise his eyes and stare off across camp toward the knoll where the Metcalf tents were pitched and feel uneasy in mind. There was no need to justify or explain anything. And yet . . .

In sheer human numbers rendezvous was big that year, bigger than Clint had ever known it to be, but though the total fur gather was sizable he did not need access to the clerks' meticulously kept account books to realize that the take of plews was spread exceedingly thin. Too many trappers in the mountains these days. Too keen a competition. And the Indians themselves were trapping a good deal more now than they used to; they were learning the true value of furs and becoming sharp bargainers.

The mountain men were upset. He heard their grumblings at every campfire.

"Whar's the beaver gone to? Why, I mind when I first come out, five year ago . . . "

"Missionaries! Goin' to be a nest of 'em in every valley 'fore long, I tell ye, an' when that happens . . . "

"Drove out hyar in a wagon, they did, jest as calm an' easy as if thar was a road all the way. Whole country'll be spiled 'fore you know it, wheel tracks an' people every way you look . . . "

"You heerd this talk Ol' Bonny's makin' about strikin' a peace with the Blackfoot? What're the mountains comin' to, anyhow?"

Captain Bonneville heard the talk, too, smiled at it and altered his plans not at all. One morning he suggested to Clint that they ride over to the Nez Perce section of camp and have a talk with the council of chiefs. As they rode across the valley, Bonneville's eyes strayed toward the rise of land where the Metcalf tents were pitched. "Paid your respects to Miss Metcalf yet?"

"No. Been too busy."

"You will, of course?"

"When I get around to it."

They forded the river. Here and there through the village, which numbered some fifty tepees, were scattered clumps of pine trees. Because the day was warm, it was in the shade of a group of these that the council was held.

During the winter he had spent with the Nez Perces, Captain Bonneville had apparently learned their ways, for he listened patiently now while each chief had his say. Two Bears, Small Crow, Eagle-With-One-Wing — each chief in turn took the full allotment of time and words due him according to his age and rank in the council. Often there was considerable hard-headed logic in the speeches, as in the one made by Eagle-With-One-Wing, a militant, suspicious old chief who had never trusted a Blackfoot and never would.

"War is a bloody business," he said. "But it keeps the eyes of the chiefs always open. If we see a trail, we know it must be an enemy. If the Blackfeet come to us, we know it is for war, and we are ready. Peace, on the other hand, sounds no alarm. The eyes of the chiefs are closed in sleep. The young men are sleek and lazy. The horses stray into the mountains. But the heart of a Blackfoot is a lie. His tongue is a trap. If he says peace, it is to deceive. When he sees us weak and off our guard, he will slay and steal." The chief made a quick, chopping gesture of rejection with his hands. "We will have no such peace. Let there be war!"

It would be no simple thing, Clint knew, to overcome such good common sense as that. Patience would be required; patience and a lot of time. So the talks went on.

Knowing that the council would consume the entire morning, Clint had stripped the saddle off his horse, a tall, well-broken sorrel, and tied it by its bridle reins in the shade of a nearby tree. Daniel, curious as any youngster, had come up and squatted beside him as the council began, but Two Bears had sharply ordered him away. From time to time during the morning Clint had seen him romping about among the tepees with another Indian boy his age, one of the youngsters straddling a stick which he pretended was a horse while the other tried to snare him with a short length of grass rope. Presently they tired of that game and disappeared. During a lull in the talks, Two Bears suddenly chuckled and pointed.

"Behold your son."

The two boys, either of whom could almost have walked under the sorrel's belly without touching it with the top of his head, were standing beside Clint's horse. Daniel apparently had decided he was going to ride it and was now puzzling over how to clamber aboard. He did not puzzle long. Going around behind the horse, he seized it by the tail, put his feet on the back of the beast's legs and started climbing up hand over hand. Clint started to get up and shoo the boy away.

"Fool kid, he'll get his head kicked off."

"Leave him alone," Two Bears said. "The horse will not kick."

"How do you know it won't?"

"The horse knows this is just a child. Its spirit tells it not to kick."

"Well, the cub's still apt to take a bad fall."

"What are a few falls to the young? That is how they learn."

All the chiefs were watching now, the serious business of the council completely forgotten now that this much more serious matter had come up. What were peace talks compared to the sport of watching a boy mount a horse alone for the first time? Had they not all done it? Would not the success or failure of the child's first effort give a sign as to what kind of man he would be?

Daniel was having his difficulties. Each time he managed to bring his head level with the horse's back, the animal would move, the boy's feet would slip, down he would slide.

Patiently he would try again with no better results. After his third failure he dropped to the ground and stood considering the animal thoughtfully, his dark eyes unblinking, his square little body motionless, then he walked to the front of the horse and conferred with his young friend. They argued for some moments, gesturing at the horse, the tree and each other. At last they reached an agreement.

Daniel climbed the tree until he reached a spot where he was higher than the horse's back. But the horse, grazing at the full length of its reins, was too far away. Daniel motioned his assistant to bring the horse closer. The boy tugged at the reins. The horse kept grazing, refusing to move. Daniel considered the distance, shifted around as if about to jump for it, then thought better of it. He motioned again to his little friend. The boy put his shoulder against the horse and tried to shove the animal into the desired position. The horse refused to budge. The boy gave up and again he and Daniel conferred.

Though not one of the chiefs had spoken or laughed aloud, all were enjoying the show hugely, their bodies shaking with silent mirth, their brown hands moving swiftly as they exchanged comments in sign language. Some were even making wagers. Still uneasy, Clint had no choice but to abide by the unspoken rules of the game, which demanded, so far as he could make out, that he let the youngster break his neck if he were clever enough to figure out some efficient way to do so.

The boy on the ground had fetched the discarded grass rope, coiled it and tossed it up to Daniel. Climbing a few feet higher, Daniel tied one end of it around a tree limb, seized the rope lower down, pushed off from the tree and began swinging back and forth like a pendulum. When the arc of his swing took him wide enough, he suddenly let go, twisted in mid-air like a cat and lit on the horse's back with hands and feet clawing for holds.

The sorrel gave a snort of surprise and shied sideways. Daniel hung on like a leech. The horse pitched halfheartedly, turned its head to look at the squirming burden on its back, then calmly went back to grazing. Daniel sat up laughing, caught Clint's eye and waved, as proud of himself as though he had just conquered a world.

The chiefs gave hearty grunts of approval. Two Bears looked at Clint, his broad, deeply lined face filled with pride. "You see? Already he masters the horse. He will be a great warrior, that boy. His blood is good."

Suddenly the quiet noonday hush of the village was broken. A murmur ran through it, like wind rising through still trees. Down the slope of the ridge to the southwest raced an Indian rider, reining his pony first this way then that, twisting his body, dipping his hands to touch the toes of his moccasins, then raising his arms over his head and moving them about in abrupt signaling motions.

The Nez Perce chiefs were on their feet, pausing only a moment to stare at the rider and read the message he was giving them, then turning to run toward their tepees. Squaws were calling to children; young men clutching rifles were swinging aboard horses staked near their lodges or running toward the plain outside the village where the main horse herd grazed; the entire camp was now alive with frantic activity. Clint, after one quick look, ran to the sorrel, jerked Daniel unceremoniously to the ground and threw blanket and saddle on the horse. Bonneville caught up with him and seized him by the shoulder.

"What is it? What's happened?"

"Blackfeet over the ridge."

"Blackfeet! Good Lord, what are they doing here?"

"Can't say. But if we're going to talk peace to 'em, we better do it quick — else we'll see some fighting."

# 9

IT WAS NOT a war party. Of that Clint was sure the moment he and Captain Bonneville topped the ridge and saw the straggling line of horses pulling laden travois, the squaws, the children, the dogs and all the other sure indications of a village on the move. A war party would not have come within miles of a camp as big as this one without knowing of its existence. But a village on the move, careless of its security because of its very size, seldom bothered with such precautions as scouts.

On the crest of the ridge Clint motioned for Bonneville to rein up, then they sat for a moment gazing down at the plain below. Armed Nez Perce bucks were swarming up the slope now but they too halted, waiting for their chiefs or the whites to signal the attack. The confusion of the Blackfeet showed that they knew they had stumbled into a hornet's nest. What had happened was clear to Clint. Traveling in loose, heedless order through heavily timbered mountain country, the Blackfeet had come down onto the flat, open plain below and had moved several miles across it in a southerly direction, completely unaware of the big camp along the river to the east of the ridge. There they had been discovered and their surprise was complete.

From their standpoint, they were in a poor position either to run or fight. Long before they could double back to the sheltering timber, hard-riding Nez Perce bucks on their fast, fresh horses could cut them off, forcing them to make their stand out on the open plain where they could be easily encircled and massacred at their enemies' leisure. And there must be no doubt in the minds of the Blackfeet now but that they had blundered into the yearly fur rendezvous of the Americans, where every man, white or red, was their sworn enemy.

Chief Two Bears reined in beside Clint and Bonneville. Clint turned in his saddle and spoke to him. "Sure they're Blackfeet?"

Two Bears nodded vigorously, giving the sign of the tribe by lowering his hands toward his feet, then making a second gesture, like that of a fat man caressing his stomach, to indicate the branch of the tribe to which this band belonged.

"Gros Ventres," Clint muttered to Bonneville. "Kind of thought they were."

"What are they doing this far south?"

"Paying a visit to their relatives the Arapahoes, likely. They do that now and then." He eyed the captain. "Do we talk or fight?"

"Talk by all means!"

"May be risky."

"I'm game," Bonneville said impatiently. "Do we ride down alone?"

Clint spoke to Two Bears in the Nez Perce tongue. The chief was silent for a time, all the lifelong hatred and mistrust for his tribe's bitterest enemy smoldering in his eyes, then he nodded. "Two Bears is no woman. He will go with you."

The chief gave his instructions to Eagle-With-One-Wing and Small Crow, who, like the young men they led, appeared to receive them with no great joy. The two white men and the Indian rode slowly down the slope, their rifles shifted to their left hands, their right hands raised with palms open in gestures of friendship. The Gros Ventres were hurriedly closing up their ranks, gathering their women, children and the horses carrying their household goods within an encircling guard of warriors. Clint guessed their numbers at around two hundred, less than a third of whom were fighting men. Still, that many cornered Blackfeet bucks must be respected, for they would fight like fiends to protect their families.

An Indian mounted on a beautifully marked brown and white horse rode out alone to meet them. He was unusually tall for his tribe, carried no arms and if there were the least bit of fear in him it did not show in the harsh, sharp lines of his face. Two Bears grunted something to Clint, which he passed on to Bonneville.

"It's Chief White Shield, he says."

"Do you know him?"

"Heard of him, that's all."

"Good or bad?"

"Bad, mostly. He's got the heart of a Blackfoot, Two Bears says. Which means he'd rather fight than eat. But we got one big thing in our favor."

"What's that?"

"No Indian likes to fight when he's got his family with him. Likely he'll talk sweet enough."

The horses stopped, the three facing the one. A hundred yards beyond White Shield his people milled restlessly, squaws shushing children, fighting men waiting in stony-eyed silence. Faintly Clint could hear the cries of the Nez Perce warriors on the ridge as white men and Indians from the camp on the far side of the river came up to join them. There must be a sizable bunch up there by now, all spoiling for a fight.

Captain Bonneville took off his hat and bared his gleaming, hairless pink head to the sun. "Tell him who I am."

Something glittered briefly in White Shield's eyes. Astonishment. Amusement. Awe. Clint wasn't sure what it was, but he had to hand it to Bonnevelle for using both the inside and outside of his head for all they were worth. Count on a Frenchman to think up a trick like that! He spoke to the Gros Ventre in sign language and presently White Shield's hands moved in reply.

"He's heard of you," Clint said. "He says you're the Bald White Chief who lived last winter with the Nez Perces."

"Has he heard that I have been talking peace to the Nez Perces and that some of their chiefs now want peace?"

"Sure, he says, he's heard it. But he thinks it's a lie."

"Do the Gros Ventres want peace?"

Clint made the inquiry, got his reply and smiled at Bonneville. "Right now, they do. Want it bad. White Shield says his heart is full of peace."

"Good! Tell him we want his band to camp with us and stay until rendezvous is over. Tell him if he does that I guarantee no harm will come to his people."

When he had relayed that, Clint waited, watching the Gros Ventre closely as the chief meditated. He could make a good guess at what was passing through the Indian's mind. White Shield would be no more apt to believe all that peace nonsense than a live-trapped wild animal would believe his captor meant him no harm. But he must make the best of a bad situation and accept what temporary protection he could get. The Gros Ventre's hands moved.

"He says he's glad the Bald Chief's heart is good," Clint said. "He will camp. But not along the river on our side of the ridge. He's afraid there's not enough grass left for his horses there. He'll camp yonder, just this side of the hills. There's water in the creek, good grass and plenty of wood." Pausing for a moment, Clint gazed at the camp site White Shield had chosen, then added, "Also, it'll be a hell of a lot better place to put up a fight, if he has to fight."

"Did he say that?"

"No. But that's what he's thinking."

"Very well. Let him camp where he likes. Tell him we want to shake hands now to show him we are his friends. Tonight we will bring him gifts, have a council and talk."

The handshaking was accomplished, White Shield

wheeled his horse around and rode back to his people, the two white men and the Nez Perce chief turned and rode back up the slope, which was swarming now with disappointed Indians and mountain men. Bonneville eyed Clint questioningly.

"Did we accomplish anything?"

"Well, nobody's shooting at anybody. That's something."

"Do you think they'll try to slip away as soon as it gets dark?"

Clint shook his head. "I doubt it. They can't travel fast loaded down like they are and they know the Crows or Nez Perces could catch them easy if they wanted to."

"We've got to make friends with them. We've got to convince them that we're sincere in our desire for peace. If we can do that with this one band of Gros Ventres, your job will be made that much easier when you talk to the Piegans and Bloods and the other Blackfeet bands."

"You don't tame a wolf with pretty speeches."

Bonneville smiled. "No. But all Indians are superstitious. Has it occurred to you that we have some very big medicine in camp in the persons of the Reverend Metcalf and his sister?"

"What can they do?"

"Why, it's perfectly obvious," Bonneville said, spreading his hands as if cupping the whole problem between them. "Metcalf is the first white missionary the Indians have ever seen. He's the first doctor. Every tribe in camp is marveling at the way he cut that arrowhead out of Beartracks Weaver's back and the miraculous way he's been curing the Indian sick."

"If he had any sense," Clint grunted, "he'd stick to saving souls and leave Indian-doctoring to the *tewats*."

"Do you suppose you could persuade him to ride over to the Gros Ventre camp with us tonight?"

"Why?"

"Just as a good-will gesture. He's the most talked-about

man in camp. If he showed off some of his religious and medical powers while you and I passed out a few gifts to the head men, it would get us off to a fine start."

Clint knew a moment's discomfort. "Why don't you put the proposition to him yourself?"

Bonneville smiled disarmingly. "As an old friend of the family, you can do the job much better than I. Besides, I think it's high time you paid your respects to Miss Metcalf. You've evaded her far too long."

## 10

AMONG the first of the mountain men to reach the ridge top had been Burn Rapp and Oswald Fram. As they sat their horses now watching the parley on the plain below, Rapp's eyelids were pressed almost together in a squint of concentration as he tried to make out the markings on the horse the Gros Ventre chief was riding. It was a paint, that much he was sure of. And there was something about the fluid, easy way it moved . . .

"By God!" he muttered, "that's it! You hear me, Oswald, that's it!"

"You got better eyes than I have. Can't even make out its color myself."

"Don't need to make out its color. See the way it moves? See how it holds its head? Hell, I'd recognize that paint twice as far away! It's mine, all right!"

"Was yours, you mean."

"Goin' to mine agin, soon as the scrap starts."

"Ain't so sure there's goin' to be any scrap. Way they're talkin', they look plumb sociable."

Rapp scowled. To his way of thinking, it would be the worst kind of crime to pass up this golden opportunity that had been dropped into their laps. Why, there wasn't a mountain man or Injun in camp that didn't have old, bitter grudges to settle with the Gros Ventres, just as did he and his partner. Harshly he spoke to Fram, his eyes still brooding on horse and rider.

"You mind well when it happened. Three years ago, up in the Gallatin country. Four packs of beaver we lost to them devils, six good horses an' every trap we owned. That's a score to be settled."

"What if Ol' Bonny won't let us?"

"Wait!" Rapp grunted. "Jest keep yore fool mouth shut an' wait!"

The parley broke up. As Two Bears, Captain Bonneville and Clint Davidson jogged up the hill, Rapp reined his horse over to meet them. Bonneville gave him a sharp look.

"What's troublin' you?"

"Who's the Gros Ventre jigger you been chinnin' with?"

"Chief White Shield."

"Figgered it must be the thievin' devil. Well, when does the fun begin?"

"Fun?"

"You ain't fool enough to pass up this chance, are you?"

"No, I'm not," Bonneville said curtly. "But the chance I see is not to butcher a band of Indians but to make peace."

"Did you notice that paint horse White Shield was ridin'? He stole it from me, 'long with a whole season's gather of plews."

"A hazard of the trade. I daresay it's not the first time such a thing has happened."

"I want that horse."

"Make him a reasonable offer and perhaps he'll sell it to you."

Other mountain men were crowding around, grumbling under their breath. Somebody muttered, "What're we waitin' fer? Let's wipe out the whole nest of 'em!"

"Only good Gros Ventre is a dead 'un!"

"Take 'em now, I say!"

Rapp grinned. "Hear that, Cap'n? All the boys are with me."

Bonneville's eyes snapped and for a moment he appeared about to make an angry reply, then Clint Davidson murmured something to him in a low voice, turned and spoke to Two Bears. The Nez Perce chief made a sign to his milling warriors, who, despite their howls of protest, wheeled their horses about and rode back down the slope toward their village. Crows, Bannocks, and Shoshones hesitated for a time, then as Clint made sign talk to them, they too reluctantly reined their horses around and followed the Nez Perces. Only the mountain men were left on the ridge top now, and as Clint's sharply questioning glance went from face to face one trapper after another rode over and took his place beside Clint and the Captain. Presently only a dozen men sat their horses on Burn Rapp's side of the invisible line which had silently been drawn. Captain Bonneville smiled.

"All, Rapp?"

"You've bought 'em off, damn you! The Injuns are afeared to lift a finger lest you cut off their trade goods an' the whites sidin' with you are all in yore pay — !"

"No, Rapp, they're just sensible men."

"What's sensible about cozyin' up to murderin', thievin' Gros Ventres?"

"If you can't see it, I won't waste my breath trying to explain," Captain Bonneville said impatiently. "All I'll say is this. White Shield has my sworn word that if he camps near us none of his people will be molested. I intend to keep that promise, do you hear? Start any trouble, and you'll get exactly what you deserve."

Rapp bristled. "Who's man enough to give it to me?"

Judd Smith shifted lazily in the saddle, his long face expressionless as he balanced his rifle on the horn. "Line forms behind me, boys. I figger t' be number one."

"Mark me down fer number two," Zack Parkins grunted.

Clint Davidson said nothing, but he kept looking at Rapp, his eyes quiet and cold. A silence held for a long moment, then Burn Rapp jerked his horse around and rode down the slope, Fram and a handful of trappers sullenly following.

## 11

AFTER he had bathed in the cold, clear water of the river, Clint shaved carefully and then donned the new buckskin clothes which one Daniel's aunts had made for him. Ever since he had learned that the Metcalfs were in camp, the temptation to splurge some of his wages on white man's apparel had been great. But this was buckskin country and he was a buckskin man. Let the Metcalfs see him as he was, not as a dressed-up imitation of what he used to be.

He had bought a white man's hat. Black felt, it was, with a bright red feather stuck into its band. Setting it on his head, he slung his rifle across his back, swung into the saddle and rode upon his errand.

The day was warm, the new clothes were stiff and he was

far from comfortable either in body or mind as his horse threaded its way through camp toward the knoll where the Metcalf tents were pitched. Stanley was not in sight but Ellen, sitting on a stool in the shade writing a letter, heard his horse's step. She raised her eyes and smiled, only a faint tightness at the corners of her mouth hinting at whatever she might be feeling. He folded his hands on the saddle horn, his face expressionless.

"Hello, Ellen."

"Hello, Clint. Surprised to see me here?"

"Thought I'd outgrowed being surprised but I admit this one did give me a turn."

"Won't you get down?"

Awkwardly he swung to the ground, feeling ill at ease under her appraising gaze. Six years had altered her appearance but slightly; the bright sparkle of youth he remembered was gone, replaced by a look of maturity and reserve.

"How's your father?"

"Father died a year ago."

Stanley came out of his tent. Quickly putting pen and paper aside, Ellen rose and called to her brother. "We have a visitor, Stanley."

"So I see." He came over. "How are you, Clint?"

Stiffly they shook hands. Clint said, "Hear you've turned missionary."

Stanley gave him a sharp look. "From the tone of your voice you don't approve."

"Oregon is no country for preachers."

"You qualified to judge that?"

"I've seen it."

"The Call came. We had no choice but to answer it."

Ellen said, "Our mission is to be among the Nez Perces. Do you know that part of the country?"

"Pretty well. They're my people."

"Your people?"

"I've spent several winters living with them. They've sort of adopted me into the tribe."

"We're anxious to see their country. Tell us what it's like."

Clint squatted on his heels, smoothed a place in the dust, took out his knife and began to draw in the rivers, mountains and valleys of the region the Nez Perces called home, becoming so engrossed in the task that he completely forgot both his initial self-consciousness and the impossibility of the Metcalf's understanding one tenth of what he was telling them.

Yet even as he talked, a part of his mind considered what their coming would mean to the Indians. Would the Metcalfs at once try to change the Indians' whole way of life? Would they attempt to impose upon the happy, easygoing Nez Perces the strict, narrow moral code, the intolerant dogma, the harsh one-God religion in which they themselves had been brought up? Or would they have the intelligence to move slowly, first trying to understand a people who, though they might outwardly appear to be savages lost in heathen ignorance, already had a well-developed spiritual life of their own? Most important of all, would they realize that it was not the white man's God that the Nez Perces wanted but his knowledge of such big medicine tricks as gunpowder and firearms, so that the tribe might master its enemies?

*Questions. Whys. Damn it*, Clint thought, *I'm beginning to think like a white man again.*

Stanley Metcalf, who had been listening with a growing impatience, waved his hand. "This is all very interesting, Clint, but you haven't yet told me what I most want to know. Where is their central village?"

"For which band?"

"For the whole tribe. Surely they must have some central location which they come to when the head chief calls a general meeting of the entire tribe."

"They've got no head chief," Clint said shaking his head. "Nor no central meeting place. And there are seventeen separate bands."

Metcalf looked irritated. Obviously it had been in his mind to establish the mission at the tribe's central village, enlist the support of the head chief and proceed from there in an orderly fashion, just as one would when establishing a new church back East. That neither central village nor head chief existed had apparently not occurred to him.

"Captain Bonneville tells me that you will be traveling with us. How soon will we leave?"

"When rendezvous is over. Couple more weeks, likely."

"You're employed by Captain Bonneville?"

"Yes."

"Trapping?"

"Sometimes. But this year the captain's thought up a special chore for me. He wants me to persuade the Nez Perces to smoke the peace pipe with the Blackfeet."

"That seems a worthy aim. But why is Captain Bonneville so interested?"

"Beaver."

A frown creased Metcalf's face. It was quite evident that he drew a sharp line between the spiritual and material world. Peace alone was a worthy aim, but it became less worthy when motivated by a desire for commercial gain. Clint gazed off at the long gray line of ridge bounding the west side of the valley. "Matter of fact, there's a band of Gros Ventres camped just over the hill yonder. Bonny and I plan to do some palavering with them tonight. Bonny says he'd be obliged if you'd come with us."

"Why?"

"The captain thinks you might have some influence on them."

"In what way?"

"Well, religious magic always impresses an Indian. So does doctoring. You're the first man the Indians have ever seen that practices either trade. Bonny thought you might like to ride over with us and put on a little show."

"I am a minister and a doctor," Metcalf said, his square face coloring with anger. "Shows, as you call them, are entirely out of my line."

"I'm sure Clint didn't mean it quite the way it sounded," Ellen broke in. "Did you, Clint?"

Clint shook his head. "Maybe I used the wrong word. Still, the captain would be obliged if you'd go over with us and do a bit of doctoring and preaching. He thinks it just might do some good."

"It would make them more amenable toward making peace with the Nez Perces and eventually trading with him, is that the idea?"

"Something like that, yes."

The missionary's eyes flashed. "What Captain Bonneville is asking, as I understand it, is that I exercise my calling purely for his financial gain. Right?"

"It might work out to be your gain too."

"How?"

"It might bring on a spell of peace between the Nez Perces and the Blackfeet. They have a bad habit of raiding each other now and then. If you and Ellen get killed, you're not going to convert anybody."

"The Blackfeet wouldn't dare attack a missionary!"

Irritation grew in Clint. He had tried to keep the conversation on purely practical grounds, but somehow Stanley kept turning it back to the religious. Bluntly he said, "Why wouldn't they? You're a white man and an American, aren't you? What is it to the Blackfeet that you're working for some being you call 'God'?"

"You're speaking sacrilege, man!"

"I'm speaking truth," Clint grunted. Avoiding Ellen's eyes, he got abruptly to his feet. "I'll tell Bonny you said no."

"Wait a minute!"

Clint paused. "Yes?"

"Tell Captain Bonneville I'll make a bargain with him. I'll go to the Gros Ventre camp with you and do what I can — on one condition."

"What's that?"

"That he, Sublette and Cerré destroy every drop of whisky in camp."

Clint stared at him for a moment in utter disbelief, then abruptly he threw his head back and began to laugh. Stanley's face turned red, then white, but try as he would Clint could not check his laughter. Cut men like Beartracks Weaver, Burn Rapp, Smith, Parkins and all the rest off from their drinking after a long year's work in the mountains? Why, they'd turn the camp inside out!

The missionary turned sharply on his heel. "Excuse me. I've promised to pay a call on a sick Indian child."

Clint's laughter subsided into a low chuckling as he watched Stanley Metcalf stalk into his tent. Ellen said indignantly, "You should be ashamed of yourself, Clint! He was perfectly sincere."

"I know he was. That's why it's so funny."

"I see nothing to laugh at."

Clint met her furious gaze and the laughter in him was stilled. She was right. There was nothing laughable in blindness, nothing funny about a lack of perception that might kill a man long before he even began the work he had dedicated himself to do. "I know this country. You and Stanley don't. And if you won't listen to me, you'll never learn." Stanley came out of his tent carrying his medical bag, and as he went hurrying off toward the Crow section of camp Clint shook his head. "Doctoring Indian kids is a dangerous business."

"Dangerous? Why?"

"If the patient dies, the parents are apt to kill the medicine man."

"Stanley is a trained, educated doctor."

"The Crows can't read his degree. If his doctoring doesn't work, they'll treat him just like they do their own medicine men."

"I can't believe that!"

"No. But it happens to be so."

Catching his horse, he picked up the trailing reins and started to mount. Impulsively she moved to him and put a hand on his arm. "Please don't go like this, Clint, not in anger. This is all so new and different to him. He'll learn. You must help him learn."

Clint grinned wryly. "Got off to a fine start, didn't we? Well, I'll try to do better."

"I haven't seen much of camp. Will you show it to me tomorrow?"

"Can you still ride a horse?"

"Of course I can! But I haven't had a chance so far. Will you get me a horse?"

"Sure. But these Nez Perce horses will take some gentling. Have you got a saddle?"

She smiled. "I bought a new one in St. Louis. It's in my tent."

"Let's have a look at it."

She showed him where it was, he carried it outside and stared at it, then shook his head. A look of concern came into her face. "Is there something wrong with it?"

"It's a handsome piece of leather. Only it's a sidesaddle. Horses out here never heard of such a contraption. It'll take some doing to get them used to it."

"Oh."

He gave her voluminous ankle-length skirts a sidelong glance. "Are those the clothes you're figuring to ride in?"

"Yes. Is there something wrong with them too?"

"Indian horses are spooky. You get on one wearing all that dry goods, he'll take off for the hills like he was shot out of a gun."

"What should I wear?"

"Buckskin would be a sight more suitable. The horses are used to that and it won't flap and billow in the wind like that stuff you're wearing. Your skirts ought to be a good deal shorter, too. Tell you what I'll do, I'll go over to the Nez Perce camp and ask some of the squaws to make you up some riding clothes."

Her face turned crimson. "If you think I'm going to dress like an Indian squaw just to please a silly old horse, you're badly mistaken! I'll walk before I'll shorten my skirts or wear buckskin!"

Clint had a sudden impulse to throw the sidesaddle on the back of a half-broken Nez Perce pony, let her mount in her long skirts and learn the facts of life for herself, but he caught hold on his temper and said, "Well, I'll see what I can do. Give me a couple of days."

Picking up the sidesaddle, he mounted the sorrel. Ellen looked up at him with a puzzled expression on her face. "Why are you taking my saddle?"

"Somebody's got to learn new ways," he said. "If you won't do it, I guess the Nez Perce horses will have to."

## 12

IT WAS after midnight when the council with the Gros Ventres broke up. To Clint's way of thinking it had gone well enough, but as they rode back toward camp Captain Bonneville seemed far from happy. Bonneville said, "Did we make any progress?"

"Kind of think we did."

"I hope White Shield appreciates his presents. They certainly set me back a pretty penny."

"He'll appreciate them. It isn't once in a blue moon he gets a chance to lay hands on even one new Hawken rifle, let alone half a dozen of them."

"Wouldn't blankets or knives have done just as well?"

"You want to wean the Gros Ventres off from the British, don't you?"

"Of course."

"An Indian knows topnotch goods when he sees them, don't ever doubt that. The Britishers have got us beat all hollow when it comes to blankets and knives. But an American long rifle — that's something else again. There's not a better gun made."

"Why did you make such a point of telling him that the Nez Perces all had American guns?"

"He'll spread the word and it'll give the Blackfoot bands further west something to worry about. If they think the Nez Perces have got better guns than they have, they'll brood long and hard before they come raiding again."

Bonneville chuckled in admiration. "You've missed your calling, Clint. You should have been a foreign diplomat. I can see you quite clearly in a frock coat at a London ball playing the British off against the French!"

"You see that, your eyes are better than mine," Clint grunted. "But the principle's the same, I guess. You buy peace with guns. At least out here you do."

"You make it sound quite simple."

The camp lay quiet now under the star-sprinkled sky, with only here and there a campfire flickering redly among the black shadows of tents and lodges. Their horses splashed across the shallows of the river ford and Clint said, "It's not quite as simple as it looks. It would be, maybe, if a Blackfoot thought like a white man. But he hardly ever does.

We mustn't crowd White Shield too much. Let him figure things out his own way. Let him wait till he sees his sign."

"His sign?"

"The right kind of dream. A rain crow lighting on his tepee. A wolf howling on a hill at moonrise. Whatever it is, it'll come to him. We won't know when, but he will."

Bonneville's voice was puzzled. "You're talking in circles. First you give me the impression that logic rules him, now you say just the opposite. Which am I to believe?"

"Both. He's cunning enough, when it comes to brains, but it isn't cunning that makes him jump. It's the wolf howling on the hill. Before he goes hunting, makes war, peace or hits a lick at anything, he's got to hear it howl."

"That sounds like sheer nonsense!"

"To us, yes. But it makes good sense to him."

The captain shook his head. "No doubt you're right, but it's all very confusing to me. As a matter of fact, I'm beginning to feel like a man taking an inventory of a powder magazine with a lighted candle in his hand. If I hold on to the candle, all will be well. But if I drop it — poof!"

"Yeah," Clint said. "That's sort of the way I feel, too. But we can't count barrels in the dark."

## 13

TWO BEARS' eldest son, Spotted Wolf, was a good-humored, mild-mannered man who had long been renowned for his skill at training horses, so it was to him Clint went, next

morning, seeking animals that could be quickly educated to
Ellen Metcalf's style of riding. Seeing Clint ride into the
village lugging the sidesaddle, Daniel laughingly followed
him to Spotted Wolf's lodge and squatted bright-eyed and
curious beside him as he tried to explain the type of horses
he needed, who they were for and in what manner they were
to be ridden. Gravely Spotted Wolf listened; gravely he
meditated; gravely he nodded. He understood perfectly, he
said, and would be honored to supply the white missionary
lady with all the horses she required.

"Gentle ones," Clint reminded him. "Very gentle."

"They will be gentle."

Pleased that the problem had been settled so easily, Clint
took Daniel up behind him, Spotted Wolf hopped nimbly
atop the horse he always kept staked out beside his lodge
and they galloped out to the spot where the main herd
grazed. Expertly Spotted Wolf cut out three animals. All
were grays and all carried the peculiar paint-splash markings
across their rumps that distinguished the animals bred and
cherished by the Nez Perces and envied by all the other
Indians of the West.

With Spotted Wolf holding one of the horses, Clint
cinched the sidesaddle on it. Knowing that the pony had
never tasted a steel bit, Clint helped the Indian tie a grass
rope bridle around its lower jaw, then he stepped back and
waited expectantly to see what would happen when Spotted
Wolf mounted. Soothingly Spotted Wolf talked to the
beast as he moved around it and prepared to mount from
the right-hand side, as was his custom. Suddenly he frowned
and pointed.

"No stirrup over here."

"It's on the side."

Puzzled, Spotted Wolf came around to the left side of
the gray, stared at the single stirrup for the left foot and the
curved leather piece higher on the saddle around which one
curled the right leg, then shook his head.

"This saddle is no good. It has only one stirrup."

"That's what I've been trying to explain to you," Clint said. "It's a woman's saddle."

Spotted Wolf smiled tolerantly. He knew what a woman's saddle looked like; it was no different from a man's. Did not his own squaw ride? Did she not have two legs, just as a man did? She rode thus — with his left hand he made the sign for a horse and straddled it with two fingers of his right hand — one leg on either side with the horse in between. That was the way everyone rode. This was a badly made saddle. It was a saddle for a person with only one leg. But no matter. The missionary lady was perfectly welcome to use his squaw's saddle. His squaw would not mind riding bareback.

Patiently Clint tried to explain, but the more he gestured and argued the more convinced Spotted Wolf became that this was some kind of joke. Daniel, seeing his uncle smile, seemed to think it funny too. Half a dozen Nez Perce boys, drawn like flies to dead meat by any scene that promised entertainment, came running over from their herding jobs to see what was going on. When they saw the queer-looking saddle, they pointed at it, shouting with laughter. As the discussion between Clint and Spotted Wolf grew heated, they covertly mimicked the men's gestures, snickering at one another. Realizing at last that there was only one way to make Spotted Wolf understand, Clint gestured in exasperation at the gray pony, then at himself, making the sign for a white squaw.

"I'll show you. I'm the white missionary lady, understand? This is the way she rides."

The gray, made no calmer by the growing excitement around him, shied suspiciously as Clint attempted to mount it from the left side, a thing its Indian master had never done. The boys hooted in derision. Swearing fervently, Clint threw himself upon the dancing horse and clawed with his left toe for the stirrup. But before he could even begin to get set, the gray's head went down, its back went up, Clint sailed through the air and hit the ground with a jolt that jarred him from head to heels.

Slowly he picked himself up, while Daniel and the other Indian boys howled with delight. Spotted Wolf's eyes twinkled. "That is the way the white squaw rides? Spotted Wolf thinks it better that she walk."

Recognizing the impossibility of ever making Spotted Wolf see how the thing was done, Clint said he would train the horses himself, took the grays in tow and, curtly ordering Daniel not to tag along after him, crossed the river and sought a secluded clearing well away from camp where he could work at his chore without benefit of an audience. All morning he labored patiently. Taking the ponies one by one he accustomed them to moving around with the queer saddle on their backs and got them used to a steel bit. Next, he taught them to tolerate his approaching and mounting from the left rather than the right side. Finally he gingerly climbed into the saddle and got them used to the idea that they must put up with a human being sitting with two heels banging against one set of ribs and none against the c⁺her.

By midafternoon he had progressed far enough to feel he could risk the final step. Tying the grays to a tree at the clearing's edge, he rode his own horse back to camp, went to one of Cerré's supply tents and purchased a sizable piece of black cotton material from a clerk, who solemnly assured him that it was exactly the sort of thing Eastern ladies were accustomed to making into skirts. As he came out of the tent he ran squarely into Judd Smith and Zack Parkins.

"Whar you been?" Judd demanded. "Bonny's been lookin' fer ye."

"Gentling some horses," Clint mumbled, hastily hiding the black skirt material behind him. "The captain have anything important on his mind?"

"Didn't say." Judd peered at him curiously. "What's that you bought?"

"Just some material."

"Looks like female dress material to me," Zack grunted. "What're you figgerin' to do, make some squaw a present?"

"You fellows ever try minding your own business?"

Looking at each other with expressions of mock hurt, the pair laughed and strolled on into the tent, while Clint hurriedly mounted and rode back to the clearing. He untied the gray pony which now carried the sidesaddle and tightened the cinch. He showed the pony the cloth, let the animal sniff at it, flapped it in front of the horse's face and rubbed it across the animal's flanks, taking his time, giving the gray ample opportunity to become accustomed to the material. At last he was satisfied that the moment had come.

He took a long, careful look around, listening intently. The willows stirred gently in the light afternoon breezes. Birds chirped as they flitted through the thick bushes, a pair of chipmunks chattered as they played tag with each other at the edge of the clearing — other than that there was nothing. Grinning sheepishly and feeling very much the fool, he wrapped the cloth around his waist and fastened it into something that vaguely resembled a woman's skirt. Cautiously he approached the gray.

"Easy, boy. I don't like this any better than you do. But we're both going to have to put up with it, seems like."

Awkwardly he swung into the sidesaddle. The horse stood trembling, rolling its eyes suspiciously. Carefully Clint urged it into a walk. A twig snapped in the undergrowth. Someone gave a subdued snicker. From another quarter there came a loud guffaw, followed by another, and suddenly the clearing was surrounded by grinning trappers and Indians, laughing and yelling and demanding that the horse show them some action.

The gray enthusiastically obliged. Clint's hands were so

full of spooked horse for the next few seconds that all he could do was hang on and swear, his curses impartially divided to include gossipy clerks, snoopy trappers, female-type sidesaddles and overmodest missionary ladies who insisted on riding as no human being was ever meant to ride.

When the gray violently humped its back like an animated question mark, Clint and it parted company with no goodbyes said by either of them. Whooping like wild Indians, Judd and Zack caught the pony before it could get clean away and led it back to where Clint sat scowling balefully at the jeering circle which surrounded him, the audience including, he now saw, the smiling Spotted Wolf and the giggling Daniel. Judd made a polite bow.

"Pardon me, lady, but did you mislay this hyar pony?"

"Never saw it before in my life," Clint grunted.

" 'Peared to me you was tryin' to ride it."

"You've got quite an imagination, Judd."

"That's a neat trick, I must say," Zack said solemnly, "that sideways ridin'. Injuns won't be able to tell whether you're comin' er goin'."

"It's easy, once you get the hang of it. Why don't you try it?"

Good-naturedly, Zack donned the improvised skirt and gave it a whirl, lasting barely three jumps before the panicked pony heaved him head over heels into the bushes. Convinced now that it took a good deal more skill to ride a bucking horse sidesaddle than it did astride, the other mountain men went at it turn by turn, for the trapper never lived that wouldn't try a new stunt if it appeared to offer him a good chance to break a leg or arm.

Come evening, all three horses were so well broken — or just plain worn out — that Clint felt no qualms in pronouncing them just what the customer had ordered.

# 14

ALL HER LIFE Ellen Metcalf had been taught that a woman must not argue with her menfolk. Just why the mere accident of maleness should bestow great wisdom upon the man and leave the woman incapable of any degree of good judgment, neither her father nor her brother had ever bothered to explain to her, seeming to feel that she should accept this fact of life as one accepted the word of the Gospel. She did not accept it. She merely pretended to, smiling quietly, putting up with it quietly, and quietly finding other means than words by which to have her way. But the morning Clint was to come and take her for her first ride she found herself forced into sharp disagreement with her brother.

"It's very unwise, your riding about camp with a man of Clint's stripe," Stanley said. "I would much prefer that you didn't do it."

"But, Stanley, I've hardly been on a horse since we left home. I must get hardened to it. Everyone says it's impossible to take the wagons any further. What am I to do the rest of the way to the Nez Perce country — walk?"

Stanley shook his head. "I've changed my mind about leaving the wagons here. We're taking one on with us — the lightest one. I'm sure we can get it through. You can ride in it."

"But a wagon is so slow and uncomfortable. Wouldn't it be best to leave it behind?"

"The plows and farming tools we brought out are indispensable. If it's at all possible to take a wagon through, I'm going to do it."

"Can't you take the plows and heavier tools apart and

pack them on horses? Captain Sublette said he thought you could."

"The wagon goes along. I'm not going to be argued out of that."

"Very well," she said shortly, "the wagon goes and the plows can ride in it. But they are made to stand more abuse more than I am. I'm going to ride a horse."

It was the first time in her life that she had ever flatly defied him, but though she knew from the tight set of his lips that he did not like it he had nothing to say other than a curt, "Do as you wish. But I still feel it's unwise."

Watching him pick up his medical bag and walk away, she was surprised at herself for having spoken so bluntly. Yet she realized that this was but one more indication of the change which each of their personalities had undergone since they had started west.

Her thoughts went back to the farewell church service she and Stanley had taken part in before leaving home. Recalling the inspired sermon Stanley had preached, the tears, the final embraces, the gifts, the flood of well-meant advice, she found herself smiling wryly at how different reality had proved from the dreams they had had then. Dedicating oneself to cheerfully endure whatever trials and tribulations the good Lord might send sounded noble and fine; enduring such down-to-earth miseries as mosquitoes, bone-chilling rain, and long days on a hard wagon seat while one's insides were cramping and churning with a flux brought on by drinking alkali-impregnated water had no quality of anything noble or fine. Promising to take the True Word to the benighted heathen of a distant land was a thrilling, soul-stirring thing when one was among friends in a comfortable church; seeing an Indian stagger up to her tent dead drunk, filthy, vermin-infested and smelling like a penful of badly kept hogs as he stared at her with unblinking, glazed eyes stirred nothing at all in her but an uneasy sense of fear and a bleak helplessness as she wondered how either Stanley or herself could ever hope to make themselves understood by wretches such as this.

And there was the matter of the church bell. The shiny, beautiful bronze church bell which the good folk of the congregation back home had purchased and presented to them as a lifetime token of their esteem. The bell, set up temporarily on a standard outside the village church, had tolled the flock into the building for that final service, then the clapper had been securely fastened and stilled. "Not to ring again," Stanley had promised from the pulpit in a firm, determined voice, "until the strong brown hands of our first Nez Perce convert in Oregon tolls the Sabbath worship hour in the church we shall build with our own hands!"

There had not been a dry eye in the house and it had seemed a wonderful thing, the pact they had made to ring the old bell in the old church in the East at a certain hour on a certain day a year hence while a continent away the new bell would ring in the new church. The thousands of miles intervening would be as nothing. Hearts and souls would hear, though ears might not . . .

Yes, it had been a beautiful bell. Crated for shipment, it weighed well over a hundred pounds, a weight which seemed a negligible thing on the stagecoaches and boats; not so negligible at Independence when the time came to find a place for it in one of the wagons; an infernal nuisance of a weight when the wagon carrying it had to be emptied before it could be dragged out of a knee-deep mudhole, an intolerable weight when there was a river to be crossed and one pound too many might make the difference between the wagon box sinking too low or floating high enough to keep the river from coming aboard when they reached swimming water in midstream.

The bell — that beautiful bronze bell with the name of

the home church and the names of the home congregation so carefully inscribed on it — lay at the bottom of the Platte now. Something had had to go. The plows were heavy, too, but Stanley had hesitated only a moment. Overboard went the bell with no more ceremony than a grunt from Stanley, "That'll lighten us some."

Lighten up, throw away the excess, get rid of all the unnecessary frills and burdens which were of no use out here. Not only the tangible things but the intangible excess burdens too. When there were sick Indian children to be treated, there was no time to debate the state of their souls. When there was carpenter work to be done on a wagon, there was no time to argue with a sister who had suddenly decided she would rather ride a horse.

Watching Clint as he rode up to her tent leading a gray horse, she knew a moment of uneasiness. If the horse did run away, if she did fall, if it did throw her, Stanley would insist that she ride in the wagon. And the skittish gray certainly looked far from tame. The smile on her face as she greeted Clint was stiff and strained, but she forced cheerfulness into her voice.

"Good morning. Is this to be my horse?"

"If you can handle him, yeah."

"What's his name?"

"Forgot to ask what his Indian name is. But I call him Gunpowder."

"Because of his color or his disposition?"

Clint smiled. "Both." Swinging down to the ground, he stood holding the gray, which eyed her suspiciously as she approached. She moved slowly, letting the animal sniff at her, trying not to startle it. As its lips touched her hand she reached up and gently rubbed its forehead. She gave a nervous laugh.

"He's trembling."

"So are you." Clint eyed her a moment. "Scared of him?"

"A little. But promise me one thing, Clint. Even if he throws me a dozen times, don't tell Stanley."

"Why not?"

"Never mind. Just don't you tell him."

He helped her mount. Stiff and uneasy as the gray danced around under her, she was frightened for a moment, sure that she was going to fall. Then Clint swung atop his own horse and steadied her in the saddle as the gray headed for the river at a canter and a measure of confidence came to her. Clint's voice was calm.

"Don't fight him — he's got a light mouth and the taste of a steel bit is new to him. Gentle does it. He's no plow horse."

That she could readily believe. Much as she had ridden back home she had never before felt the explosive energy of a really spirited horse such as this one under her. It was a terrifying feeling at first, but gradually as they rode along the grassy, open flat next to the river the easy rhythm of the smooth-moving muscles under her seemed to flow into her own body, to become a part of her. It was a glorious, wonderful feeling, and she found herself laughing aloud in sheer exuberance.

The morning passed quickly and it was by all odds the most enjoyable morning she had spent since she left home. As her confidence grew, she began to look curiously around her. They had ridden several miles downstream, leaving the camp behind. Ahead, the river glittered in the sunlight as it wound southward toward a line of hills faint in the haze of distance. The horses stopped at the edge of the stream to drink. Turning in the saddle, she gazed toward camp, where the tents and tepees looked dwarfed beneath the rugged immensity of the snowcapped mountains behind them. She smiled at Clint, who was quietly watching her.

"There's nothing like this back home."

"No."

"Where is the Gros Ventre camp?"

He inclined his head toward a ridge to the northwest. "Over yonder."

"I want to see it."

He hesitated a moment, then nodded. "All right."

He led the way to a spot where the river widened and shallowed, the gravel bottom showing clearly beneath the swirling surface of the water. "Don't look down," he cautioned. "It'll make you dizzy."

Some perverse impulse in her did make her look down just as they reached midstream. Though the current was swift, the water did not appear to be moving at all. But the gravel bottom was moving, undulating, going out from under her. A queer feeling that she was losing her balance made her suddenly sway in the saddle. Gasping, she closed her eyes, then she felt Clint's hand steadying her, heard his laugh as the horses plunged up out of the ford on the far bank.

"Don't you ever do as you're told?"

She gave him a sharp look. "All my life men have told me what I should or shouldn't do. It grows tiresome after a while."

"I can't recall that you ever paid much attention to me."

"You were different."

"How?"

"You didn't resent my arguing with you. You acted as though I were a person with a mind of my own and not just a woman who wasn't even entitled to an opinion."

"Most men don't do that?"

"None that I've ever known."

He shook his head. "Truth is, I never could figure out any way to keep you from having your say, short of taking a club to you."

She smiled. "Is that the way Indian men make their wives behave — by beating them?"

"Some of them try. But I can't say it works too well."

"Do the Nez Perce husbands beat their squaws?"

He evaded her eyes and his voice was suddenly cold. "No."

"Stanley says he's heard they do. He says that's to be one of the first things we must put a stop to."

"Stanley doesn't know what he's talking about."

"Tell me about their family life. Are the women ill-treated? How are the children disciplined? What kind of marriage ceremonies do they have?"

There was a strange veiled look in his eyes as he stared off into the distance while their horses walked slowly along.

"They're not white people, I'll say that. If a man and woman want to live together, they arrange the thing with the girl's father, have a feast and the thing's done. If the woman misbehaves, the man throws her out; if the man misbehaves, the woman walks out. As far as the children are concerned, they don't know what a cuff or a beating is. They just grow up with the fool notion that their parents love them and that they're supposed to respect their parents."

"Then they have no discipline?"

"I said they weren't white people. The parents have never caught on to such white tricks as boxing a hungry kid's ears because he's filched a piece of meat out of the pot or raising welts on his back with a leather strap because he's gone swimming without asking permission. They're just poor dumb savages when it comes to raising their kids. But maybe you and Stanley can teach them civilized ways."

The bitterness in his voice was unmistakable and it shocked her. "You wish we hadn't come, don't you?"

"What does it matter what I wish? You're here."

"You could be a great help to us, if you would."

He shook his head. "Saving souls is your trade, not mine. I'll see you through to the Nez Perce country. After that, I'm afraid you'll have to look out for yourselves."

The pleasure she had been feeling was suddenly gone.

For a while she had forgotten herself and had slipped back into the old easy, comfortable relationship with Clint which they had once both enjoyed. But the completeness of it was missing now and perhaps would always be. They could ride together, they could talk, they could travel together as they would in the days to come, but always there would be a point beyond which they could not go. She believed in what she and her brother were doing. Clint did not. Perhaps that was part of it. But she sensed that his sudden coldness toward her went deeper than a mere difference of opinion as to the wisdom of trying to Christianize the Indians. There was a remoteness in him now which she could not penetrate. A door was closed to her. A piece of his life that must remain his alone seemed to stand like a solid wall between them.

She was hurt. It was foolish that she should be, she told herself angrily, yet the mere physical proximity of the one person whom above all others she had once felt close to brought her an overpowering desire to go back to the deep and wordless understanding which they had formerly shared. But the wall was there.

As they rode down the slope and into the Gros Ventre camp, Clint said, "They've never seen a white woman before. Likely they'll be curious. Don't be frightened if the squaws paw at your clothes and rub at your face to see if the white comes off."

"It will take more than that to frighten me."

Clint spoke little during their brief stay in the village. Despite all the terrible things she had heard about them, she did not feel frightened, merely curious, and she sensed that the timid squaws who fingered her clothes and gingerly touched her face were far more in awe of her than she was fearful of them. Outwardly the Gros Ventres looked no different from the Indians she had seen in the main camp. They were quieter, more wary, more suspicious. In spite of their name they seemed to have no bigger waistlines than any other Indian, and she made a mental note to ask Clint why they had ever been given such a vulgar tribal name as "Big Bellies."

Clint talked for a while with a tall, harsh-faced Indian who was apparently chief of this band. He did not introduce her, which she thought strange. In fact it angered her that the two men should so completely ignore her, leaving her surrounded by a group of squaws who rubbed their greasy hands over her face, tugged at her skirt, fingered the side-saddle and gabbled with one another, while Clint and the Gros Ventre chief stood exchanging meaningless gestures, appearing completely unaware of her existence. As they rode out of the village Clint looked at her and grinned.

"I know what you're thinking."

"Do you? Then why didn't you introduce me?"

"Because you're a female. But don't be insulted because White Shield didn't kiss your hand and invite you into his lodge for a cup of tea. You made quite an impression on him."

"How could I have? He never once looked at me!"

"You just think he didn't."

"Couldn't he at least have said hello?"

"He's not in the habit of saying hello to squaws."

"So I'm just another squaw to him!"

Clint laughed heartily. "No, he thinks you're pretty big medicine. But it strikes him as real queer that a white squaw would ride over to visit his village when her brother won't. Which is the man and which is the woman? he wonders. He's not sure but he thinks he's being snubbed. That's why I cut our visit short."

"Stanley was wrong in not coming, wasn't he?"

Clint shrugged. "It's his affair."

"Please, Clint, be patient with him. He'll learn in time. But he's got to do things his way."

"Yeah, I know," Clint said, his smile fading. "Even if his way is dead wrong."

They topped the ridge. His quick eye catching the way she was shifting uncomfortably in the saddle, he reined up. As a grin spread slowly across his lean face, she flushed.

"It isn't funny."

"Don't have the least notion what you're talking about."

"You most certainly do."

"A wagon might be best for you after all."

"A wagon seat is just as hard as a saddle," she said hotly, then winced. "Only the calluses seem to be in slightly different places."

"You didn't ride the wagon seat sidesaddle."

She pointedly ignored that. "I've a week yet to get used to it. I'm going to ride every day if it kills me — until I'm as hardened to it as a squaw!" Blushing furiously, she nodded at the Indian village on the slope below. "Isn't that the Nez Perce camp?"

"Yeah."

"I want to see it."

For a moment she thought he had not heard her. Taking out his pipe, he filled it and sat gazing off at the tall peaks on the far side of the valley. Then he said quietly, "No reason you shouldn't."

This was no silent village. From the moment they rode into its upper end the difference between these friendly, happy people and the sullen Gros Ventres was strikingly evident. Children ran laughing toward their horses, squaws looked up from their chores, smiled and called out greetings, men waved to them and exchanged jests with Clint; even the hordes of dogs yapping around them seemed to be making their noise more out of good spirits than in challenge. She looked curiously at Clint. He appeared strangely relaxed, the distance-seeking look gone from his eyes, the quiet alertness usually present on his face replaced by a look of being at peace with himself and all the world. It was just such an expression as she had observed many times on her father's face when he had come into the parsonage after a long, exhausting day, unbuttoned his coat, loosened his tie and sunk back in his favorite leather chair by the stove with his eyes half closed. This was home to Clint, that was quite evident. And the secret of his remoteness, the strangeness she had sensed in him, the answer was here.

She could not explain how she knew that. But the knowledge was as positive as though Clint himself had given it to her.

Directly ahead, some sort of celebration seemed to be going on, for a large mass of shouting, laughing Indian men, women and children were gathered around an open place among the tepees watching performers whom she could not yet see. Their horses edged into the crowd. Dark faces looked up. Hands went quickly to cover open mouths. Indians swirled around them, still grinning but suddenly silent. The horses stopped, unable to move because of the pack of people around them. She got a glimpse of Clint's face and saw it go tight and grim. Harsh anger flooded it and he made a gesture as if he would violently sweep the Indians blocking the way from out of his path. Then as swiftly as the anger had come, it vanished and he sat relaxed, a wry smile beginning to lift the corners of his mouth.

Now she could see the performers in the center of the circle. One was a man, the other a small boy. The man was down on all fours, bouncing around on the packed earth with jerky, twisting motions for all the world like those of a wildly bucking horse. He would suddenly stop and be perfectly still for a few moments, save for the ludicrous rolling of his eyes and the twitching of his nose. He would then be aproached by the boy, who from the waist up was naked but from the waist down wore a ridiculously long skirt improvised out of red cloth.

Apparently the boy was putting on some sort of act of mimicry. One moment he would be walking with short, mincing steps, then he would stop, make big boastful gestures with his hands, and suddenly he would appear to become an entirely different character, this time taking huge, swaggering strides, pulling the improvised skirt up to his knees, throwing his chest out and looking for all the world like some drunken white trapper. At his every gesture, his audience roared with laughter and shouted its approval.

"*Aah taats! Aah taats!*"

Puzzled, she nudged Clint and whispered, "What is it?"

He seemed to ponder for a moment, then he said, "Why, it's a kind of ceremony. Yeah, that's what it is — a symbolic ceremony. Been in the tribe for generations."

"Is the man on his hands and knees supposed to be a horse?"

"Yeah."

"And the little boy — what is he?"

"Him? Why, he's a sun spirit. Just come out of the east, he has, and he's met this here wild horse and now he's trying to ride it."

"Why is he wearing the skirt?"

"He's a female sun spirit."

"Clint, you're teasing!"

"Just watch. Maybe you can figure it out for yourself."

The boy, after making innumerable boasts, suddenly seemed to lose all his confidence and went tiptoeing gingerly up to the man on all fours, who now was rolling his eyes, baring his teeth and giving every indication of being a bad horse indeed. The boy eased a noosed rope between the man's jaws, hesitated, then with a shrill war cry leaped aboard his back, sitting sideways. That drew a huge peal of laughter from the crowd. The man-horse bucked, the boy tumbled off, then both man and boy rose and did a fast-tempoed, stomping dance around each other, while the crowd cheered madly.

"*Aah taats! Aah taats!*"

"What are they shouting?" she asked Clint.

"Good show." Swinging to the ground, he muttered, "But I'll give 'em a better one."

Completely baffled, she saw him throw back his head and give a piercing, animal-like howl that instantly stilled the noise of the crowd. A way opened magically before him, hands flew to mouths, then as he stepped out into the circle everyone began pointing at him, then at the man and boy. This pair now stood frozen, staring at Clint as he slowly approached them. She saw Clint stop, take his knife out of his belt and stand for a moment thoughtfully running one thumb over the glittering blade, as if testing the keenness of its edge.

Someone in the crowd giggled. The grownup Indian who had been playing the part of the horse smiled, then his face grew solemn and he looked down at the boy standing beside him and mournfully shook his head. The boy stared at Clint, who pointed a finger at him, then made a circling motion around his own head which even to Ellen's inexperienced eyes could only mean the act of scalping. Involuntarily she shivered. The boy slid around to hide behind his man-horse as Clint stalked toward him, the knife glittering in the sunlight. A chant started in the crowd, eerie and weird and chilling, and grew in volume until all the Indians were slowly nodding forward and back in time to the singsong chanting. Clint gestured to the man-horse, who, with apparent great reluctance, pulled the boy loose from his leg and thrust him forward.

In one lightning gesture, Clint whipped the knife through the air a foot above the boy's head, lifted an imaginary scalp for all to see, sheathed his knife, picked up the boy with a whoop of laughter and tossed him high in the air. Catching him as he came down, Clint swung the child astride his own neck and went galloping around the circle while the boy shouted in glee. The crowd roared its appreciation.

Enthralled and strangely touched, Ellen sat watching as Clint carried the boy toward her through the laughing crowd. She was beginning to understand what had happened. Boy and man-horse had been re-enacting some of the troubles Clint had gone through in breaking the horses for her, and the fact that she and Clint had appeared in time to witness the mimicry was to the Nez Perces the best kind of joke. But how odd it was to see Indians laugh. Somehow she had never thought of them as having the least sense of humor.

Clint was standing beside her horse now. He had taken the boy off his shoulders and set him on the ground, where the child stood clinging tightly to his hand, his brown eyes shining and bright as he gazed curiously up at her. Clint said quietly, "Do you understand it now?"

She laughed gaily. "I think so." She extended a gloved hand to the boy. "A magnificent performance, sir. May I shake your hand?"

The boy glanced quickly at Clint, who murmured something to him in the Nez Perce tongue. Briefly the small brown hand touched Ellen's, then the boy resumed his attitude of quiet watchfulness. Clint was watching her, too, not speaking, and an odd constraint came to her.

"Such a fine looking child! What is his name?"

"I call him Daniel. He'll get his Indian name when he's a few years older."

"He certainly seems fond of you."

Clint kept looking at her and so did the boy. There was something about the way each held his head, something in the way each stood, something in the configuration of each one's body that suddenly struck her with their similarity. The eyes, one pair gray, the other brown, yet . . . Her hand went to her throat. She felt dizzy, faint. Even before Clint's gentle voice penetrated her consciousness, she knew.

"He should be fond of me, Ellen. He's my son."

## 15

RENDEZVOUS was beginning to show signs of breaking up when Captain Bonneville conferred with Clint a few days later. "Are you all set?" he asked.

Clint noded. "The Nez Perces are getting ready to travel. Likely we'll hit the trail in two or three days. Are you going to keep us company for a ways?"

Bonneville shook his head. "Indians travel too slow to suit my taste. Besides, the Nez Perces will probably swing north and make for the Salmon River country as soon as they hit the Portneuf. I plan to follow the Snake on westerly."

"That's mean country this time of year. Dry and dusty and hot as the hinges of hell."

"It's mean country any time of year. But it's flat and we'll be traveling light."

"Once you pass the mouth of the Boise and swing north the land stands on edge. Are you figuring to tackle Snake River Gorge again?"

"Not if I can help it. The Indians tell me there's an easier route across the Blue Mountains than the one I took the last time I went down to the lower Columbia. I want to give it a try. Do you know it, by any chance?"

"Heard talk about it, that's all. It's Cayuse country out there and they're related to the Nez Perce. My guess is they'll be friendly enough and you can hire 'em to guide you through."

Captain Bonneville's restless eyes strayed to the ridge on the far side of the river, beyond which White Shield and his band of Gros Ventres were still camped. Abruptly he rose. "Let's ride over and see White Shield. I want to bid him goodbye. While we're at it, we might as well make one last effort to convince the old devil that a policy of peace toward his neighbors is best."

They mounted and rode toward the Gros Ventre camp. All during rendezvous, the Gros Ventres had kept to themselves, watchful and wary. They had accepted Bonneville's gifts; they had listened passively as he talked of peace; they had smoked and talked and exchanged bland lies with the Nez Perce, Crow, Shoshone and Bannock chiefs whom Clint and Bonneville had brought to their council lodge; they had pretended to agree to everything that was said on the subject of peace, yet they remained as suspicious and sullen as they had been that first day.

It was Bonneville's feeling now that nothing had been accomplished. Clint wasn't so sure. Look at the thing from White Shield's angle. He'd pulled a damn fool stunt leading his people into a trap yet he'd gotten out of it without losing a soul. Why? Because a white man had saved his hide. An American. Being an Indian, he wasn't going to get down on his knees and thank Bonneville for that. Nor was he going to go home to his relatives and tell them what a fool he'd been to get into such a fix. No, the way he'd tell it he'd come out the hairy bear. He'd make it out he'd been so cunning and brave that he had saved all his band. And he'd have the long rifles the Bald Chief had given him to prove how much the Americans respected him.

But he had eyes and he'd had two long weeks to use them. He'd seen more Americans gathered in this valley than he ever dreamed existed. He'd learned how much they hated the British. He'd seen how friendly the Nez Perces were toward the Americans, learned about the long rifles with which they were being equipped, and seen that they hated the British too. He'd seen the Crows being friendly toward the Americans and being armed by them. And likely he was beginning to wonder.

Clint told Captain Bonneville all that, concluding with the warning, "Don't make the mistake of judging an Indian by what he says. Hell, an Indian can lie just as good or better than a white man can. Judge him by what he does. That'll show you what he's thinking."

"If he cuts my throat, I'm to assume he's unfriendly, is that what you mean?" Bonneville said dryly. "While if he doesn't, he's on my side?"

"Something like that, yeah."

"Excellent advice. I'll try to keep it in mind."

When they reached the Gros Ventre village they were greeted by the usual stolid sullenness, the silent suspicion in the eyes of the women and older men, the smouldering resentment in the faces of the warriors. It was as if these people felt they were captives, held here against their will, and there was no gratitude in their hearts that their lives had been spared; instead, there was only pent-up hate.

White Shield led the two men to the council lodge in the center of the village, where for an hour or so they sat and smoked and talked with the chief and half a dozen of the head men. With Clint interpreting for him, Captain Bonneville told his intentions to establish a trading post on the lower Columbia and of the white missionaries' plan to settle at some central spot among the Nez Perces. The assembled head men listened with no show of expression, save for the medicine man, Ta-tu-ye, The Fox, who from the beginning had not bothered to conceal his hatred and contempt for Americans and who had grown more hostile with each meeting. He was a thin, sharp-eyed Indian of middle years with some kind of spinal ailment that made him keep his head constantly cocked to one side. During previous parleys he had always sat at White Shield's right hand, from time to time leaning close to the chief to spit out a word or two meant for the chief's ears alone; but today he was as far removed from White Shield as the confines of the lodge would permit and no matter how often he tried to catch the chief's attention White Shield ignored him.

"The hearts of the Nez Perces are strong for peace," Captain Bonneville said. "You have seen it. You have smoked with their chiefs and with the chiefs of the Crows, Shoshones and Bannocks. The hearts of the Americans are strong for peace. When you return to your own land after visiting your cousins to the south, I want you to give this message to your Blackfoot brothers. Tell them that the Bald White Chief would trade with them and be their friend."

White Shield was silent until the pipe had made its rounds, then he answered, "I have heard the words of the Bald Chief and I will remember all he has said. I have seen a sign. I have had a dream which tells me that the time is not good to visit our cousins to the south, the Arapahoes. My dream tells me we must return to our own country now. There I will tell my Blackfoot brothers what the Bald Chief has said."

"This is good. But you have not yet shown me your heart."

"My heart is good. I am glad that the Nez Perces say their hearts are good. But this may be a lie. When we meet next time in the buffalo country we will know what is true and what is a lie. If all is peaceful there, then the Nez Perces have spoken true. If blood is shed, they have lied. We will wait and see."

The Fox spoke bitterly. "This is the talk of fools. When Nez Perce and Blackfoot meet in the buffalo country they will fight, as they always have. It is meant to be. The advice of the Bald Chief is bad. We will not take it."

"You would be wise to take it," Bonneville answered.

"You speak of wisdom," The Fox said contemptuously. "Yet you are so weak and lacking in manhood that you listen to squaws. I have seen this and know it to be so. I have seen She-Who-Rides-Sideways go about with your head men and talk to them as if she were a chief." The Fox spat. "Men who let their squaws rule them in council are weaklings and fools."

When Clint translated that to Captain Bonneville, the captain's face colored and he snapped, "Let The Fox listen to the voice of the American long rifles. Then let him say, if he is still alive and able to speak, who are weaklings and fools."

It was the first time an insult had been directly given and bluntly answered, and as Clint's hands moved there was a sudden murmuring among the head men, a sudden grunting and gesticulating in which hate and passion and fear bubbled like the sticky seething of tar in a pot. White Shield cut in sharply.

"Is The Fox the head chief now that he may speak out in council while all others remain silent? No! He is a whirlwind full of air and dust, fit to roll small tumbleweeds but of no worth in a talk between head men. Let him be silent!"

The parley broke up after appropriate pipe-smoking and polite speeches of farewell. Riding back to camp, Bonneville said, "That was an unexpected explosion, wasn't it? What do you suppose it meant?"

"Hard to tell. But my guess is The Fox is jealous of all the big medicine he's seen the past two weeks. Likely he's had quite a say up till now on how White Shield ran things. But his grip has slipped and he's sore. He's got so green-eyed he overstepped himself today and White Shield put him in his place good and proper."

Bonneville chuckled softly. "Maybe it's just as well the Reverend Metcalf didn't accept our invitation to visit the Gros Ventres. If he had trespassed on The Fox's field of doctoring and healing, we would really have had a fire to put out."

"That might have been easier to handle than fixing the dent he made in White Shield's pride," Clint said, shaking his head. "If Metcalf is going to get along out here, he's got to be a sight less stiff-necked."

"What do the Nez Perces think of him?"

Clint shrugged. "Ask me that a year from now when they have gotten to really know him."

"Well, stiff-necked or not, do what you can to help him. It's for the best, I'm convinced. A successful American mission in Oregon may prove more troublesome to the British than any number of trappers, trading posts or re-alignment of Indian tribes we can manage. It will be one more stone rolled into their garden."

Clint studied Bonneville curiously. "You're rolling a lot of stones into their garden, it seems to me. A man's bound to wonder why. Where's the gain to you?"

Captain Bonneville smiled, shook his head and made no reply.

# 16

ALWAYS toward the end of rendezvous each year there came a time when Burn Rapp suddenly stopped drinking. It was never a conscious choice; it simply happened. A man got enough. One minute whisky tasted fine and did exactly the things to him he wanted it to do; the next the terrible stuff gagged him, poisoned him, made him plumb sick to his stomach. Staggering out into the dark, he'd unload everything inside him, reel bat-blind to his blankets and fall into a black, dreamless pit of oblivion. For sixteen hours he would sleep like a dead man. When he woke up he would feel as cleansed inside as an Indian just out of a sweat bath, all his appetites for drinking, wenching, talking, fighting and general hell-raising completely satisfied. The fun was over. Time to think of the next year's work.

When he opened his eyes now, daylight was fading. A stillness lay over the valley, an empty hush that told him the scattering of mountain men, Indians and traders had already begun. Not moving, he lay on his back breathing slow and deep, watching a fair-weather cloud directly above him lose its fluffy whiteness, turn pink, flame-red, then purple, while around it stars blinked on one by one. Good traveling weather tomorrow, looked like.

His head felt light, his mouth dry, his tongue thick and fuzzy. Somewhere nearby he could hear a fire crackling and the odor of broiling antelope meat made magpies dance in the pit of his sore belly. He sat up. Squatting in front of the fire slowly rotating a green willow stick covered with skewered meat chunks over a glowing red bed of coals, Oswald Fram turned and grinned at him.

"You still alive?"

"Water," Rapp grunted. "Gimme some water."

Fram tossed him a nearly full canteen and he drank greedily, draining it to the last drop. That helped. He stood up and took stock of his surroundings. Few were the fires winking in the valley now; few the tents and lodges. Fram took a piece of meat off the stick, cooled it by tossing it around in his hand for a moment, then took a tentative bite of it. "Done, I reckon. You hungry?"

Hunkering down on his heels before the fire, Rapp helped himself to the meat. The first swallow gave him trouble but he got it down, kept it down, and shortly the magpies quit dancing. He grunted, "Sublette gone?"

"Couple of days ago."

"Bonneville?"

"Pulled out for the Columbia yesterday mornin'."

"Clint Davidson?"

Fram jerked his head toward the dark ridge to the south-west. "Moved over to camp near the Gros Ventres. Got the Metcalfs and the Nez Perces with him. Goin' to bring the Injuns together for one last peace parley tonight, then he's makin' fer Salmon River."

"That's a fool thing, talkin' peace with White Shield."

"So I say. But who listens to us?"

They finished the meat in silence, Rapp staring glassy-eyed into the fire while he sorted through the whisky-hazed jumble of happenings of the past few weeks and viewed the prospects for the season ahead. Nothing to cheer a man. No fat cash wage this year. Turndowns from Bonneville, turndowns from Clint. A murdering, thieving Gros Ventre who owed him a blood debt camped yonder over the ridge with the whites talking sweet to him and giving him guns. Bill Sublette acting mean and stingy, laying the law down to him like it'd never been laid down before, putting a limit on the credit he'd give, nam-ing a miserable price for next year's plews and telling him exactly what he could do if he didn't like it. A sorry busi-ness all around.

Fram wiped his greasy hands on his thighs, filled his pipe and fished a live coal out of the fire. When he had the pipe going, he said, "Do we pull out tomorrow?"

"Might as well. There's no beaver here."

"Which direction do we travel?"

Which direction? An ornery question to answer, these days. Time was, all a man had to do was pick him a river, follow it uphill into the mountains to where the aspens began and start trapping. Couple of months work in the early fall, couple more in the spring and he got him-self all the plews he could handle, with traders fighting one another at rendezvous, come summer, to buy them from him at good prices. But no more. The lush, easy days were gone, and a man had to scratch hard and scratch deep even to pay for his fixin's now, what with the mountains lousy with white and Indian trappers and the traders organizing into big companies and squeezing every dollar till the juice ran out of it.

Raising his eyes, Rapp gazed out into the dark. From the talk he'd heard among the mountain men, the only chunk of country they were shying clear of this season was the Three Forks region, northwesterly. Beaver there, they all agreed. The headwaters of the Gallatin, the Jefferson, the Madison, all that upper Missouri River country had beaver aplenty. But it had Blackfeet aplenty, too, and a man was apt to spend more time fighting, hiding and running than he did trapping.

Up until a few years ago the Blackfoot had shown little interest in doing any beaver-trapping themselves, preferring to let some fool white man wade the cold mountain streams, set his traps, skin and rough-cure the hides, then along about the time he'd baled his gather of plews and was ready to set out for rendezvous they'd ambush him and take over his pelts, his horses, his traps, even his topknot if they could. Then they'd trade with the British, who had no scruples as to where the pelts came from so long as they were prime. They had waylaid Rapp and Fram that way once and he wasn't anxious to have it happen again. But the thought that came to him now was that if the Blackfoot wanted beaver to trade for guns they'd have to do some stream-wading themselves this year. And the trick they'd pulled on him and Fram could work the other way.

"The Wind River country, maybe?" Fram said.

Rapp shook his head. "Won't be a plew left there, time Bonny's crew and the Crows work it. The Three Forks'll do fer us."

"Be swarmin' with Blackfoot, that country will."

"Bees swarm, bears steal their honey."

"You mind what happened to us up there three year ago."

"I mind it well. And I mind what I lost."

"You'd best forget that paint. The world's full of horses."

Rapp's eyes lingered on the dark line of ridge which blocked out the lower portion of the star-studded sky to the southwest. All the frustrations he had suffered lately suddenly focused upon a single tangible object; all his anger, all his cunning, all the animal energy that drove him suddenly joined to demand accomplishment of a single act of retribution.

"That paint was the best horse I ever owned. The Injun bastard that stole it is camped jest over the ridge yonder. Things break right fer me, I'll git it back. With some Gros Ventre's hair to decorate its bridle."

"White Shield's?" Fram said, looking at him uneasily.

"His'd do," Rapp grunted. "His'd do jest fine."

# 17

WHEN THE rising sun topped the ridge next morning, it lighted a strange scene. The Nez Perce tepees were all down, folded and lashed on travois. The wagon which Stanley Metcalf had insisted on taking along was piled high with plows, luggage and camping gear, and the two teams of horses which were to pull it were fidgeting in their harness.

The pack animals belonging to Clint and the ten mountain men in his party, the horses they were to ride, Ellen's horse, all were saddled and ready to take to the trail.

But at this moment all was quiet. There was no talk, no movement, no sound save for the strong fervent voice of the Reverend Metcalf, who, head bared, knees on the ground and arms wide spread, was sending a plea up into the brightening blue of the wide and empty sky that the journeyers gathered around him be given such blessings and protection as the Almighty in His infinite wisdom saw fit to provide.

Though Clint knelt too, his head was erect and his eyes were open — not from irreverence but from habit. The responsibility for the party's safety was all his now. Daybreak and the confusion of camp breakup made this time a fine one for trouble to strike.

As Metcalf prayed on, a paint horse came loping across the grassy flat from the Gros Ventre village. The Indian riding it was Chief White Shield, Clint saw. An uneasy restlessness ran over the Nez Perces. Judd Smith and Zack Parkins, kneeling directly opposite Clint, glanced quickly at the nearing Indian, then shot questioning glances at Clint.

The prayer went on and on. Seeming to sense that this was big medicine and not to be interrupted, White Shield reined up and sat immobile, waiting, his observant eyes filled with superstitious awe and respect. At last Metcalf said, "All these things we ask in Thy Son's name, amen."

The mountain men rose and donned their hats. A low murmur of talk ran through them, ran through the Nez Perces too, then a hush fell as Clint and Judd Smith walked out to meet White Shield. Clint became aware that Stanley Metcalf was striding beside him, and he heard Metcalf murmur, "Who is he?"

"Chief White Shield."

"What does he want?"

"Hard to tell. A look at you, maybe."

"A look at me? Why on earth would he be interested in me?"

Clint gave the minister an irritated glance. "Ever since White Shield made camp here he's heard stories about the Big Medicine Talker — which is what the Indians call you. He's seen your sister and he's wondered about you. He asked about you again last night, wondering why you hadn't paid him a call. He was some insulted you hadn't. Now maybe his curiosity has got the best of him and he's come to have himself a firsthand look."

When Clint greeted the Indian in sign talk, White Shield's supple brown hands moved quickly in reply. Reading the talk as aptly as Clint did, Judd Smith looked at him and murmured, "Here's a bad thing, boy. Best shy clear of it, I say."

Not answering, Clint gazed across the flat toward the Gros Ventre village. It was bad, all right. Bad as could be. His eyes caught movement off to the east, and turning slightly he saw a pair of riders trailing pack horses top the ridge and move down the slope. They were white men from the look of them, trappers, likely, belatedly heading for beaver streams. At his elbow, Metcalf said impatiently, "What is it? What does he say?"

If he lied, Metcalf would never know. But something in Metcalf's very earnestness made a lie seem a poor answer.

"His wife is sick. He wants you to make her well."

"Ask him what's wrong with her."

Hands flashed question and reply. "It's her belly, he says."

"How long has she been sick?"

"Three days."

"Any pain?"

"Bad pain, he says. First high up on the right side, now it's spread all over."

Lost in thought, Stanley Metcalf was silent a moment,

then he turned abruptly to Ellen, who had come up to stand beside him. "Would you get my medical bag out of the wagon, please."

"You're going?"

"Of course."

"I'm going with you."

"If you like. I may need your help." She hurried off and he turned back to Clint, speaking as casually as if he had just agreed to have a look at an ill white trapper. "Tell him I'll go. May I borrow a horse from one of your men?"

"How bad off is she, do you think?"

"It doesn't sound good. But I'll know more when I've examined her."

"Can you save her or is she likely to die?"

"I can only do my best. The rest is up to the Lord."

"What I'm getting at is this," Clint persisted stubbornly. "If you're pretty sure you can save her, then it's all right to go over there. But if the chances lean strong to her dying, you'd better skip it."

"Why?"

"Because if she dies while you're doctoring her, there's a good chance you won't get out of that village alive."

As Ellen came up with the medical bag, Metcalf gave him an irritated look. "Are you trying to tell me I should let her die unattended simply because of some foolish Indian superstition?"

"Yeah. That's exactly what I'm trying to tell you."

"If I took your advice I'd be a disgrace to my calling."

"If you don't take it you're apt to be dead."

"How would you explain my refusal to White Shield?"

"You're a white medicine man, I'd tell him, and your tricks work best on white people."

"He wouldn't believe that."

"Maybe not. But we'd be rid of him."

Anger flashed in Metcalf's eyes. "Is there no compassion

in you? When you thought my going to the Gros Ventre camp would make it easier for you and Bonneville to trade with them, you begged me to go. But now that a human life is at stake, you insist that I not go."

"There's a difference. The first time you weren't risking your own life. This time you are."

"Isn't it my duty to accept that risk?"

"I can't tell you what your duty is. But mine is to keep you alive. That's just what I'm trying to do."

Ellen's face was pale but her voice was sharp. "Our lives are in stronger hands than yours." She turned to her brother. "I'm ready, Stanley."

Grimly silent, Clint watched Metcalf help Ellen mount, watched him go over and borrow one of the mountain men's horses and climb awkwardly into the saddle, watched the two of them join White Shield and ride out of camp. He turned and spoke quietly to Judd Smith and Zack Parkins. "Look after things here, Zack. Judd, I guess we'd best tag along with them. Comes trouble, maybe we can pull 'em out of it."

Mounting their horses, the two men caught up with the Metcalfs and the Gros Ventre chief. Stanley shot Clint a brief questioning look but did not speak. The pair of trappers which had topped the ridge a few moments ago had kicked their horses into a lope and were angling across the flat with the obvious intent of intercepting them midway between the two camps. Making the men out to be Burn Rapp and Oswald Fram, Clint muttered to Judd, "More trouble, maybe. Keep your eyes open."

Maneuvering their horses and pack animals in such a manner as to block the party's way, Rapp and Fram reined up in front of them. Rapp had unslung his rifle, balancing it across the saddle horn as he gestured for them to halt. They reined in and Clint said, "What's eating you, Burn?"

Rapp pretended not to hear. Addressing himself to the

Reverend Metcalf, he grunted, "Where's this dirty Gros Ventre takin' you?"

"To his village. His wife is ill."

"We got a thing to settle, him and me. An old debt."

"Can't it wait until later?"

"This'll only take a couple of seconds. I want that horse he's ridin', that's all. He stole it from me a few years back. I want it. I want it now."

Clint moved forward, past the Metcalfs, intending to edge in between White Shield and Rapp. The muzzle of Rapp's rifle swung toward him. He stopped. Rapp said, "Stay where you are. I'm dealin' the cards, this round."

"You're asking for trouble, Burn."

"No. I'm jest askin' fer what's rightfully mine." His eyes shifted to the Reverend Metcalf and he said sardonically, "You know what the Bible says about stealin', Parson. Suppose you do some preachin' to White Shield now. Tell him what a black sinner he is an' why he'll go plumb to hell if he don't git off that paint horse and give it back to me right now."

A wary, trapped look had come into the Gros Ventre's face, but Clint knew that Metcalf neither saw it or recognized the potential danger in the present situation.

"I suggest that you come to the village with us," Metcalf said. "After I've looked at the sick woman, I'll do what I can to help you settle your difficulty."

"No," Rapp grunted, swinging his rifle muzzle to bear on White Shield. "We settle it now. Get off that horse, you thievin' devil!"

White Shield moved. Jerking the paint around, he tried to ride clear of the tangle of horses hemming him in. Rapp made a grab for the paint's grass bridle reins, missed and caught White Shield's legging. Quick as a cat, White Shield drew a knife and slashed at him. Rapp shied away, swinging his rifle to bear.

Spurring his horse directly into Rapp's, Clint grappled with the man, tearing him clear of the saddle, falling to the ground with him. The rifle barked harmlessly at the sky. The two men rolled over and over on the ground, heedless of the horses rearing and pitching around them, clawing and pounding at each other, using knees and elbows and feet with the silent fury of animals.

Rapp got his knife out. Clint kicked it out of his hand. Rapp came at him in blind rage, reaching for him with his huge hands. Clint slid to one side, tripped Rapp and sent him tumbling to the ground. Rapp bounced up and came at him again. Clint got his pistol clear, lifted it high and clubbed Rapp to the ground. Rapp rose, staggering blindly. Clint hit him with the pistol again, knocked him down, seized him by the collar of his shirt, pulled him to his feet and brought the heavy pistol barrel down again and again on a face that had suddenly become a solid mass of blood.

There was a rage in Clint such as he had never known before, a rage like a blinding red mist that dimmed hearing and sight and judgment until only the need to strike and strike again until all resistance and all life was gone out of this animal-like thing before him was the only thing that mattered. Somewhere far away he seemed to hear a woman screaming; somewhere men were yelling; somewhere the hoofs of many horses were making the earth tremble. But in his world there was only . . .

"Easy, boy, easy," Judd was saying. "No need to kill him, much as he does deserve it."

Hands were restraining him, pulling him back. There was a weariness in his right arm. He let his arm fall, let the senseless man slide out of his grasp and huddle in a grotesque bulk on the ground. He looked around. Mountain men were rounding up the scattered horses. Outside the Gros Ventre village fifty or sixty fighting men were milling restlessly, while in the Nez Perce camp an equal number of edgy bucks were running their horses back and forth. He drew a long breath and put his pistol away.

"Any harm done?"

"Only to him that asked fer it. But it was touch an' go fer a minute there. Thought we had a first class fight on our hands fer shore."

"Where's White Shield?"

"Yonder. He cut an' run fer home, then when he looked back an' saw you two rasslin' here he pulled up an' watched it from a safe distance. Guess we got him to thank fer clampin' the lid down on his young bucks."

Clint walked over to where Stanley Metcalf stood with his arm around Ellen, who was white-faced and trembling. For a single brief instant her eyes met Clint's, eyes filled with stark horror. Patting her shoulder soothingly, Metcalf stared at Clint. "I've seen some brutal things in my life, but none quite as brutal as that. What on earth came over you?"

"This is a brutal country," Clint answered. "A man does what he has to do."

"But to attack a man with no provocation — "

"If you didn't see the provocation you're stone blind."

"It was trivial. A mere bit of scuffling over a horse that would have settled itself if you hadn't interfered."

A bit of scuffling. Yes, Clint thought wearily, likely that was all Metcalf had seen, missing the knife slash, the rifle muzzle swinging around, the finger tightening on the trigger. Turning to Oswald Fram, who was kneeling over Rapp, Clint made an impatient gesture.

"You can do one of two things with him. Load him on his horse and head out for wherever you're going. Or take him to the Nez Perce camp yonder. Dr. Metcalf will patch him up as soon as he's tended to White Shield's squaw." He turned back to Metcalf. "Or do you want to skip that now?"

"I — " Metcalf ran a hand over his eyes, as if just now recalling the errand on which he had set out, then his jaw tightened and he snapped, "Of course I want to see her. That's what we started out to do, isn't it?"

"Let's ride, then."

# 18

THE MASS of Indians milling about on the plain just outside the Gros Ventre village appeared to include every male member of the band capable of bearing arms. Chief White Shield sat his paint horse in the forefront of the seething group, studying the approaching whites with silent suspicion.

A figure which appeared to be more animal than man was weaving and dancing its way among the Gros Ventres, and wherever it went it created momentary frenzy of sound and movement. It was a grotesque, fiendish-looking figure whose shape and identity Clint could not make out at first, then as his group drew nearer he saw that an Indian had taken the skinned-out pelt and head of an immense white wolf and cunningly made it into a costume which covered him from head to toe, concealing face and body and arms so that it appeared that a snarling wolf was dancing about on its hind legs through the crowd. Medicine bags, skins of small animals, dried bones, strands of human hair and charms of all kinds depended from the costume.

"What on earth is that?" Metcalf exclaimed.

"Their medicine man, Ta-tu-ye," Clint answered.

"Why is he dressed so outlandishly?"

"That's his doctoring costume. Likely he's been dancing and chanting and saying magic words over White Shield's woman all night. Now he's showing off for your benefit and daring you to to put on a better show than he's doing."

"I'm afraid I must decline his challenge," Metcalf said acidly, "and put my faith in calomel, quinine and God."

Chief White Shield suddenly quieted the crowd with a wave of his hand, kicked his horse forward and rode out to meet them. He stared at the Reverend Metcalf for a moment, stared at Clint, then wheeled his horse around and led the way through the crowd and into the village. The Fox danced around the whites, chanting and rattling his charms, croaking insults and curses at the missionary man and woman which were so obscene and foul that even Judd's calloused sensibilities were stirred.

"Suppose I was to accidentally shoot this jigger 'tween the eyes," he muttered to Clint. "Would White Shield regard that as an unfriendly gesture er as good riddance of a public nuisance?"

"Pay it no mind. The Fox is just venting his spleen."

"Blamed if I wouldn't admire t' put a vent in his spleen you could throw a dog through," Judd grunted.

Clint shot a quick glance at Ellen. The chalky whiteness of a few minutes ago had left her face and she seemed to have control of herself now. Without looking at him, she said, "If the worst happens, what do you want us to do?"

"Don't panic and don't try to run. Judd will stand guard outside the lodge. If we get in a tight, you stick close to him. I'll look after Stanley. Don't either of you interfere, no matter what I do."

The lodge in which the sick woman lay was next to the central council tepee where the previous peace-talks had been held. Several old women stood outside. The party dismounted, Judd taking the reins of all four horses and positioning himself to the left of the tepee entrance. White Shield spoke sharply to the women, who, after frightened glances at the Metcalfs, stooped and scuttled into the lodge. The chief made a curt gesture to the Reverend Metcalf, then disappeared within the lodge. Stanley Metcalf looked questioningly at Clint.

"Keep your head," Clint said. "Look her over without touching her first. If you see it's hopeless, stall."

"Are you coming in with us?"

"Yeah. But White Shield may run me out."

Ducking low, they entered the lodge. After the bright sunlight outside, the interior seemed dark and gloomy, but in a few moments their eyes adjusted and they could make out the chunky figure of a woman lying wrapped in blankets with only her face showing, while around her a dozen or so squaws squatted on their heels, rocking and moaning as if they themselves were sharing her pain. White Shield had crossed to the far side of the tepee, where he squatted apart from the others, saying nothing but eying the Reverend Metcalf with harsh black eyes.

Ignoring Clint's advice, Metcalf went to work without the preliminary of even a brief prayer. He put a hand on the woman's forehead, muttered something to Ellen about a fever, then turned down the blankets and picked up a limp wrist to test the pulse. A low growl of suspicion came from White Shield's throat and Clint saw him suddenly rise, fingering his rifle. Metcalf paid him no heed. When he had checked the pulse, he stripped the blankets to below the woman's waist and began prodding at her abdomen with skilled fingers. The woman, who appeared to be in a coma, twisted her head from side to side and uttered a half-conscious moan. White Shield took two quick strides forward, his face black with mistrust. Clint signed for him to have no fears and he stopped, but suspicion still lingered in his eyes.

"The Big Medicine Talker causes her to cry out in pain. This is a bad thing. I will have no more of it."

"It is not your woman who cries out in pain. It is the bad spirit which has crept into her. It is frightened because the Big Medicine Talker has discovered its hiding place."

"How could he discover its hiding place? He did no spirit dance. He made no talk with the unseen ones. He chanted no medicine magic as our own healers do."

"His medicine magic is in his fingers. He passes them over her body and his fingers tell him where the bad spirits dwell."

White Shield fell silent. Metcalf glanced across at Clint, a shadow in his eyes, and Clint said, "What's her trouble?"

"There has been an acute intestinal obstruction which has ruptured," Metcalf said shortly. "The poison has spread all through her abdomen. There is nothing I can do for her."

"She's bound to die, then?"

"I'm afraid so."

Metcalf replaced the blankets, then sat gazing down at the Indian woman with a look of infinite sadness and compassion on his face, as if he were extending her his mute apology because the skills of his profession were great enough to recognize her illness but powerless to effect a cure. Bowing his head, he began to pray. Seeming to sense the white man's sincerity, White Shield questioned Clint no more. He motioned for Clint to leave the lodge. Clint went outside, hunkering down on his heels to the right of the tepee entrance. Judd eyed him quizzically.

"How bad off is she?"

"Too bad to be helped, I'm afraid."

"Where does that leave us?"

Clint shook his head. "That all depends on how White Shield takes it. If the worst happens, we can put a gun to his head and use him as a hostage to get us out of the village."

"Which will make Bonny real unhappy," Judd grunted, "after all the trouble he's gone to tryin' to make friends with these jiggers. Not that I'm objectin', understand. I'd a sight ruther see Bonny unhappy than us dead. But I'm a man with a fondness for statin' facts when there's no other type of amusement handy."

They waited. For a long while they waited, while the Reverend Metcalf's voice murmured on, while the Gros Ventres moved restlessly about, while The Fox chanted and danced and mumbled to the unseen ones. Suddenly Clint was aware that silence had fallen within the lodge. He exchanged looks with Judd. They got to their feet. Ellen Metcalf came outside, her face pinched and white, and after a moment Stanley followed her. Clint looked at him inquiringly. Metcalf shook his head.

"She's dead."

Inside the tepee the squaws were chanting the death song now and a visible stir ran over the waiting Indians, a rumble of sound that rose angrily and then died into abrupt silence as the tall figure of White Shield came out of the lodge entrance and straightened. There was grief on his face as he stood for a moment staring unblinkingly into the sun, the deep, stricken grief of a savage whose loves and hates pulse through him like the blood of life itself, unreasoning, blind. This was no moment in which to try to reach him by logic, Clint knew, for there was no guessing how words could affect him.

Without speaking, Clint motioned for Ellen and Stanley to mount their horses. Beside himself with triumph, The Fox came shuffling out of the crowd and launched into a jeering tirade directed at Stanley Metcalf. The minister turned and stared at the Gros Ventre, not understanding a word but recognizing the insulting tone of the medicine man's voice. Making a visible effort to control himself, he looked at Clint.

"What is this fool saying?"

"That your medicine is weak. That you wanted the woman to die. That you breathed an evil spirit into her body and made her die."

"Does White Shield believe that?"

The tirade of the medicine man had registered on the Gros Ventre chief, that was evident, for he was staring at Metcalf now and listening intently as The Fox harangued the crowd. Bad things would come to pass if the Gros Ventres gave ear to the council of the Bald Chief, The Fox had told them, and now he claimed that his prophecy had come true. White Shield had smoked and talked and sat in council with his enemies against the advice of his medicine man; he had accepted their gifts; he had rejected the healing services of his own kind and brought the Big Medicine Talker into the village to make his wife well. The unseen ones were angry with him and had punished him for his lack of wisdom. Now he could make peace with the unseen ones only by killing the whites — all of them.

The crowd pressed closer, grunting its approval. White Shield was scowling, staring first at The Fox, then at the Metcalfs. Turning away from the crowd, The Fox spoke directly to the chief.

"Does blindness still cloud your eyes? Your woman is dead. Why do you not kill those who made her grow sick and die?"

Still White Shield neither moved nor spoke. In the moment's silence Clint made a sign with his hands that he had something to say. The chief's eyes moved questioningly to him, and after a pause Clint spoke.

"Who is head chief of the Gros Ventres? It is hard for me to know. Many nights I have sat in the council lodge and talked with a brave man with a good heart who said he was the chief. His name was White Shield. But now I am puzzled, for I see a wolf dancing and hear foolish, empty

words from a coward who hides under a head which is not
his own yet talks as if he was the head chief. Who is the
chief of the Gros Ventres? I would like to know."

White Shield's hands flashed and his eyes, filled with a
sudden venom, flicked to The Fox and then moved scorn-
fully off to focus on the horizon. Clint nodded his head.

"Good. White Shield is the chief now, as he always has
been. He is the man who listened to the promises which
the Bald Chief made him. He is the man who accepted the
Bald Chief's gifts. I would have him tell me if the promises
made him by the Bald Chief have been kept or if they have
proved to be lies."

"The words of the Bald Chief have stood on straight legs."

"White Shield owns a paint horse which a white trapper
would have taken from him. When the trapper tried to kill
him, who saved White Shield's life? Was it The Fox? Or
was it a white man who had made White Shield a promise
that no harm would come to him as long as he and his
people camped here in peace? Let White Shield think and
remember."

From the look in the Gros Ventre's eyes, he was doing just
that. Clint dropped the butt of his rifle to the ground,
leaned on its muzzle and stared off at the distant mountains.

"I have had a dream. In this dream I saw a medicine man
whose heart was filled with hate because his chief was making friends with a people whose magic powers were greater
than his own. But the chief was wise. He understood that
the words of the medicine man were foolish words, like a
whirlwind in the dust that rolls dead tumbleweeds along the
ground but affects no man. So he moved the medicine man
away from his right hand and set him on the far side of the
council lodge where no one could hear his foolish words."

White Shield gave a grunt which could have meant anything. Not looking at The Fox, Clint went on.

"In my dream, I saw the medicine man thirsting for revenge. I saw him sitting late at night over his medicine fire, talking with the evil spirits, until at last they agreed to slip into the chief's lodge and breathe a deadly seed into the mouth of the chief's woman while she slept. I saw the seed grow inside the woman until it made her sick. I saw the medicine man come to the chief's lodge and dance around her and say his charms, pretending to heal her, but instead putting a spell on her so that soon she must die. Then I saw the chief angrily cast the medicine man aside and come to his true friends, the whites, and beg them to make her well." Clint paused. "Then I awoke and my dream ended."

The silence was so complete that it seemed no one breathed. Making a sign that he had no more to say, Clint moved toward the horses Judd was holding and murmured, "Let's go while he's still chewing on that."

The Fox went mad. Breaking into an impassioned jabbering, he danced toward Clint with a stiff-legged frenzy. Whirling around, Clint shoved him away. The Fox tumbled to the ground, leaped up and ran to the Metcalfs, shaking his medicine bags in Stanley's face, clutching frantically at Ellen's skirt as she started to mount, raining curses upon them. Clint saw Stanley's face go livid. He heard White Shield grunt a guttural order which The Fox ignored. He saw Stanley reach out, seize The Fox by the breast of his outlandish costume with his left hand, lift the medical bag which he held in his right hand and strike the Indian just under the wolf-head mask with all the strength that was in him.

The Fox went spinning backward, tripped and sprawled at full length. The wolf head had twisted sideways until it was pointed at right angles to his body and as the Indian leaped to his feet one arm was clear of the costume. A knife was in his hand — a knife which he got no chance to use, for before he had taken two strides in the Reverend Metcalf's direction a Hawken barked. The Fox collapsed, twitched once in the dust, and then lay still. White Shield, who had swung his rifle around and shot the medicine man at point-blank range, stared down at him for a moment in bleak hatred and contempt, then he raised his harsh eyes to Clint and the Metcalfs.

"The lying one is dead. It is good." He waved them away. "Go in peace."

# 19

ELLEN METCALF had learned long ago that she could not afford to indulge herself in such purely feminine luxuries as fainting or going into a fit of hysterics whenever she happened to witness something unpleasant. So she did neither now, but as they rode back to the Nez Perce camp her mind was numb and dazed with shock. Little more than an hour had passed since Stanley had finished his prayer for a safe journey, yet during that hour she had seen more brutality and violence than she had experienced in her entire lifetime prior to this day.

She had seen two white men fight like animals, with one clubbing the other into insensibility. She had seen her own brother strike a fellow human being in anger for the first time in his life. And she had seen one man kill another.

It was so much to absorb in such a brief space of time that she momentarily lost her grip on reality. For no reason at all she suddenly recalled a church social back home when a young lady parishioner of delicate sensibilities had gone into a nervous frenzy because an overboisterous, clumsy young man had enticed her to go for a stroll with him, paused in a shadowed spot, grabbed her and tried to embrace her. What a scene that had brought on!

Ellen could recall every detail of it even now: the girl running into the parlor, screaming hysterically; the party stopping dead and all eyes turning to the girl as she collapsed in a chair, her body rigid with shock, her eyes closed tight, her face completely without color as she screamed over and over, "He tried to kiss me! He tried to kiss me! Oh, I think I'm going to faint!"

And faint she had.

Ellen restrained a foolish impulse to giggle. So silly to faint because a man tried to kiss you! Now if he had tried to kill . . .

Sitting straight and rigid in the saddle, she suddenly became aware of the wide spill of sun-splashed land around her, the Indians restless to be on the move, the mountain men making last-minute adjustments to packs, the teams hitched to the heavily loaded wagon, the injured trapper lying on the ground while his partner fussed over him. She took a deep breath. She knew why she had remembered that silly girl and she was not at all proud of herself for it. She had been desperately seeking the moral strength to bolster her own faltering courage and had found it in the most contemptible of ways — by reaching into the past and finding someone weaker than herself on whom to heap scorn.

Her horse had stopped and Stanley was giving her a hand down, anxiety in his eyes. "Are you all right, Ellen?"

"Yes."

"That was a terrible thing for you to see."

"You can't shelter me from things any more, Stanley. Please don't try."

"You're a brave woman, Ellen."

"No. But I can do what has to be done." Her eyes went to the man on the ground. "We must tend to him."

Burn Rapp was in bad shape, for his scalp and face had been viciously bruised and lacerated by the pistol barrel, but

except for his partner no one seemed to care. She helped
Stanley cleanse, stitch up and bandage his wounds. An Indian
child wandered over and squatted beside her, watching with
alert curiosity as Stanley's skilled hands worked. When Stanley momentarily laid his needle down on a clean cloth beside him, the child reached out with a grubby, dirty hand,
picked it up and examined the shining piece of curved steel
with absorbed fascination. Oswald Fram snatched it out of
his hand and gave him a shove.

"Git out of here!"

The child went sprawling. Ellen started to rebuke Fram
sharply, then as the boy got up, grinning amiably, she
recognized him. Her tongue froze in her mouth. The wide
brown eyes were staring straight into hers, trusting and
friendly, and she knew that the boy remembered her. Her
voice faltered.

"You may watch, Daniel. But you mustn't touch things."

The boy grinned, not understanding her words nearly as
well as he understood the gentleness in her voice. Stanley
looked up with a frown. "Were you speaking to me?"

"No, — I was speaking to Daniel."

"Daniel?"

Her brother's gaze moved from her to the boy, then back.
He smiled. "You have a little Indian friend already, I see.
Where did you pick him up?"

She bit her lip. "Daniel is Clint's son. We met several
days ago."

The smile left Stanley's face. "Clint's *son*, you say?"

"Yes."

"The mother?"

"She's dead. That's all I know."

"Why haven't you told me this before?"

"Because I — " She broke off. "It isn't in the least important, Stanley. Not to me, at any rate. Let's finish our
job here. Everyone seems anxious to travel."

She helped Stanley put the dressings in place and bind

them there with strips of white cotton cloth wound around Rapp's head so that only his eyes and mouth showed. He was conscious now but seem stupefied and only vaguely aware of his surroundings. Thinking it best that he be kept quiet for a time, Stanley mixed a draught of laudanum, lifted Rapp's head and spooned it between his unresisting lips. The opiate took effect almost at once and Stanley gently lowered the trapper to the ground as his eyes closed and his body sagged.

Ellen heard a step and looked up to find Clint gazing down at the unconscious man. Daniel jumped up and ran to him, laughing, pointing at the bandages which swathed Rapp's head and chattering in the Nez Perce tongue as his quick hands made motions imitating the way Stanley had sewn up the wounds. Clint gave the boy a quiet command and Daniel went scuttling off. Clint looked at Stanley.

"All finished?"

"Yes."

"Let's hit the trail, then. We've lost a lot of daylight."

Turning on his heel, he was starting to walk away when Stanley got to his feet and angrily caught him by the shoulder. "What about Rapp?"

"You've patched him up, haven't you? That's more than he deserves. We'll leave him here."

"With no one to look after him?"

"Oswald can tend to him."

"Oswald is no doctor. The man is badly hurt and is going to require professional care for a long time. If you callously go off and leave him, you're no better than a murderer."

Even that seemed not to touch Clint. She saw him turn and gaze at Oswald Fram, who was squatting sullenly on the ground beside Rapp. "Where were you heading?"

"The Three Forks country."

"Think you can behave yourself if I let you trail along with us as far as the Portneuf?"

"Git one thing straight, Clint. This was Burn's play, not mine. I warned him it'd buy us nothin' but trouble."

Crossing to Rapp, Clint stooped and seized the unconscious trapper under the armpits. "Get his feet. We'll dump him in the wagon."

Seething with an anger that was close to hate, Ellen watched Clint as he and Fram picked Rapp up and carried him to the wagon. Stanley mounted to the wagon seat and unwrapped the reins from the brake handle. Someone had tied her horse to a rear wheel of the wagon and as she walked toward it Clint untied it and then turned to her, eying her quietly.

"You look a bit upset."

"I'll be all right," she said stiffly.

"Sure you will. But I think it'd be best if you rode in the wagon and rested for a while. Your horse can trail behind."

Because she did feel weak in the knees and was none too sure she would not suddenly burst into tears as a relief from the fiddle-string tension within her, she had been considering doing that very thing. Now she felt she would rather die.

"I prefer to ride the horse."

He offered his hand to help her up. She ignored it, awkwardly got her foot in the stirrup and swung up, almost falling as the gray shied, then clumsily finding her seat as Clint expertly snubbed the horse up short. He handed her the reins.

"Easy does it, Ellen. We've a long piece of trail ahead of us."

She would not look at him, and after a moment he strode away. She sat staring fixedly down at the hoof-slashed turf, the anger in her slowly fading until all she felt was an uncaring numbness. This was a moment she had long looked forward to, this setting out on the last leg of their journey west, with the Indians among whom she and her brother were to spend the rest of their lives all around her, with a fine horse under her, with new and interesting country ahead. This was a moment to lift the heart and soul.

But she felt nothing, nothing.

Far ahead, she heard a faint cry. She raised her eyes. There was movement. Mountain men, Indians, pack animals, horse herds, milk cows. Movement beginning some distance away then spreading like wind-ripples over a still pond. Stanley leaned forward on the wagon seat and shouted at the horses, slapping their backs with the reins. Leather creaked, harness chains clanked, muscles strained, then the wooden wheels were turning, turning.

The gray moved under her, breaking at once into a smooth jogtrot that took it past the wagon and straining teams, past the ponies laden with lodgepoles and tepee coverings, past the fat squaws holding children on placid horses, past the trappers' pack animals, on out toward the forefront of the party where the gray seemed to feel it was his duty and privilege to travel.

Something stirred within her. Sitting straighter in the saddle, she took a long, deep breath and fixed her eyes on the rolling gray line of the horizon to the southwest. She wondered what lay beyond.

# PART TWO

# the alien flag

## 20

STANLEY METCALF was too practical-minded a man to waste either time or energy speculating on what might lie beyond the next rise of land. The wagon wheels were turning. That was enough. Just keep the horses moving, the wheels turning.

This was dry, treeless sagebrush country, with the river lost behind them now and foothills to the west rising into a distant line of mountains. As the morning passed the route swung more and more to the left, until by noontime the angle of the sun told him that they were heading directly south across a rolling, barren country which seemed to have no end to it. He was puzzled. Knowing that the party would be guided by men who knew the lay of the land intimately, he had paid little attention to the maps Clint had drawn for him on the ground or the details of trails, mountains and river valleys which Captain Bonneville had explained to him, but he did recall that there had been much talk about the Snake River. It lay westerly and it ran westerly, he knew, yet the direction in which they were now traveling was consistently south.

He saw Clint, Two Bears and Eagle-With-One-Wing

sitting their horses on a knoll, staring off toward the west, the hands of the Indians moving in animated argument. He stopped the wagon and got down to stretch his legs and quench his thirst with a couple of swallows of water from a canteen. Clint and the two Indian chiefs rode over to the wagon, still arguing amongst themselves. Metcalf looked up at Clint inquiringly.

"Something wrong?"

"They're raising a fuss over the direction we're going. They want to cut straight west over the mountains."

"Isn't that the way we ought to go?"

Clint jerked his head at the wagon. "Dragging that contraption along, the way we'd ought to go and the way we have to go are two different things."

"I was under the impression that we would follow Snake River and that it ran through flat desert country."

"We should and it does," Clint said, nodding. "But first we got to get to it." Turning in the saddle, he pointed at a blue line of mountains to the north and west. "Yonder's the Snake. If we were traveling Indian fashion we could reach it in three, four days by riding due west across the mountains. But no wagon will make that trail unless you figure out some way to put wings on it."

"I won't part with the wagon. You know that."

Clint turned and spoke to the two Indians, who argued with him for a few moments, then wheeled their horses around and rode off. They did not appear at all pleased. Metcalf watched them go, then looked up at Clint and said, "Well?"

"They'll stick with us till we hit the Snake at the mouth of the Portneuf. After that — well, we'll see."

## 21

THE CATTLE were a nuisance. Even Stanley Metcalf admitted that, though it had been his idea to bring them along in the first place. Originally he had bought ten head in Independence, a mixed lot which included three cows of a good milking breed, three more of a beef strain, two yearling heifers and two sturdy young bulls. The animals were to be the progenitors of the beef and dairy herds which in a few years he hoped would supply the mission with milk, butter, cheese and beef, thus teaching his Indian wards the practical value of animal husbandry. From his readings he knew that the Nez Perces were already experts at raising and breeding horses; the Lewis and Clark journals had praised them highly for their skills in that field. It seemed logical to assume that a people and a country so admirably suited to horse-raising would adopt dairying and beef-growing with little or no trouble.

He had expected an animal or two to be lost on the way out, even with the best of care. That was why he had made sure that there were two bulls and a pair of young heifers as well as the cows, which the seller in Independence assured him had already been bred and would be dropping calves in the fall. If an animal should die, it would in all likelihood be one of the mature cows, he reasoned, for they were the least suited to the hardships of the trail. But his assumption proved faulty, as any assumption is apt to do when it concerns such contrary beasts as domesticated cattle. Every last cow reached rendezvous safely, thin as rails, dry as stones, but alive. The pair of sturdy young bulls and the two healthy, frisky young heifers had all been lost along the way.

The first bull had died back along the Platte, having made the fatal mistake of challenging a buffalo bull twice its size. The second had gotten bogged down in quicksand at a river crossing and was so badly crippled by the time it could be pulled out there was nothing to do but kill and butcher it. One of the heifers had had an unfortunate meeting with a bear in a plum thicket on the Sweetwater. The other had been converted into a veritable pincushion of arrows by a boisterous band of young Crow bucks two days short of rendezvous, their excuse being that they had mistaken the animal for some new variety of antelope.

But the six cows lived on. Three placid weeks of good grazing, plenty of water and rest had filled out the wrinkles in their hides and erased from their bovine memories every single good traveling habit that had been pounded into them on the trail from Independence to rendezvous. They had developed an intense dislike for Indians. This was probably because the Indian boys in camp had pestered them constantly during rendezvous, riding them, roping them, swinging from their horns and tails, goading them into making awkward charges which the nimble-footed youngsters gleefully evaded at the last instant. They disliked the searing heat of noonday, the sagebrush which scratched their flanks, the cactus spines which stuck in their lips when they reached down for an all too infrequent mouthful of tinder-dry grass. They bawled because the sharp lava rocks which underlay the fine-powdered gray soil cut their feet; they bawled because there was no water to drink during the day-long dry drives; they bawled at the end of the day because the water that was found was so impregnated with alkali that it burnt their mouths.

Keeping them moving was a full-time job for one man, but Metcalf was not long in discovering that the task was one which neither Nez Perce nor mountain man would endure for more than an hour at a stretch. Both classes of men seemed to regard cow-herding as beneath their dignity. Indian boys could not be trusted, for a cow to them was of even less importance than a dog and was so treated. Metcalf himself was tied down to the wagon, except on those rare occasions when he was able to persuade Ellen to drive it for an hour or two, or when he grew so desperate with concern for the cattle that he turned the reins over to a mountain man. This he did on three different occasions — and regretted every one.

Beartracks Weaver, Hugh Marlow, Luke Young — each in turn obligingly took over the wagon when requested to. Each trapper tried to outdo the others in sheer recklessness, setting a beeline course through the waist-high sagebrush, lashing the teams into a run and pounding pell-mell toward the forefront of the party. Rocks, gullies, sidling slopes meant nothing at all to them. All had the bravado, if not the skill, of born stagedrivers. The fact that they lacked a stage road only served to make the sport more fun. When they mounted the wagon seat, they wanted action — and action they got, let shattered wheels and broken reaches fall where they might.

If Metcalf had been a man of a more suspicious nature, he would have soon reached the conclusion that there was a conspiracy afoot to lose the cows and wreck the wagon so that those two impediments to faster travel would no longer be hinderance to the party. But he was fair-minded enough to realize that there was no malice in either the Indians or the mountain men. It was simply that neither cared a hang whether or not cows or wagon got to Oregon. If he persisted in bringing both along, that was all right with them. Let him look after them. If he wanted their assistance, they would hustle the fool things along in their own haphazard way, and if cows and wagon couldn't stand the gaff why that just proved the things weren't made for this kind of country.

They had been on the trail a week now, still bearing south across a gray-green sea of sagebrush that stretched interminably ahead. Reaching a creek with a dribble of brackish but drinkable water in it, they made camp in mid-afternoon, and as Metcalf halted the wagon he was exasperated to discover that the cows were missing again. Burn Rapp, who was mending slowly, had sat up these past two days, resting on the seat beside him, not speaking, brooding on the sun-hazed distance with an unnatural lack of interest that made Metcalf suspect the blows which had rained down on his head had seriously injured his brain. There had been a dullness in his eyes, a film, as if he saw what passed before him but understood none of it. His condition had worried Metcalf, for he knew that if Rapp ever were to become his normal self again he should soon be showing signs of making a recovery.

Swinging down to the ground, Metcalf held out a hand to assist Rapp down, speaking to him as gently as he would have to a child. "Get down, Burn. We'll camp here."

Surprisingly, Rapp ignored the hand. "I ain't no cripple," he grunted, put a hand on the wheel and vaulted to the ground.

He lit on his feet fair enough, but lost his balance and sank down on a knee and a hand. Metcalf watched him closely. Rapp crouched there for a moment, rubbing his eyes, shaking his head as if to clear it of a sudden dizziness. Metcalf moved to him and took him by the elbow.

"Better go easy. You're not up to such acrobatics yet."

"I stumbled."

"Yes."

"I — " Rapp broke off and stared at him, an odd light in his eyes. Metcalf smiled reassuringly, crossed over to the horses and began unbuckling their harness. Suddenly Rapp strode toward him, shoved him roughly away from the horses and muttered, "Reckon I can do that."

Metcalf watched Rapp work. The trapper's hands were clumsy and awkward and Rapp seemed to have trouble making them behave as he wanted them to. But time would remedy that, Metcalf felt sure. Time, rest and the inexplicable way God had in making the body heal its own hurts.

Recalling the missing cows, Metcalf decided it would be less trouble to ride back and look for them himself than to ask some of the Indians or mountain men to do it. He went to the back of the wagon and untied Rapp's saddled horse, which, with the four pack animals belonging to Rapp and Fram, had trailed behind the wagon all day while Oswald Fram rode off from the line of march in search of fresh meat. As he started to mount, Fram rode up, steadying the gutted carcass of an antelope slung over the saddle horn before him. The trapper's eyes flicked toward the front of the wagon, then came back to Metcalf.

"You put Burn to work, I see."

"No. It was his own idea."

Fram's plain, stolid face showed pleasure. "Isn't that a good sign?"

"A very good sign."

"Way he's been actin' lately, I been 'feard fer him. 'Feard somethin' inside his head was busted so bad he'd never come out of it." Fram grinned and patted the antelope carcass. "I kilt us some fresh meat."

"So I see. It will certainly be welcome."

"You ridin' off someplace?"

"The cows have strayed again. I'm off to find them."

"Who was supposed to be tendin' to 'em?"

"That's precisely the trouble," Metcalf said dryly. "Everybody promises to look after them — but no one does."

"Want me to go back an' look fer 'em?"

"I really don't mind the ride. A saddle is a welcome change after sitting on that hard wagon seat all day."

"Well, if you're set on goin' the least I can do is keep you company. Burn can dress out the meat and git supper started. Jest you sit tight till I tell him."

Fram rejoined him presently and they rode back along the trail, searching for more than an hour before they found the missing cows. The animals were lying down in a draw, resting, and it was only with considerable urging that the two men were able to prod them to their feet. As they stood bawling plaintively, Fram swung to the ground and examined each animal closely, looking at its mouth, lifting each hoof. Mounting his horse again, he shook his head.

"Less'n we take care of them critters soon, we'll lose 'em shore as sin. Their mouths are so full of cactus spines they can't hardly eat an' their feet ain't nothin' but a plumb mass of cuts an' bruises. Let's see if we can't ease 'em on to camp. I'll work on 'em this evenin' an' try to get 'em in shape to travel."

"What can you do?"

"Oh, I know an Injun trick er two."

"I'll be grateful for anything you can do."

Darkness came late at this time of year and Fram used the remaining daylight hours after they got the cows to camp to mix a salve of bacon grease, gunpowder and tobacco. He cut and shaped socklike leather shoes for the cattle's sore feet. Roping each animal in turn, he tied it down, pulled out the cactus spines with a pair of wooden tweezers, applied salve liberally to both mouth and feet, then tied on the leather shoes.

"Injuns shoe their horses thisaway sometimes when they're ridin' over rocky country," he explained. "The shoes don't last more'n a few days but a man kin always make more. Cows ain't got much sense, but I reckon these here fool critters will learn to shy clear of cactus. Anyhow we'll be out of this ornery dry country 'fore long. They'll be able to git good grass an' water when we hit Bear River."

"Will they last that long?"

Fram grinned. "Shore, Doc. Jest you leave 'em to me."

The piece of Bear River that ran northwesterly made for a week's fine going. A wide, flat valley winding among tall mountains. Good rich soil, belly-deep grass, plenty of pure, sweet water. Game aplenty. Thickets filled with berries. Wood for the camp fires.

The Nez Perces were content to loaf along, letting their horses eat their fill after the lean days of the barren country they had just crossed. The cows began to find life worth living again now that their mouths and feet had healed. And Oswald Fram, who had quietly taken over their care, brooded as he had not brooded in years.

Riding along under the warm sun with the cattle moving slowly before him through the wind-rippled grass, he found himself troubled by strange thoughts. Queer to see cows out here. Made a body realize how big and empty the country was. Seeing horses or trappers or Injuns or wild game moving across the valley, he'd never gave any thought to the land's size or emptiness before, because he was used to seeing such things here. But unfamiliar objects like cows and wagons made him recollect the East, where he'd come from, and suddenly he saw the whole view on a different scale.

Take the chunk of valley reaching from here to off yonder where the river took a left hand bend between them two blue-hazed peaks. Twenty mile, it'd be. Back in Kentucky where he'd been born and raised there'd be a hundred fenced-off farms and a sizable village dotting the space from here to yon bend, roads leading every which way, churches and schools, bridges over the river and boats on it, more livestock and people than you could count, and a courthouse in the village with a roomful of records just to keep track of who owned which square foot of ground. Out here there was nothing but twenty miles of grass. And twenty more beyond the bend. And twenty more beyond that. And a thousand more valleys like this one scattered all over the West, just as fertile, just as empty.

He got to thinking about the Reverend Metcalf and his sister and the job they'd tackled. Sure wasn't much hymn-singing, hell-and-damnation preaching or like foolishness about that pair. Far as he could see, neither one of 'em had tried to do any converting yet. Sure, Miss Metcalf was spending most all her time with the Injuns, but the main thing she seemed to be up to was making friends with 'em and learning to speak their lingo. Had a notion she was going to get the Nez Perce tongue down in writing, he'd heard her tell her brother, put some religious tunes to it and learn the kids how to sing like young 'uns did back home in Sunday School. Next she was going to translate a chapter or two of the New Testament into Injun jabber and learn them as showed a knack for it how to read, so's they could see for themselves what the Good Book had to say.

As for the Reverend Metcalf himself, it'd had always been a problem for Fram to figure out what to call him, him being both a doctor and a parson. But whatever you called him, you had to admit he was sure a man with a good, sensible head on him, a strong pair of hands that he wasn't too proud to dirty at any chore, and gumption enough to stand up for what he thought was right no matter what odds were lined up against him.

He was sure totin' a sizable load in that wagon. A queer assortment of stuff it was, too, for a preacher to be hauling. A couple of plows, a dozen hoes, half a dozen axes and shovels, a full set each of carpenter and blacksmith tools. And seeds of all kinds. Wheat, barley, corn, vege-tables, melons. Why, packed away in sawdust he even had a whole boxful of dried-up potato slices, each one with an eye in it, which he claimed would keep fine till next spring and would sprout and grow when he stuck them in the ground. That was a trick Fram had never heard of before; he wasn't at all sure it would work and had told the parson so, but Metcalf had just smiled.

"Drop around next fall and you'll see. I'll serve you all the baked potatoes you can eat, smothered in butter, with sweet milk to wash them down and fresh hot bread made from wheat we have raised and ground into flour ourselves."

Fresh bread. Milk. Baked potatoes smothered in butter. Fram thought back, trying to recollect just when it was he'd last eaten such things. Years. Too many years. He couldn't help wondering how the Nez Perces would take to such civilized stunts as farming and cattle-raising. And how on earth would Metcalf ever get all the work done he had lined out for himself, with nobody around to help him but Injuns? How would he get trees cut and a cabin and church and school built, ground plowed, crops in and tended, cattle looked after and milked, while at the same time he kept up with his preaching and doctoring, and nobody there to give him a hand but his sister and a pack of wild, ignorant Injuns whose language he was only beginning to learn? He wasn't counting on Clint or any of the mountain men for help, that much Fram was sure of, because they had other fish to fry. Soon as they'd seen the Metcalfs through the Nez Perce country, they'd likely just dump 'em there, leaving 'em to fend for themselves while they went chasing off for beaver plews and whatever other chores Bonny had laid out for Clint to do.

Fram squinted off into the sun-splashed distance. Metcalf would likely welcome another pair of hands, all right. Maybe be glad to pay out some cash wages. But there was no point thinking about that. Not when Clint had made it clear that the Portneuf was as far as he intended to let

him and Burn tag along with the party; not when him and
Burn owed Sublette a season's trapping; not when Burn
had this fool notion in his head he was bound to risk the
Three Forks country, Blackfoot or no . . .

Hell! Might as well face up to it — it *was* a fool notion.
At the piddling price Sublette had offered to pay them for
pelts, they could take all the horses they owned and load
'em down with plews till their legs bowed and the best they
could hope for would be to break even. What sense was
there in risking their topknots for that? None at all, that
he could see. He shifted uneasily in the saddle. Trouble
was, Burn was so damned bull-headed, once a notion
stuck in his craw. Yet maybe if the thing was put to him
the right way. . . .

That night, after supper was over and dark had fallen
and the Metcalfs had gone wandering off to the Nez Perce
section of camp, he made his try. Waiting till Rapp had
settled himself down in front of the fire and had his pipe
going, Fram poked at the embers for a spell, then without
looking at Rapp he muttered, "Reckon we'll make the
Portneuf in a week or so."

"Yeah."

"You feelin' better?"

"Nothin' wrong with me."

"I'm glad to hear that. Real glad." Fram stared into
the fire, finding it hard to go on. It had always been Rapp
who had the ideas when it came to making plans, Rapp
who had spoken out and said what they were going to do.
You got used to a thing like that, it was hard to turn it
around. "I been thinkin', Burn. This notion we had to
try the Three Forks country . . . "

"The hell with that," Rapp grunted.

Fram stared at him. "What'd you say?"

"To hell with trappin' the Three Forks country. I got
other plans now."

"Like which?"

Absently Rapp touched his face with gently exploring fingers, a habit he had fallen into of late, tracing the network of healing flesh ridges on his forehead and cheekbones. "I been talkin' to Doc Metcalf. He wants us to go on to Oregon with him. He done me a favor. I figure it's only right I do him one."

"You know it's queer, but I was thinkin' that same way."

"Sure. I've knowed that fer days. It's been wrote on yore face, plain as print."

"What about Clint?"

"What's he got to do with it?"

"He says the Portneuf is as far as he'll let us go. We can't buck that, less'n he changes his mind."

"No, we can't buck Clint. But Metcalf can. An' will."

There was one thing Fram had to know. "Jest tell me this, Burn. Is it on account of Clint you want to go on to Oregon?"

"Supposin' I said it was?"

"Guess it wouldn't matter. But I wanted to know."

Burn Rapp stared across the fire, out into the darkness in the direction of the mountain men's section of camp, and he was silent for some moments. Then he said, "He knows it's goin' to happen, soon or late. Jest me an' him, alone somewheres. Guns er knives er bare hands, it's all the same to me. But we got to be alone, with nobody near to stop it till it's done. I'll wait a long time fer it. A long time."

## 22

THE LAST time Clint had passed this way the only signs of human habitation on the plain where the Portneuf River joined the Snake had been half a dozen ragged tepees. The Indians had been Bannocks, he recalled, a thin and hungry lot after a long hard winter and so desperate for food that they had just that morning killed a gaunt old he-grizzly bear that had come wandering down out of the hills after its winter's nap.

He'd been more than a little meat-hungry himself, he remembered, and had been glad enough to trade a couple of handfuls of the pemmican he was carrying for a small chunk of bear haunch. Wasn't much question who got the best of the trade. Dirty and old and rock-hard though it was, the pemmican, which had been made out of dried salmon and berries, at least had some nourishment in it, but the bear meat — from whence all fat had long since vanished — could have been boiled, roasted or fried for a month and still would have remained as tough and tasteless as a chunk of saddle leather. Other than exercising his jaws, it had been a miserable excuse for meat.

The Indian tepees were gone now. But there on the first rise of land back a way from where the two rivers met sat the new trading post, square, ugly, its timber and mud walls as solidly uncompromising in appearance as the bleak hills beyond. Over it, whipped to and fro by the hot wind, fluttered a homemade American flag.

"Wal, I'll be damned!" Zack Parkins grunted. "Ole Nat went an' done it, didn't he, jest like he swore he'd do!"

"Looks that way."

"How come him to call it Fort Hall?"

"Named it after one of the men backing him, I hear."

Zack spat thoughtfully. "Blamed if I can see any sense in buildin' a post hyar. Kin you?"

There was sense to it, good sense. The post had been built by Nat Wyeth a year ago as a gesture of anger and defiance, Clint knew, after the fur company which had contracted for the load of trade goods and supplies he had brought out from St. Louis reneged on their promise. Like Bonneville, Wyeth had a passion for rolling stones into the gardens of his rivals, and because of the strategic location of this post he had succeeded in making a pile of trouble not only for the American traders who had tried to cut his throat but also for the Hudson's Bay Company. Like water running downhill, trade drained to the nearest outlet. This was the only post on the entire Snake River watershed, which was a sizable piece of fine beaver country. If Wyeth could stick it out long enough the trade would be bound to come to him.

"Let's go down and pay our respects. Maybe they'll have news of Bonneville."

Captain Thing, the New Englander whom Wyeth had left in charge of the twelve men who made the post their trapping and trading base, was delighted to see them. The fort boasted a few crude comforts. Seating his visitors on stools before an ax-hewn table in his living quarters, Captain Thing dug out tin cups and a jug of rum. A genial man whose normal tone of voice was a bull-like roar, he walked about the room with feet widespread and body hunched forward, as if constantly fearful that the ground under him would heave upward or sway sideways in the next instant. In fact he looked so strikingly like a man who had spent more time on a quarter-deck than on dry land that Clint could not keep from asking the question that had been in his mind from the moment they first shook hands.

"Have you ever been to sea, Captain Thing?"

"Aye, that I have." Captain Thing drained his cup, set it down on the table and grinned as he reached for the rum jug. "I came by my title honestly, lad, which is more than ye can say for the dry-land captains which this benighted land is so blasted overrun with."

"How did you happen to trade salt water for sagebrush?"

Captain Thing drank deeply, setting his cup down with a sigh. "'Tis a long story. Likely ye'd not believe it anyway if I told it just the way it happened, so I'll not trouble ye with details. All I'll say is this: Nat Wyeth has a way about him, once he sets his mind to a thing. I love a dollar as well as the next Yankee and there seemed to be money in it."

"In what?" Zack asked curiously.

"Why, there was talk of furs, as I recall, and cargoes of salmon to be salted and shipped from the Columbia to New England, an' brigs to be sailin' back and forth around the Horn, 'twixt Oregon and Boston. There was a scheme that had to do with boats on wheels which could cross plains and rivers with equal ease. It all seemed to call for a seafaring man." The captain fell silent, his head cocked to one side, his eyes focused on invisible distances where wide seas rolled. "And here I lie becalmed in a benighted desert." He reached for the jug. "Ah, well, so long as the rum holds out . . . "

"Where is Wyeth now?" Clint asked.

Captain Thing gestured vaguely to the west. "Out there. He's gone to the lower Columbia, the bucko has, where they do say the great sea tides can be felt a hundred miles up the river. Gone an' left me becalmed —"

"What's he doing?"

"Saltin' salmon, skinnin' beaver an' pesterin' His Sovereign Majesty in every way he can thing of. His scheme was to set up shop directly across the river from the Hudson's Bay Company trading post so's the Britishers could get full enjoyment watchin' him steal fish an' beaver right out from under their stuck-up noses. Oh, he's a brash one, Nat Wyeth is! And I wish to Heaven I was with him!"

"He has a ship in the river?"

"Aye, that was the plan. A brig out of Boston. An' I sit here becalmed — "

"When did you see Captain Bonneville?"

"A week past. He only stayed the night." Captain Thing chuckled. "He's a fit mate for Nat, your Frenchman is. Did ye hear of the brawl him an' his boys had with the band of Britishers they met two days west of here?"

Clint shook his head. "No. What happened?"

"Why, the way I got the tale from one of my men that chanced by in time to partake of the fun, your Captain Bonneville was headin' down the Snake when he ran smack into a band of Hudson's Bay Company men cruisin' east for what beaver they could steal or trade the Indians out of. They'd come from that new British post Hudson's Bay just built at the mouth of the Boise — "

Clint frowned. "The company has a new post on the Boise, you say?"

"That they have. Started buildin' it just as soon as they found out Nat had built this place. Oh, he's throwed a scare into them, lad, make no mistake about that. There's a fine brawl shapin' up in Oregon 'twixt John Bull an' Uncle Sam. I'll lay you odds it'll come to war, soon or late. But as I was sayin', Bonneville met this party of Britishers two days west of here. They made camp side by side. An' that night the fireworks began."

"There was a fight?"

"Well, there was an' there wasn't, if ye know what I mean. That is to say, Bonneville and the Britisher which happened to be leadin' the company party was as sweet as sweet could be to each other when it come to talkin' face to face. But the minute one's back was turned, the other went right to work. The Britisher did his unholy damndest to hire away Bonny's men, an' Bonny did likewise. They was each itchin' to find out what the other one was up to, an' the lies that were spread around were a wonder to behold. The way it came to me, it was a stand-off, both ways."

"Ol' Bonny kin lie with the best of 'em when he puts his mind to it," Zack said loyally. "Yes sir, he kin lie real good. But I shore didn't know he could keep up with a Britisher." He grinned at Captain Thing. "When did the fightin' start?"

"I'm comin' to that, lad. Pass me your cup." When he had replenished the cups again, Captain Thing leaned back on his stool and squinted off into the distance. "It was the honey that started it, you might say."

"Honey?" Clint said.

"Aye. That and the alcohol. There's a potent mix, if ever I heard tell of one."

"Sounds like it would be."

"What happened was this. The Britisher invited Bonny and his men over to his camp for supper. Not to be out-done, Bonny said he'd bring something to warm their bellies. All he had was a gallon or two of alcohol which was so low-grade an' ornery he hadn't even dared feed it to the heathen Indians, for fear they'd scalp everybody at rendezvous. But he had a keg of honey, too, an' he got to thinkin' that maybe the sweet would take out some of the poison, so he mixed the stuff together an' went to the party."

"An' that was when the fightin' began?" Zack said.

"Aye, that was the start of it. Oh, it was just friendly fightin', you understand, with nobody hurt permanent. But it was one fine night of howlin' and brawlin', of that ye can be sure."

"Who got the best of it?"

"Why, the Americans, of course, who else? At least they were able to travel next day whilst the Britishers wasn't. Last my man saw of Captain Bonny, he was headin' west next mornin' with all hands aboard, though there did appear to be some achin' heads and tall moanin'. The Britishers were still lyin' in camp, greener than seasick pigs. Died there, for aught I know. At least nobody's raised sail of 'em since."

From the looks of the captain, Clint guessed he would be quite happy to rattle on for the rest of the day, and from the looks of Zack *he* would be content to sit and listen for just as long as the rum held out. But it was high time they were getting on. Shaking hands with Captain Thing and promising to talk more with him later, Clint prodded Zack to his feet, nudged him out to their horses, and they mounted and rode back up the valley of the Portneuf to meet the slow-moving party they had left behind. Glancing at Zack, who was looking quite mellow and at peace with the world, Clint decided it would be best to camp a couple of miles up the valley from the fort. More firewood, grass and shelter from the hot, dust-laden winds there. And a sight less rum.

Jogging along beside him, Zack slouched comfortably in the saddle, squinting ahead at the rising streamers of dust which marked the slow movement of the party down-valley toward them. He belched, then grinned at Clint. "Mighty fine rum the cap'n served us, wa'n't it?"

"Don't let Stanley Metcalf get a whiff of your breath."

"Wal, don't you let Miss Metcalf whiff yourn."

Clint laughed. "It wouldn't matter much if she did. I'm afraid I'm lost beyond redemption as far as she's concerned!"

"That's a fool thing to say. Why, from the things I've heard her say about you an' the way I've seen her look at you — "

"What has she said and how has she looked at me?" Clint asked sharply.

"Oh, you know how women are," Zack answered vaguely.

" 'Tain't so much the words they say as it is how them words come out of their mouths. An' how's a body to describe a look? It's — wal, it's jest a look."

"You're not making much sense."

"Reckon the rum's addled my tongue some," Zack muttered. He scowled thoughtfully, as if not quite sure the words had come out right. He tried again. "Rum's addled my tongue some. Now thar's a mouthful fer ye. Jest try it an' see iff'n ye can make it come out straight."

"What would that prove?"

"Nothin'. Nothin' at all. Jest happened to be a stray thought that come to me. Rum fills a man with stray thoughts, seems like. Why, jest now I had another one, which was what a real interestin' year this past 'un has been. Think of all the sights we've seen. Californy an' the Spaniards. Milk cows an' missionaries at rendezvous. A wagon goin' whar no wagon never went before an' a real live sea captain becalmed in the middle of a benighted desert. Why, this country out hyar is gettin' so plumb run over with all sorts of curiosities a body's bound to wonder what in tarnation will turn up next."

Zack was still talking when they met the Nez Perces, though what he was saying Clint had long since ceased to pay any mind. Because it was a habit of Zack's, Clint knew, to lead a man off on a wild conversational goose-chase right after he had dropped some small remark that was mighty apt to give that man food for thought for some days and nights to come.

# 23

EVERYBODY was overdue for a rest after the trials of the past few weeks, Clint knew, so they camped on the Portneuf for three nights. He himself was dead weary. He couldn't recall when he had tackled a worse chore than the one he'd had bringing the party from rendezvous to Fort Hall. Keeping such ill-assorted elements as cows, pack animals, the wagon, the loose horse herd, Indians, missionaries and mountain men traveling together in some semblance of order was a well-nigh impossible task. White men liked to travel one way, Indians another, and there was just no reconciling the two. The whites preferred to rise with first light, snatch a hasty breakfast, travel steady till noonday, take a two-hour break to eat, rest and recruit the animals during the worst of the day's heat, then press on for a few hours more before camping for the night. But the Nez Perces got up when they felt like it, took their time eating and packing, traveled without a break for eight straight hours no matter how hot the day got, then made camp.

Each morning Clint had detailed a pair of mountain men to take to the trail shortly after daylight, riding ahead unencumbered by pack animals so that they might spot sign of hostiles, should there be any in the neighborhood, and kill game before it had been frightened away from its drinking and grazing places by the main body of the party. The cows followed, with Fram pushing them along at as fast a pace as they would undertake during the early morning hours when they were still fresh and rested. Then came the wagon, with three or four mountain men to help lower it down or heave it up the steeper slopes. Behind it came the pack train, led and guarded by the rest of the mountain men.

The Indians and their loose horse herd followed whenever they got good and ready to travel.

If all went well, the same order of march was maintained until time came for the noonday halt. Packs would be dropped, a piece of canvas would be stretched from the wagon to a pair of sticks stuck in the ground so that Ellen might have shade while she ate and rested, and everybody would partake of a cold snack. The animals would graze, if there was grass, and drink, if there was water handy. The mountain men would seek whatever shade they could find — willow thicket, bush or clump of sagebrush, put their hats over their faces and fall asleep.

Invariably the Nez Perces would catch up with the whites before they were ready to move on. Even if the plain or river valley afforded plenty of room for the Indians to swing out and around the party, they never did so. Laughing, whooping, yelling, in the best of good humor despite the tongue-parching heat, they would come charging right through the middle of the whites' resting place, loose horse herd and all. Nothing Clint could do would stop them, for it was all a great joke to them, this white man's habit of rising early to travel and then stopping to rest all through the middle of the day, and to show how wrong the white man was and how right they were seemed a point they must laughingly prove over and over again.

When the Indians moved on, they would leave the fine, choking dust stirred up by their horses' hoofs to settle slowly, while the mosquitoes and gnats roused from their dozing places in the thickets and marshy grasses along the river swarmed angrily over animal and human, ending all thoughts of sleep. Yet the whites would lie by for a while longer, letting the animals rest and the Indians get a good way ahead, so that their dust would not be quite so bad once the whites did take to the trail. Around two in the afternoon, cows, wagon, pack animals and mountain men would again move out. The dust would not be too bad at first, though the heat often was ovenlike, particularly when the trail led close to the face of a bare basaltic bluff which had soaked up blazing sunlight and now was radiating it back into the air in shimmering waves.

By now, the Indian horses would be tiring. Their pace would slow, the gap between the two parties would close as the fresher animals of the white party rapidly began to overtake those ahead, the air would fill with choking dust. For two hours or so the whites would endure this torment, then, just about the time the afternoon began to cool off so that traveling became endurable, the Nez Perces would make camp. Being in the lead they of course pre-empted the best grass, water, wood and camp sites and could not be persuaded to move a mile further along the trail no matter how many hours of daylight remained.

Such was the pattern of the better days. Many were worse. Some days the weary cattle fell so far behind that it was long after dark before they could be driven forward to rejoin the main camp. Time and again the wagon broke down, had to be unloaded and repaired, reloaded, and then pulled and heaved and pried by brute animal and man power through uncertain twilight or moonlight or dark up and down lava-strewn hills which gave even lightly laden pack animals trouble. Twice it overturned and went careening to the bottom of gullies, with its driver barely managing to leap clear in time to save his neck. Each time Clint breathed a long inward sigh of relief, certain that this time the thing was shattered beyond any possibility of repair. But each time Metcalf, with Rapp's help, found some way to fix it and keep it rolling.

Every mountain man in the party had come to hate that wagon, Clint knew, and no one hated it more than himself. Yet he marveled at Metcalf's dogged, untiring persistence. And so did the mountain men.

"Bound to take that fool wagon through, the parson is. Never thought he'd git it this fur, but he has. Goin' t' take it further, 'pears like."

"Got a knack fer patchin' things, Metcalf has. 'Course he's got that wagon in a two-way bind — if he cain't fix it with his hands right off, he can pray fer the Lord to help him out. Seems to beat cussin' a damn sight, 'cordin' to the results he gits."

"What's he goin' to do if he busts an axle? Listen, he'll keep that blamed contraption rollin' jest as long as they's a piece of it left big enough to drive a peg into. An' he'll peg the pegs, when it comes down to that. When the pegged pegs give out, he'll take his pocket knife, whittle him out a new wagon from the nearest tree an' start all over agin. No sir, you ain't goin' to git past the parson. N'r over, under er around him, neither."

The day after they made camp was a Saturday. Ellen washed and mended clothes. Some of the Nez Perces and mountain men went on a hunt, bringing back enough fresh buffalo and antelope meat for a feast Saturday evening to which Clint invited Captain Thing and the men stationed at the fort. Having heard of the Metcalfs' presence, Captain Thing came into camp respectably sober and had the good sense not to bring any drinkables along, though Clint was well aware of the fact that the mountain men had all managed to find some excuse or other to drop by the fort during the day and exchange civilities with the captain.

Before the evening ended, Captain Thing extended Clint's party, a dozen of the Nez Perce head men and the Metcalfs an invitation to dine at the fort at noon, next day, following which he said he would be deeply honored if the Reverend Metcalf would preach a sermon. Metcalf graciously agreed. Captain Thing somehow forgot to mention to Metcalf that after the preaching the trappers and Indians were planning to liven up the afternoon with a bit of horse-racing, and Clint judged it just as well to let the oversight pass.

The hour was late now. The camp had grown quiet. Smoking one last pipe before seeking his blankets, Clint sat staring into the dying fire, thinking on the conversations he had had the past few evenings with the Nez Perce chiefs. He heard a step out in the darkness, glanced up and saw Stanley Metcalf pause just within the circle of firelight. His face was thinner, the bone structure of it showing clearly now, and there were lines of fatigue around his eyes.

"I'd like a few words with you, Clint."

"Sure. Sit down."

Metcalf squatted on his heels. While rendezvous had lasted he had tried to preserve some semblance of dignity, going about camp most of the time dressed in a black suit, hat and tie. They were gone now, carefully packed away in the wagon against some future day when he might have need of them again, and he was wearing grease-stained, shapeless gray pants, shineless boots, a filthy shirt open at the throat with sleeves turned up above the elbow, and a hat whose better days were far behind it.

"What's this I hear about the Nez Perces leaving us?"

"They're talking of it, yeah."

"Why?"

Clint picked up a stick and drew a few lines in the dust. "Every summer they cross the mountains and go to the Bitter Root Valley to lay in their winter's supply of buffalo meat. That country lies due east from Salmon River. From here, it lies due north. The way the Nez Perces see it, if they're going to kill any buffalo this summer they've got to head north right now."

"Before they go home?"

"That's their idea, yeah."

"Ellen says they want us to go with them. She says they're afraid that if we don't go with them they'll never see us again."

Clint nodded. "They're worried, no denying that. The way you'll have to go if you're to take the wagon through will swing you a long piece west of the Nez Perce country. They're afraid you'll see some Indians you like better than them and will settle downriver amongst the Hudson's Bay Company people."

"We'd never do that!"

"Well, it's worrying them anyhow."

Metcalf looked troubled. "What do you think we ought to do — go north with them to the buffalo country?"

"No sense to that. Likely that country'll be swarming with Blackfeet. It usually is. There may be some fighting. No point in your getting mixed up in that. Besides, you'd never be able to take the wagon through the Bitter Roots."

"What are you going to do?"

Clint poked aimlessly at the ground with the stick. He had his orders from Bonneville. Trouble was, if he obeyed them to the letter he would have to ride off in two directions at once. Not seeing any way to do that, he guessed he would have to settle for the next best thing.

"Split the party. Judd Smith and four of the boys will ride north with the Nez Perces and try to make them and the Blackfeet act friendly toward each other. I don't hope for much, but Judd will try his best. The five of us that's left will stick with you and Ellen."

"What about Rapp and Fram?"

"You heard what I told them. The Portneuf is as far as they go with us."

"I wish you would reconsider. Splitting the party as you plan to do will leave us short-handed. You say there's some bad mountain country ahead. Rapp has been a great help with the wagon. And I don't know how I would ever have brought the cows through without Fram."

"They're troublemakers. I want no part of them."

"They've made no trouble so far, have they?"

Clint shook his head. The truth was splitting the party would leave them short-handed but he still did not like the idea of taking the two men along. "Fram I don't worry about too much. It isn't in him to make trouble unless he's led into it. But he leads easy. And Rapp is an ornery breed of cat — mean clear through."

"Suppose I were to guarantee his good behavior?" Metcalf said, eying him closely. "Would you take them along then?"

"I'm not so sure you could guarantee it."

"I am. Very sure."

"You've already talked to him, I take it?"

"Yes."

Clint hesitated a moment, then nodded. "All right. They go along. But I'm counting on you to keep them in line."

Metcalf was silent for a time, as if wanting to say more but not quite sure how to go about saying it. The light was poor, the night still save for the wind prowling among the tepees of the sleeping camp. Clint found his mind wandering back to other nights, years ago, when as boys together he and the man squatting on the far side of the fire had counted it the greatest of adventures to camp out somewhere in the hills a few miles above the village. While the fire burned low they would talk and dream boyhood dreams aloud, both maybe a little afraid of the dark around them and drawn closer to each other because of it. Now they were older and wiser; too old to fear the dark, too wise to share dreams. Yet for a few moments things seemed almost the same.

"Clint," Stanley said softly, "why didn't you tell me you had a son?"

"Guess I didn't figure you'd understand."

"Ellen said the mother is dead."

"Yes."

"Ellen was hurt for a while — I guess you know that. But now she's beginning to understand. And so am I. But one thing I've got to know, Clint. Do you intend to raise Daniel as an Indian or a white man?"

Clint stared off into the darkness. "It's got to be one or the other, hasn't it?"

"I'm afraid so."

"Why did you have to come out here?" Clint said harshly. "Why couldn't you let us be?"

"Clint, what we're doing wasn't thought up as a personal affront to you," Metcalf said earnestly. "The entire religious world in the East is afire. Ellen and I happen to be the first, that's all. Next year I suspect there will be several parties of missionaries setting out for Oregon. And it doesn't end with the missionaries. All over the East people are thinking and talking about Oregon. Why, there isn't a city or village of any size that doesn't have an emigration society. You've been gone six years, you know. You've no idea of what's been happening back home."

Clint was silent. Metcalf stood up. "You're a thinking man, Clint. I want you to keep thinking. Think about Daniel and how you want him to grow up. Think about home and the way you were raised and the things you used to believe in. Most of all, think about your own immortal soul and what you intend to do with the rest of your life."

Clint looked away. "Did you come out here to convert Indians or white men?"

"Both, if I can," Metcalf said softly. "Good night, Clint." He turned to go, then paused. "I just want you to know how deeply I appreciate all you've done for Ellen and me so far — and all you're going to do."

He was gone. Clint stood for a long while staring into the darkness after him, his pipe dead and cold in his hand, then he turned and sought his blankets. He lay for a long time staring up at the stars.

# 24

ELLEN could not remember when she had ever enjoyed a meal as much as she did the one at Fort Hall that Sunday. She had had a bath, bathing as the Nez Perce women did in a brush-covered wickiup filled with live steam. It was wonderful to feel completely clean again, to be wearing clean hose, clean petticoats, her best black silk dress, sleek-fitting dress-up gloves rather than the coarse leather ones she used for riding, and a wide-brimmed hat that was serious enough for Sunday yet still had a few softening touches. It was good to see Stanley washed, clean-shaven and wearing his handsome black Sunday suit and cravat, just as he always did for dinner back home. It was amusing to watch Captain Thing as he enthusiastically played the host, his graying hair and beard newly trimmed and combed, his blue serge suit brushed, pressed and its brass buttons gleaming, his eyes glowing with delight as he made sure that the guests seated at his table missed none of the delicacies he had provided for them.

Luxury, Ellen mused, was a relative thing. The plates were tin, the spoons wooden, the forks nonexistent save for the three or four badly battered ones Captain Thing had managed to dig up for those of his more civilized guests whom he felt would know how to use such implements. The tablecloth was a piece of nondescript muslin which looked as though it had recently been laundered without benefit of soap or hot water after having been dug out of some dusty storeroom. The table had been extended by laying planks over wooden blocks. Indians and mountain men perched gingerly on more planks balanced on lower blocks, while she, Stanley, Clint and the captain himself

were privileged to sit on backless wooden stools. Walls and
roof were of dried mud crudely smeared over wooden poles,
windows were merely square holes with dried skins to drop
over them in case of bad weather, and the floor was the
earth itself, carefully dampened to lay the dust. Yet luxury
it all seemed to her after the complete lack of such comforts
on the trail these past few weeks.

The captain sat at the head of the table, dignified as a
baron; Ellen was on his right, Stanley his left, with Clint
and his men ranged further down on Ellen's side of the
table and the Nez Perce guests on Stanley's side. None of
the fort employees was seated, for all were busy doing their
awkward and self-conscious best to carry out their duties as
waiters and cooks. One of them, a good-looking, blue-eyed
young man of twenty or so, seemed to regard it his sole task
to look after her, for he never left her side except to run out
of the room for some fresh dish of food. He was so attentive
that she asked him his name.

"Matthew, ma'am," he blurted, blushing furiously. "Matthew Flaherty."

"You're very kind, Matthew. I'm not used to such gra-
cious service."

"Oh, it's a pleasure, ma'am! A great pleasure!"

Captain Thing winked at Stanley, grinning broadly. "The
truth is, the lad's that lovesick an' lonesome for the girl he
left back home, he just can't take his eyes off Miss Metcalf.
Says she reminds him of his sweetheart." The captain
reached out and slapped Matthew on the back. "That's the
way of it, eh, me bucko?"

Grinning sheepishly, Matthew leaned past Ellen and took
an empty bowl off the table. "I'll get you some more potatoes."

Captain Thing roared with laughter as the young trapper
hurriedly left the room. Ellen kept her eyes on her plate.
She had gotten an unmistakable whiff of a rum-scented

breath, though whether it had been the captain's, Matthew's or both she could not say.

The variety of the menu amazed her. There was fresh buffalo and antelope meat, cooked as only a mountain man could cook it. There was coffee and tea, with sugar or honey for sweetening if one so desired. There was ice. There was hot corn bread. But it was the wonderful array of garden-fresh vegetables that was the greatest treat to her, for not since they had left civilization months ago had she even seen a vegetable. Yet here were tender young carrots and beets, crisp radishes, fresh lettuce, and — treat of all treats — new potatoes and peas. As she declined a second helping of meat but gladly accepted seconds of every vegetable dish offered her — with what she cheerfully admitted to be an unlady-like appetite — Captain Thing beamed upon her.

"Ye'll accept my apologies, Miss Metcalf, that we can offer ye neither butter nor milk. 'Twas a sad oversight, fail-ing to bring a cow or two along, and ye may be sure I've scolded Nat Wyeth in my mind for it many's the time this year past. 'Tis to be hoped I can trade your brother out of one of his cows once his own herd's well started."

"Oh, Captain, don't apologize for anything! It's a won-derful dinner! You raised the vegetables yourself?"

"Aye, that I did. I've a fine little piece of garden down by the river. I'll show it to ye later if ye're of a mind to see it."

After such a meal a bit of leg-stretching seemed called for. As they rose from the table to go outside, the moun-tain men groaned cheerful complaints about being too stuffed to walk, dug out pipes and tobacco pouches and pre-pared to smoke. What food was left on the table magically disappeared as the Nez Perce guests unashamedly appropri-ated everything edible, intending to take it to their families, Ellen supposed, so that wives and children might sample the kind of fare served at a white man's feast. No one objected, so she guessed that this cleaning of the dinner table by the guests was an accepted custom.

Outside, the courtyard of the fort was filled with curious Nez Perces. Though not invited to the dinner, the entire village had moved en masse to the plain below the fort. Horses, dogs and children were everywhere, scampering about, eating, lying in what little shade could be found, acting for all the world like white people back home on a Fourth of July picnic. When Stanley expressed a desire to see the garden which had produced such a bounteous supply of vegetables, Captain Thing proudly led him, Ellen and Clint to it.

The plot covered a couple of acres and had been surrounded by a zigzag split-rail fence. It had been a month's work to clear the spot of sagebrush and build the fence, Captain Thing declared, and another month had been required to set up the irrigating system. Stanley seemed intensely interested, and as he asked question after question the captain became so engrossed in explaining his pet project that he completely forgot his manners and left Ellen to trail along with Clint while he and Stanley argued out the virtues and faults of water wheels, flumes, soils, seeds and planting times with the dedicated single-mindedness of a pair of philosophers settling the fate of the world.

When Stanley and the captain wandered off to inspect the water wheel, Ellen, weary of trudging around in their wake, paused to rest just outside the fence. The contrast between the rich greenness within the enclosure and the dreary brownness outside was striking. Even the color of the soil seemed different. Outside, it was powdery, a light yellow-brown, puffing upward like smoke at every step. Inside the fence, where the long shallow ditches had carried water between the rows of plants, it was very dark, almost black, with a look of richness to it. As she leaned against the fence, she became aware that Clint was squatting down on his heels nearby, absently shifting a handful of dust from one palm to the other as he stared at the garden. Something about the look in his eyes arrested her gaze. She could not put a name to what she saw: a bleakness, an intent peering at something tangible and near while his mind tried to translate it into something intangible and distant. It was so odd a look that she could not tear her eyes away from his face, and after a moment he suddenly glanced up and caught her staring at him. Embarrassment made her say the first conventionality that came to her mind.

"It was a good dinner, wasn't it?"

"Better than I had the last time I passed this way."

"Oh? And when was that?"

"Year or so back." His head inclined toward a spot beyond her. "Yonder was where I camped. There were half a dozen lodges of Bannocks camped right near and we shared what food we had. Poor pemmican for worse bear meat. But look what a man can do with a few seeds and a bit of water. Thirty people ate dinner off that little garden spot and you can't see that anything much is missing."

"God is generous to those who are willing to till His fields."

"Yeah, that's the catch to it, all right."

"Stanley thinks the Nez Perces can be taught farming. Once we have converted them to Christianity and taught them to read and write, Stanley is sure we'll be able to show them the value of growing their own food."

Clint shook his head. "Maybe you've got the answer there. But if you have you've got it backwards, to my way of thinking. You better feed your Indian first. Then educate him. Make a white man of him, or a reasonable imitation of a white man. When you've done that you can start converting him to a religion that was made for the white man alone."

His bitterness puzzled her, but before the argument could go any further Stanley and Captain Thing returned from their inspection of the irrigating system. The water wheel was an adaptation of a device Captain Thing had seen in the Holy Lands, Stanley said, the wheel being turned by the force of the current and lifting water from the river to the flumes which led to the garden by means of a set of pivoting wooden cups. There was not a nail or piece of metal in it and Stanley was positive he could construct a similar device if irrigation were needed for their mission garden in the Nez Perce country.

It was midafternoon now and the heat was beginning to abate. The services were held in the open, with the Indians and mountain men seated in a semicircle on the ground facing the brush arbor which had been erected to give shade to the minister and to the half dozen favored individuals who sat beside him looking out toward the crowd. These included Ellen, Captain Thing, Two Bears, Eagle-With-One-Wing and Judd Smith, who had agreed to pass the sermon on to the Nez Perces in sign language after Clint, whom Ellen had assumed would undertake that task, begged off. A prayer was offered. A few hymns were sung, with Ellen leading, Captain Thing following in a loud but off-key bass and the mountain men self-consciously croaking out what few phrases they remembered of the old songs of their youth. Then Stanley rose and began his sermon.

It was difficult for Ellen to concentrate on his words. There was nothing new in them, no message that she had not heard many times before, and she found her interest concentrating more on the circle of attentive faces in front of her and on the expressive movements of Judd Smith's hands as he stood off to one side and slightly behind her brother, drawing pictures in the air for the benefit of the Indian listeners, rather than on the content of the sermon itself.

She was proud of Stanley. And seeing the mass of Indians listening so quietly and reverently she suddenly felt uplifted in spirit and serenely confident that with such a receptive group of people as these the mission could not possibly fail.

Even handicapped as he was by not being able to speak their tongue, Stanley was somehow finding a way to pierce the language barrier and reach their hearts. They understood. God was making them understand.

The service ended presently and for some moments after Stanley's closing prayer the Indians and mountain men sat in silence, then as Ellen and Stanley strolled with Captain Thing toward the fort and the refreshment of a cup of iced tea the assemblage began to break up. It was four o'clock now, with the most pleasant of the daylight hours still ahead. As she drank her tea, Ellen mused that the perfect way to end this quiet Sabbath would be to go back to camp and write a long letter to the congregation back home telling them about the inspiring events of the day. Captain Thing smiled and pushed back his stool.

"It's been a great honor and pleasure having ye with us today. An' now, if ye're so minded, we'll stroll outside an' give eye to the entertainment my boys have prepared for ye."

"Entertainment?" Stanley said.

"Aye. Come, 'twill be beginning soon."

She could see by the way her brother's lips had tightened that Stanley had not liked the sound of the word, but he made no comment as they walked out the fort gate. Many of the Indians and trappers still lingered on the slope near the brush arbor, but they were no longer reverently silent. Family groups talked and laughed together. A pair of supple-bodied Indian boys, stripped to their breechclouts, were warily circling each other in a wrestling bout, while relatives and friends urged them on. Two middle-aged Indians were arguing vehemently over something Ellen could not quite make out, though apparently it had to do with the two boys and the display of strings of beads, knives and other trinkets piled on the new red blanket between them.

Further down the slope they passed a knot of twenty or

so braves who squatted chanting in unison, their eyes intent on one of their number who was rapidly shuffling something back and forth between his hands. As Ellen watched, the brave extended his hands, fists closed, another pointed at the left one, the brave opened it to reveal the hand empty while at the same time he gleefully dropped a piece of bone to the ground from his right hand. Shouts of triumph went up from some of the watchers, others howled in anguish, and there was a sudden frenzied scramble for the trinkets lying on the ground. She turned to Captain Thing in astonishment.

"Why, they're gambling!"

"Aye," Captain Thing said imperturbably. "They're great ones for any kind of gamblin' sport. Why, they'll play that fool game all day an' all night, 'long as they've got a blanket or a horse or a wife left to their name."

Ellen shot a quick glance at Stanley. His face was stony but he kept his peace. A large crowd was gathered on the knoll just ahead. Captain Thing led them through it, blasting a way with voice and hands. Indians and whites laughingly jeered back at him, though as soon as they saw whom he was escorting they courteously stepped aside. The smell of rum was overpowering.

As the crowd suddenly shifted, a burly trapper lurched against her. She found herself staring directly at two laughing mountain men who were just in the act of passing a canteen from one to the other. Beartracks Weaver was one of the men; the other was young Matthew Flaherty. Both trappers grinned in the friendliest possible fashion, doffed their hats and bowed clumsily.

"Beg pardon, ma'am," Beartracks said. "I shore didn't go to bump ye." He nodded to Stanley. "Howdy, Parson. Say, you're as sharp at preachin' a sermon as you are at hackin' out Injun arrers! That was a ring-tootin' dilly of a sermon, I'll take oath to that!"

"Hello, Miss Metcalf," Matthew Flaherty mumbled. "Hope you liked the dinner."

"Yes — yes, it was fine."

They were at the forefront of the crowd now, standing where they could see the stretch of flat just below. A number of horses and riders were milling there. She heard a pistol shot, and suddenly a black and a sorrel leaped forward, a mountain man on one, an Indian on the other, and went pounding across the flat with their riders belaboring them with quirts for all they were worth. Amid the bedlam of shouting around them, Captain Thing turned to Stanley, seized his arm and pointed excitedly.

"Watch that black, Parson! He'll take the sorrel sure as ye're a foot high!"

She saw the color leave Stanley's face. She saw his eyes flash with sudden anger. She saw him gaze around at the frenzied crowd, in which whites and Indians alike were shouting for the favorites on which they had bet their all, and he seemed bewildered, as if wondering how so quiet and reverent a congregation could so quickly change into as wild and heathen a crowd as had ever made mockery of the Sabbath. The look in his eyes frightened her and impulsively she touched him.

"Stanley, I know it's wrong. But please don't — "

Her voice was drowned by the crowd's roar. Oblivious of her and of everything else, Stanley stared bleakly down at the ground. The crowd noise drew Ellen's gaze to the flat. A quarter of a mile away from the starting point a stake had been driven into the ground. Her heart leaped into her throat as the two horses reached it together and swung sharply around it, the riders swaying far over to the inside of the turn, the horses skidding and half falling, then righting themselves amid a great cloud of dust and racing back toward the finish line.

The black was two lengths behind now. Captain Thing was

bellowing encouragement at the top of his mighty lungs, swinging a great fist back and forth in rhythm, as if he himself were atop its back and applying the whip to its glistening flanks.

"C'mon, bucko! C'mon! C'mon!"

Frowning, Stanley raised his head, prudently moving a step to one side in order to stay clear of the captain's piston-like elbow. His body now blocked Ellen's view. Impatiently she clutched his shoulder, using her grip on it to pull herself up on tiptoe. Now she could see. The black was moving up, closing the gap. Its muzzle was abreast of the sorrel's tail, its mid-section, its neck, its . . .

The black swept home, winner by the narrowest of margins. The crowd went wild. Ellen sank back on her heels and closed her eyes, trembling in every muscle. When she opened her eyes a moment later, she found Stanley gazing at her quizzically. She flushed.

"Stanley," she murmured. "I think we'd better go."

"Why?" he said dryly. "You appear to be enjoying it."

"Aren't you?"

"A man who doesn't enjoy a horse race has no blood in his veins."

"But it's the Sabbath. We have no right to enjoy it. Please, we must go."

"All right. But first I want a word with Captain Thing."

"Don't scold him," she said quickly.

She could have bitten her tongue off for that. Stanley gazed sternly at her. "You know it's wrong. I know it's wrong. Yet you want us to slip away, saying nothing. Wouldn't that be rather cowardly, Ellen?"

She dropped her eyes. "I'm sorry. Do what you think best."

Beaming, Captain Thing turned to Stanley, looking as pleased and excited as a child on Christmas morning. "Ah, lad, there's a sight to warm the heart of a seafarin' man. How I do love to watch horses run! But it's few the chances

I got when I was at sea those thirty long years. Now that I'm becalmed ashore I cannot get my fill of watchin' the wonderful things spurn the earth's dust with their burnin' hoofs!"

"I know, Captain. But — "

"Now would ye look at that skinny gray yonder? Does your eye show ye a spark of spirit in him? No, I'll lay it doesn't! But watch him go when the pistol barks. Why, he's nothin' but a jack rabbit, I tell ye — "

They stayed until the last race, not speaking, not even looking at each other. What kind of peace Stanley had made with his conscience Ellen could not guess. Perhaps he had done as she had, making no peace at all, merely striking an uneasy truce for the time being, with the reckoning to come later.

There was an accident during the last race. Just how it happened no one could say. One instant the two trappers were bending low over the necks of their mounts, quirts flailing, dust flying, hoofs pounding, the crowd screaming; the next, animals and men were tumbling over and over in a wild melee, and the crowd was suddenly still.

She was so limp from the long period of constant excitement that it all seemed like a dream. She saw men running toward the spot where the fall had occurred. She saw Captain Thing stride swiftly down the slope, with Stanley close behind him. She saw both horses and one of the trappers struggle to their feet and limp away, while the other trapper sprawled in the dust unmoving.

She was not aware of how she got there, but presently she found herself on the outskirts of the crowd gathered around the fallen man, found the crowd opening up to let her through. Captain Thing knelt on one side of the injured trapper, his broad back toward her, while beyond him she could see Stanley's grave face as he loosened the man's clothes. She saw Stanley look up and shake his head.

"I'm afraid he's dead. His neck was broken in the fall."

"Ah, that's a cruel thing!"

There was a moment of silence. She could see Stanley's eyes, dark and inward-looking and tormented, as if he were searching his own soul and finding it not without blame. She heard Captain Thing speak in a low voice.

"Would ye say a burial service over him, Parson? I'd take it as a great favor."

"What was his faith?"

"That I don't know. Catholic, likely. But does it matter so much now?"

Gazing at her brother, Ellen was suddenly struck by how much his face had matured these past few months, how much it had thinned down, so that now it held the same gaunt bleakness that had been in his father's face. He had never struck her as nearly as strong-willed a man as his father had been. His father never hesitated, as he was doing now; his father never searched deep into his own soul for the answer to any question, as he now appeared to be doing. His father had been a strong man where matters of will and mind were concerned.

And she knew beyond any shadow of doubt what her father would have done, had he been here. The lesson was so plain. *Quote the commandment which has this day been broken. Look at the silent, humbled men standing before you; look down at the dead man; then say no more.* It would be a lesson remembered by these violent men for a long time to come.

Stanley got slowly to his feet. The valley now lay in shadow, but beyond him she could see low angle sunlight painting the bleak hills starkly yellow. But all she could see in her brother's eyes was compassion and sorrow.

"Of course it doesn't matter," he said gently. "Carry him up to the brush arbor, please. We'll have the service there."

Beartracks Weaver and Captain Thing picked up the

dead man and carried him through the crowd. Seeing her, Beartracks mumbled apologetically, "Excuse us, ma'am."

She stepped back out of their way, and it was then that she got her first glimpse of the dead trapper's face.

Matthew Flaherty.

Stinging, blinding tears filled her eyes. She covered her face with her hands and wept silently. Stanley's arm went around her shoulders.

"There, now, Ellen."

She turned and buried her face in his breast, murmuring words meant for his ears alone, for only he would understand their true meaning.

"Stanley, I'm glad . . . I'm glad . . ."

# 25

THE NEZ PERCES were greatly impressed, Clint knew. If ever there had been a doubt in their minds as to the genuineness of the white man's magic, the weekend at Fort Hall had dispelled it. They had been shown a lot of powerful medicine. The water wheel, the strange new vegetables, the sermon, the funeral service — all were awesome, wonderful things, fuel for campfire meditation and discussion for many nights to come. But Two Bears had done his meditating alone. Clint learned of it when the chief came to him early next morning.

He had been deeply troubled, Two Bears said, ever since he had learned that the Big-Medicine-Talker and She-Who-

Rides-Sideways were traveling on down Snake River while his own people went north to the buffalo country. He had sat far into the night thinking about it, and over and over his heart had said to him: *This is not a good thing.*

"The Sent Ones came to bring light to my people," he went on, "yet we part with them here and go to hunt buffalo. Three moons will pass before we see them again. Perhaps they will forget us. Perhaps they will come to believe we do not want the light they carry and will take it to some other tribe of Indians. My heart would be sad if such a thing happened."

He fell silent for some moments. Clint waited patiently. At last Two Bears raised his head. "Now I know what I must do. I must not go to the buffalo country this year. I must go with the Sent Ones and show them the way to the country of my people. That is all I have to say."

Clint welcomed the prospect of the chief's company, for Two Bears knew the trails across the Blue Mountains far better than he did. "I am pleased. The Sent Ones will be pleased too. Do you ride alone or do you take your family with you?"

"My wife comes with me to tend my lodge. Also my youngest girl child."

"What about Daniel?"

"My son, Spotted Wolf, and his wife have been caring for him like one of their own. They wish to take him with them to the buffalo country. But you are his father. It is for you to say."

Clint gazed out over the stirring camp. The cub was his, damn it, not Spotted Wolf's, with as much white blood in him as Indian. No need for Two Bears to remind him of that.

"We'll take him with us. Got your lodge down?"

"We are ready."

"Good. We'll move out shortly."

Shrugging off his irritation, Clint walked over to the

wagon, where Burn Rapp was harnessing the teams. Two days of rest had restored the strength and spirits of the horses, and the wheel pair, always ornery, was giving Rapp considerable trouble. And Rapp seemed clumsy, ungodly clumsy. In a hurry to roll out, Clint lent him a hand. When the job was done Rapp grunted a curt word of thanks and was starting to turn away when Clint spoke to him.

"Let's have an understanding, Burn. I didn't want you along. Metcalf did. That's why you're still with us."

"Reckon I know that."

"Why did you change your mind about trapping the Three Forks country?"

Not answering for a moment, Rapp lifted a hand and fingered the ridges of scar tissue on his forehead. Apparently he had had a big night at the fort, for his eyes were bloodshot and he was scowling as though drums were thumping inside his head. "Doc done me a big favor, patchin' me up. He needs help. Givin' him a hand with the wagon seemed a good way for me to pay back my debt to him."

"Don't you think we can take the wagon through?"

"Depends on how the hosses hold up. They ain't really big enough fer the job. The grass'll be poor 'tween here an' the Boise an' the heat will wear 'em down. Time we're ready to tackle the Blues they won't be in very good shape. But Doc Metcalf's got his heart set on givin' it a try. I'll do the best I kin fer him." He paused, staring at Clint. "I pay my debts — all of 'em."

"There's some you'd do well to forget," Clint snapped, turned on his heel and walked away.

Watching him go, Burn Rapp stood unmoving for a time, wishing the pounding in his head would stop, wondering how much longer it would be before the feeling of weakness in his legs and the clumsiness of his hands would leave him. Three weeks it had been now. Three weeks.

The sun, edging up over the dark line of mountains to

the east, lanced through the rising haze of dust. The glare of it hurt his eyes. Covering them with a hand, he massaged his temples gently. Three weeks — and he was far from mended yet.

"All set to go?" a voice asked.

He raised his head and shook it hard, trying to clear his blurred vision. The figure standing before him at last swam into focus and he nodded. "Sure, Doc. Any time."

"You don't look it. Aren't you feeling well?"

"Got a headache, sort of. An' my eyes are botherin' me some. Lot of dust at the races yesterday afternoon. Guess maybe that's what done it."

"How drunk did you get?" Metcalf cut in.

"Drunk? Why, I — "

He stopped. He did not know why, but suddenly he simply ran out of words and stopped. Metcalf gave a snort of disgust and turned away. "That's what I thought."

Rapp stared down at the ground, puzzled at the way his tongue had suddenly turned wooden in his mouth. What he'd started to say was he'd had one drink, sure, but it had made him sick as a dog and he'd drunk no more. Yet from the way he felt today, he might just as well have drunk a whole gallon of the stuff. But Doc Metcalf thought . . .

He rubbed his eyes. His head hurt. It hurt like hell.

After Clint had brought in and saddled Ellen's horse and his own, he gave Judd Smith, who, with four of the mountain men, was to accompany the Indians to the buffalo country, a few last-minute instructions. The main thing troubling him was the fact that the most influential chief among the Nez Perces traveling north would be Eagle-With-One-Wing, whose feelings toward the Blackfeet were well known.

"The old booger would sooner trust a rattlesnake than a Blackfoot," he told Judd. "Try to keep his mind on buffalo instead of fighting."

"Jest how d'ye suggest I do that?" Judd asked.

"Small Crow and Spotted Wolf pack some weight. Not as much as he does, but some. Likely he won't listen to you. But they'll listen to you, and he'll listen to them. That's the only handle I can give you to the thing."

Judd spat thoughtfully. "Wal, a nub of a handle is better'n none. S'posin' we do meet some Blackfeet which are willin' to gab 'stead of fight? What kind of sermon do I preach to the jiggers?"

"Tell them Bonneville wants to trade. Tell them we all want peace. Likely they've heard gossip about how cozy the Gros Ventres got with us at rendezvous. Likely they'll be curious about the Metcalfs. You can make a big thing of that."

"D'ye think it is a big thing?"

"You can make it out to be. Tell them the Metcalfs are going to settle in the Nez Perce country and build a Big Medicine mission that'll outshine anything Hudson's Bay has got in Oregon. Invite some of their head men to pay us a visit at the mission, come fall."

"Where will it be — in the Salmon River country?"

Clint shook his head. The Metcalfs were out here to trap souls, not beaver; to raise cattle, not kill wild game. The Salmon River country was a mountainous region, hard to get to, heavily timbered, subject to deep snows and bitter cold and lacking the easily tilled valley land Metcalf would need for his farming operations. But a hundred and fifty miles to the northwest lay a flatter, more open country at a considerably lower altitude. It wasn't country a mountain-loving man could have much fondness for but it was well suited to Metcalf's purposes.

"I'm going to show Metcalf the country near the mouth of the Clearwater. The Lapwai valley. It's central to all the Nez Perce bands, the winters are mild, there's good soil and grass. I've got a notion it'll be what he's looking for."

"You want me to meet you there, come fall?"

"Yeah."

Judd rubbed his chin, his eyes squinting off into the distance. "Where do we go from there, Clint? Trappin'? Er was you figgerin' to settle down an' turn missionary?"

It had been said half in jest, Clint knew, but as he glanced quickly at Judd he knew that the lanky trapper had seen the vague shape of things to come, just as he had, and was troubled. He shook his head. "We'll see. Maybe I'll have word from Bonneville by then. You know how he works — when one scheme blows up in his face, he's got two more ready to take its place." He smiled and held out his hand. "Luck to you, Judd."

"Same to you, Clint. You may need it more'n I do."

"Try to keep things peaceful."

"Shore will." He paused. "But s'posin' I can't?"

Clint swung into the saddle. "Then the hell with it. Just try to keep your hair. You're apt to need it, comes a cold winter."

# 26

EVER SINCE Ellen had left home she had kept a journal. It was a tie with home, a daily reminder that no matter what great distances separated her friends and herself they were still together in spirit. She wrote a few lines in it each day, describing the country, the interesting white people she met, the Indians and their strange customs — anything which she thought would entertain her friends and give them some idea of what a trip across the continent was like. When the opportunity offered itself she tore out the sheets she had written, sealed them in an envelope and entrusted them to eastbound travelers.

At first her writings had been a complete outpouring of her mind and heart. There was no reason to hold back anything. Her cause and that of her friends in the church was one and the same. But they had stayed at home . . .

It was at rendezvous that she first began to realize there were some things she could not put down in black and white. She described the wild savagery of the Indians and the riotous carousals of the mountain men in a general way, but she could not bring herself to detail some of the scenes she witnessed. The parishoners would be horrified, she knew. They would condemn all trappers as hopeless brutes and all Indians as besotted animals lost beyond redemption. Which was not the truth at all.

She wrote: "Everyone is most helpful. We're being furnished a guide, an experienced trapper who knows the country and the Indians. He and several of his men will accompany us . . ."

She failed to mention the guide's name.

During the twenty-three days it took the party to travel from Fort Hall to the Boise River, her journal entries became briefer, her descriptive passages more terse. The country itself certainly required few words.

". . . a gray, flat, dreary sameness that dulls the eye and mind. Nothing but miles and miles of sagebrush. We follow the Snake. It carries a great deal of water, though often its canyon is so deep and vertical we cannot drive the stock down to it to water them . . ."

That was all she could find to say about the look of the land. Yet even that little would be beyond their understanding, she feared. The bleak immensity of the country was not a thing to be captured by words. It must be seen and felt. And her former desire to share her experiences was waning with each passing day. Home ties seemed thin now. Fort Hall had been the last American outpost, Clint said, and it would be most unlikely that they would meet any traveler eastbound for the States until Captain Bonneville or some of his men returned from the lower Columbia months from now.

So there was no great hurry to write, even if she had had something of importance to write about.

The weather was hardly worth mentioning. Say that the sun shone from dawn to dusk in a blue, cloudless sky. Say that there was no rain and that from the look of the land there never had been any rain here. Say that it was hot and dusty. Say that the wind blew. You had said it all.

Twice she noted the fact that she had seen waterfalls. She mentioned the natural curiosity called Thousand Springs, where countless underground streams burst out of the north canyon wall and tumbled down to the river below. It did not occur to her to compare either falls or springs in size or uniqueness with natural marvels back home. They were there, she saw them, recorded the fact, then forgot them.

Sometimes the evenings were pleasant, particularly if they happened to camp where there was good grass, a bit of wood and a cool night breeze to blow the mosquitoes away. She got her first taste of salmon and liked it, despite the fact that earlier that day she had seen the filthy river Indians from whom Clint had bought the fish and had glimpsed the indescribably dirty hovels in which they lived. Dirt meant nothing to her any more. How could it? when hour after hour, day after day choking dust rose from her horse's hoofs with each step, coating face and body and hands with a gray-brown film as fine as talcum powder? Stanley jokingly said that that kind of dirt was probably good for a person because it formed a protective layer over the skin which shut out the burning rays of the sun and lessened the drying action of the wind. If dirt coated the food too — well, perhaps it would soothe the stomach just as it did the skin.

Of evenings she frequently sat in front of Two Bears' lodge, talking to the children. No one bothered them. Clint and the mountain men would be at their own fires, off a ways; Two Bears would sit back in the shadows, listening but saying nothing, while his wife puttered away at her endless woman's tasks. The girl was around nine, Ellen judged, smart enough and willing to learn, but always subdued and a bit fearful, as if she had been given strict instructions by her parents on how to behave and had her mind more on that than on the lessons at hand.

Ellen tried to treat Daniel as just another Indian child. Two Bears made it quite clear that in his estimation a grandson was of far more importance than a daughter and should be so regarded by her. The chief made it clear, too, that he wanted Daniel to be made aware of and to take pride in his white blood.

"Suyapo," Two Bears would say, pointing proudly at Daniel, then at her. He would hold up a hand, placing two fingers together side by side to represent herself and the boy. "Suyapo, suyapo."

The word meant "white person," she knew. And the chief's meaning was unmistakable. He loved the whites; it was the pride of his life that a white man had fathered his grandchild, and he wanted the boy taught all the great medicine to which his white blood entitled him.

In her journal Ellen wrote: "The Indian children are a delight to work with, so well behaved, so quick to learn . . ." But she did not record the unwanted thoughts that came to her as the bright eyes in the dark-skinned face watched her intently.

*Daniel. That was the name of Clint's father. But he's a child to be taught, nothing more. I must not think about whose blood runs in his veins.*

As the tiring days passed, her journal entries became cryptically factual. Of their first crossing of the Snake, which had frightened her badly because Stanley had nearly drowned, she wrote: "Crossed the Snake sitting atop an elk-hide like a squaw . . . the wagon tipped over and would have been swept away if the men on the far bank had not had a rope tied to it . . . the plows and most of the seeds lost . . ."

She did not have the heart to record Stanley's despair.

Later she made another brief entry: "Our guide saved my life today when my horse tried to run away . . ."

Someday she might be able to tell her friends about that and laugh, for it had been as embarrassing and comical as it had been frightening. But she need not write down the details, for if she lived to be a hundred the memory of those awful moments would be etched indelibly upon her mind.

*My horse was walking along as peaceful as you please. I was daydreaming. I remember looking down at the ground and seeing a little hole — a gopher hole, I think it was — with some kind of an insect flitting around it. Then my horse stepped on the hole, it caved in, and thousands of hornets came swarming out. My horse went insane. Next thing I knew I was falling. My head and shoulders were dragging on the ground, my foot was caught in the stirrup, my skirts were flying — and I was screaming . . .*

*And suddenly my horse stopped. I looked up and there stood Clint. He was holding my horse by its bridle with his left hand, trying to make it stop pitching, and in his right hand he held a pistol. I asked him who in the world did he think he was going to shoot — me? He grinned down at me, the most unconcerned, exasperating grin, and said, "No, but I'm sure going to kill me a horse if he don't settle down mighty quick."*

Someday it might seem comical. But not for a while.

Nor was there anything comical about the way she had made a spectacle of herself in the middle of the desert one

day in full sight of the whole party. That she would remember for the rest of her life and feel shame for, though
she had expressed no shame in her journal. All she wrote
was: "The horses grow weaker and Stanley keeps discard-
ing things to lighten the wagon . . . today he threw out my
wooden chest with Mother's best linen, china and silver-
ware . . . all I have to remember her by . . . I sat down on
the ground and cried . . . then our guide . . ."

*Our guide. Oh, bless you, Clint, with all your tough-
mindedness, all your outward callousness — you still have
a soft spot in you someplace!*

"Guess a woman's got a right to some things of her own.
Dump half the load that bay horse is carrying, Zack, and
cache it. We'll pack the chest along."

As the body grew calloused and numb, so did the mind,
the nerves and all one's finer sensibilities. She knew Stanley was growing frantic with concern for his precious wagon,
knew that he almost never rode in it any more, knew that
he was exerting himself far beyond his strength. But it
did not seem to matter. One evening she wrote the starkly
brutal entry: "Stanley fainted twice today . . ."

It seemed superfluous to explain why he had fainted, how
he had been revived, how he got up and went on until he
fainted again, was revived again, went on again. Such matters were things to be taken for granted.

Three days later she made another entry: "Broke an axle
tree on the wagon today . . . made camp at noon . . . wagon
was made into a two-wheeled cart, which we'll take as far as
Fort Boise . . . our guide says we may have to leave it there,
though Stanley doesn't agree . . ."

Why write more? A dream was ending in failure short
of the final goal. That was all. Buried somewhere deep in
her weary mind was a sympathy for the braveness of the dream
and a sorrow for its death, but the tombstones which marked
its resting place set not in this bleak spot where the dis-

carded wheels, broken axle tree and excess wagon fittings were being left behind. They were strung along a thousand miles of trail behind, buried in the sands of the Platte where the church bell had been dumped overboard, sunk under the waters of the Snake where the plows had been lost, scattered at a dozen places in the trail-side dust. The loss of each item had been mourned; a small piece of grief had been left behind with each. Now there was no more grief left than there was wagon.

They went on. And on the evening of the twenty-third day, she wrote: "Reached Fort Boise today, where we were well received . . . the desert is now behind us, they say, for which Heaven be thanked . . . I know how Moses and the Israelites felt . . ."

Fort Boise. And over it floated the twin flags of the Hudson's Bay Company and Great Britain.

## 27

THEY STAYED at Fort Boise two days. The factor in charge of the post, Thomas McKay, was hospitable enough, treating the Metcalfs as honored guests, advising Clint about the mountain passage ahead, giving him news of the Bonneville party. There had been bad forest fires up in the Blues two weeks ago, he said, which had blocked Bonneville's way, delaying him for several days while his scouts futilely sought some way around them, forcing him finally to swing north and cross the rugged Wallowas, as he had done on his previous trip, over trails fit only for a goat. But there had been rain lately and though the forests were still smoldering in spots McKay thought Clint's party could get through.

This was the twenty-fourth day of August. Clint reminded Metcalf of that. They still had a long way to go, he pointed out, much to be done before winter set in, and time was growing short. The desert crossing had so exhausted the teams that it would be sheer folly to attempt taking the wagon any farther, even abbreviated and lightened as it was.

"Your plows are gone," Clint said. "Most of your seeds and tools are gone. What little you've got left we can carry on pack horses. There's no sense in taking the wagon any farther — it'd only be a millstone around our necks."

"McKay has horses," Metcalf said stubbornly. "Why can't we trade him mine for fresh ones? I'd pay him liberal boot."

"He won't trade."

"Why not?"

Clint shrugged. "Try him."

Metcalf did try — and quickly learned that McKay's hospitality did not extend to business matters. He would buy the teams. He would buy the cows. He would buy the wagon. But he would not trade or sell anything — not even so much as a pinch of gunpowder or salt. His attitude puzzled Metcalf. Clint explained it with a grim smile.

"Company orders. Don't fight Americans. Feed 'em if you have to. But don't do a thing to help 'em on their way."

"That extends to missionaries too?"

"Seems to."

The battered, much repaired wagon sat in the fort yard. Metcalf's eyes sought it out and lingered on it a moment, bitter with disappointment. He gazed off to the west, where the yellow-brown foothills on the far side of the Snake lifted into the smoke haze covering the higher crests of the Blues.

"Very well, we'll leave it. But there will be other years."

McKay's outward friendliness and inward coldness were shown in other ways. He made sure that the mountain men in the party were well fed and entertained. Of evenings there was rum for those who wanted it. Tobacco was passed out with a free hand. The post employees went out of their way to be convivial, and if late at night when everybody was in a mellow mood some rather extravagant statements were made as to the size of the yearly wages the Company was willing to pay its employees and none too subtle efforts were made to persuade Clint's men to desert him — well, that was just part of the game.

Nor did McKay neglect Two Bears. Presents, promises of good beaver prices, vague hints of how much happier and better off the Nez Perces would be trading with the British rather than with the Americans. All in the game too.

But it was on Ellen that McKay exercised most of his considerable charm. Clint was aware of it but he had no idea of how shrewdly McKay was playing his game until Ellen came to him fresh from a long talk with the Hudson's Bay Company factor.

"Mr. McKay is not at all like I thought he would be. Why, from what I had heard, I expected him to be surly and resentful of our coming. But he isn't that way in the least. He's sincerely glad we've come."

"Why?"

"Because he's interested in seeing the Indians converted to Christianity. All the Company factors are, he says. The more peaceful the Indians become, the more the fur trade can be developed. The Company is quite anxious to have the Indians Christianized and is eager to help missionaries of any faith, he says. Dr. McLoughlin, the head factor at

Fort Vancouver, has given his employees strict orders to that effect."

"That's news to me."

"It's so. Mr. McKay says he has sent a courier to Fort Walla Walla to tell the factor there that we're coming. The courier will take the news downriver to Fort Vancouver too. Mr. McKay says he's sorry he doesn't have enough stores to equip us with all the things we'll need to establish the mission, but he's sure that if we will only go to Fort Vancouver Dr. McLoughlin will give us everything we need."

Yes, McKay was playing the game well. The Metcalfs had only a vague comprehension of distance and terrain and did not realize that Fort Vancouver was four hundred miles west of the Clearwater country. After their long overland trip, the fort would be bound to impress them, for it was a big post, stocked with all the comforts and luxuries that the land and a yearly supply ship from England could provide. Dr. McLoughlin was a kind man and a fine host and a good Christian gentleman. He would have a house available for the Metcalfs, no doubt, with a tight roof on it and furniture in it and rugs on the floors. He knew the country as no other man, therefore could give advice that would be sound beyond dispute.

At Fort Vancouver the autumn rains would be beginning shortly after the Metcalfs arrived, steady, dreary rains that would continue for months to come. But there would be snow in the colder interior country, McLoughlin would quietly point out, and this was no time of year to leave a tight roof and a warm fire and go four hundred miles up-river into an unsettled land where the best shelter they could hope for would be the uncomfortable one of an Indian tepee. Wait until spring, he would say.

*But we came to minister to the Indians. We must not be idle.*

No need to be. Across the river in the Willamette Valley are many Indians who are eager for the word of God. A sizable settlement of white people, too, retired fort employees with their Indian wives and half-breed children. Why not start a mission there while you're waiting for spring to come? It would be a great blessing. And we need a school . . .

It was not Clint's place to point out these things, so he said nothing. But he saw the way McKay's stick was floating. And so did Two Bears, who listened uneasily to the factor's speeches, accepted his gifts, but grew increasingly restless during their stay at the fort. He said nothing to Clint or the Metcalfs, but toward evening of the second day Clint saw him conversing earnestly with a straight-limbed young Cayuse buck who had drifted into the post that afternoon. All Clint caught of the conversation were a few bits of guarded hand-talk as he chanced to stroll by — signs meaning a far place and a long ride and don't-let-any-grass-grow under-your-pony's-feet. A while later, he saw the Cayuse buck go galloping off into the dusk. He smiled to himself.

Two Bears was sending his own courier across the mountains.

When they left Fort Boise, next morning, the sky was gray over the Blues and smoke haze paled the sun to a wanly yellow disk. They crossed the river Indian style, the horses swimming free, the men in the water behind them clinging to their tails, the women and children, tepees, tents and supplies ferried across on rafts of cottonwood logs. The cows had forded and swum too many rivers to balk at one more, and gave no trouble.

For three days they traveled in a general northerly direction along the left bank of the Snake, then on the fourth day they deserted the river, swinging northwest and beginning the long climb toward the crest of the Blues. It was a relief to be shut of the wagon but it had been with them so long Clint found himself mentally judging each difficult stretch of trail, calculating how a slope could be negotiated here, a stream forded there, a narrow rock-strewn canyon threaded, a dense thicket cleared enough to bull the wagon through. Indian ponies wouldn't do for these steep grades, he knew, nor would the light draft animals Metcalf had used to pull the wagon as far as Fort Boise. Mules might be the answer. Or better still, oxen.

It was Two Bears who guided the party now, for this was a piece of country Clint had but a sketchy knowledge of. Day and night the smoke haze stayed with them, limiting visibility, giving the air a biting acrid smell, making them cough constantly. The stream valley up which they were traveling was a twisting snake track, with the trail first on one side of the shallow trickle of water, then on the other, forcing them to cross it dozens of times each day.

McKay had said it had rained lately up in the Blues, but there was no evidence of recent moisture in these parched hills. Dry gray sagebrush gave way to drier-looking yellow bunch-grass. Lava bluffs and boulders had a burnt, cinder-black look to them, and the heat of midday was stifling. Yet when they camped and night fell, darkness brought chill currents of air down from heights hidden by smoke haze, a sure indication of the nearness of tall mountain peaks.

The stream left them and the country opened up into a wide valley, and for a day or so the going was level and easy. They began to climb again. Now timber appeared as they crossed a low ridge, then it vanished as they made a slight descent into another valley. Then up again, with the smoke thickening and the timber growing denser and taller. Time and again they passed patches of burned trees, many of whose naked trunks were still smoldering. Traveling became a nightmarelike feeling forward through eye-smarting gloom so intense that Clint marveled at Two Bears' ability to keep to the trail.

They were seldom without Cayuse company now. Groups

of Indians appeared and disappeared at all hours of the day, sometimes bringing gifts of fresh meat or newly picked berries or dried roots which were welcomed by all, for in this smoke-choked haze the risk of getting lost was too great for Clint to permit any hunters to leave the party. They crossed yet another broad valley where the soil was black and rich-looking. There was a lake here whose waters were so hot that steam rose from them and a strong sulfurous smell added its stench to that of the burning forests. A ways further a clear cold stream crossed their path, a stream which Two Bears indicated ran north and east through a wide and beautiful valley and alongside of which ran an old trail the Cayuses were accustomed to follow whenever they went to visit their Nez Perce cousins. No, he did not intend to lead this party by that route; their way led yonder — he gestured off into the blank wall of smoke haze — over the mountains and then down to the plain where the King George men had built their fort at the junction of the Walla Walla River with the Columbia.

"Is the fire worse up ahead?" Clint asked.

"It still burns in places, the Cayuse say. But we can get through."

Again they climbed. That day smoke was so thick that sunrise, noon and sunset all seemed one. Sleep was impossible that night, for the only way they could breathe was by keeping their faces covered with cloths soaked in water. Choking, coughing and miserable, the whole party huddled along the banks of the stream on which camp had been made, keeping the cloths soaked, breathing the somewhat purer air which the stream carried down with it from the higher slopes.

Toward midnight, a breeze began to blow. Clint heard it stirring the tops of the pines overhead long before it made itself felt on the ground. Knowing what wind could do to a forest fire, he sought out Two Bears, whom he found sitting nearby, a wet rag tied around his face, dozing imperturbably. Though Clint's footfall had made no sound, the Nez Perce chief woke as Clint squatted down beside him. Before Clint could speak, he said, "The trees whisper. There will be wind."

"I know there'll be wind. The question is, which way will it come from? And which way is the fire from us?"

Two Bears gestured in one direction with his left hand. "The fire is there." He paused for a moment, then waved his right hand in the opposite direction. "The wind will come from there. It will be Lo-ki-ye-wah — the Hot Wind — which roars much but does no harm."

"I hope you're right."

"I have said it."

"Will it bring any rain?"

"It will bring thunder. It will bring lightning. As for rain — " Two Bears spat on the ground. "It will bring no more than that."

The Nez Perce chief was right. Minutes later Lo-ki-ye-wah struck, a torrent of wind, filling the night with a great bluster of thunder and lightning and dust scooped up off distant desert lands, but only a few scattered drops of rain fell. Within an hour's time the storm was done. The smoke was gone, leaving the air clean and cool. Most of the members of the party fell into an exhausted sleep, but Clint and Zack Parkins climbed to a rocky spur of ridge a few hundred yards above the camp, from whence they got a clear view of a sizable piece of country.

In the direction from whence the wind had come lay the dark folds of forested mountain slopes. In the opposite direction the entire sky was aflame; tongues of fire danced along ridge lines as far as the eye could see, and entire mountains were ablaze.

"Now thar's Hell's back porch, I'm thinkin'," Zack grunted. "We'd be fried fer shore, had that wind come from t'other way. Pays t'have a preacher along, I'd say."

"Do you think he arranged it?"

"Wal, he'd shore of been embarrassed good, wouldn't he, if he'd let us all be burnt to crisps? Least it would seem to me a mighty poor recommendation fer him out hyar whar he's a stranger. Sort of git him off on the wrong foot, so to speak."

Next day, the way still led upward. Shortly after noon they paused to rest and eat beside a spring which welled out of the base of a wall of lichen-covered rocks. They were in deep forest now, with the red-brown boles of huge pines all around them and the sun screened off by interlaced limbs overhead. Along the course of the stream which the spring formed was a scattering of alder and aspen, a sure sign that they had reached a substantial altitude, and even at noonday there was a welcome coolness in the air. Two Bears made a rippling sign with his hands, then facing the northwest he spread his arms and made a sign meaning a wide country and a big river. Ellen asked Clint what the Nez Perce chief was saying.

"That we've reached the top of the Blues. That the streams all run northwest now toward the Columbia, which we'll be seeing before the day's over."

"It's that close?"

Clint smiled. "No, but we'll be seeing it."

Puzzled by his answer, she rode beside him for the rest of the afternoon's travel, which for a time was a slow winding across a high plateau among great trees. Then gradually the timber began to thin, the way to drop. Aspen and alder disappeared. The pine trees became smaller, appearing only in clumps now, with the clearings between filled with breast-high thickets of sumach and elderberry bushes, on the latter of which hung clusters of purple fruit. Clint sensed her growing excitement and guessed its cause. The last river was ahead. The Columbia. The last river. It gave meaning to all the months and miles behind; it was a goal longed for and talked about and dreamed of, and now it was about to be seen for the first time.

Two Bears arranged it well. Less than an hour of daylight remained when he signed that this was the spot where camp was to be made, here in a grass-filled swale near a clear-flowing stream with a few low, gnarled pine trees on a rise of land close by. The mountain men started to unpack the horses but Two Bears motioned for them to let it go for the time being and said, "Come."

The entire party followed him as he strode up a slight slope, around a clump of screening bushes, out to a bare promontory of hill from which the view was unobstructed in all directions save that from which they had come. Waving a hand at the reach of space visible before them, he said, "Look!" and then was silent.

Standing beside Ellen, Clint saw her catch her breath sharply. He smiled but did not speak. Out yonder lay the biggest piece of country she had ever seen from one spot, he knew. From this height the mountains fell sharply away, dark-timbered heights melting into foothills yellow with autumn-dry bunch-grass, blending into plains gray with sagebrush, plains reaching out toward a horizon so distant and wide that the world's rim showed as a distinct curve.

In the middle distance glittered a thin silver line, running from north to south, then disappearing behind a bluff that looked to be no bigger than a thimble though he knew it was a thousand feet tall. He pointed toward it.

"Yonder's your river."

"The Columbia?"

"Yeah."

"But it looks so tiny."

"It's a mile wide, right there."

"How far away is it, for goodness' sake?"

"Two good day's travel. Fifty miles, I'd guess, at least."
He swung his arm around slightly and pointed directly
west. "See that nubbin sticking up over the horizon line
just to the right of where the sun's going down?"

"Yes. What is it?"

"Mount Hood. It's a couple of miles high, they say —
and two hundred miles away."

"It doesn't seem possible!"

No, it did not. But there it was — the long look and
nothing like it anywhere in the West that he knew of. A
person could stand here looking, thinking about how he'd
get up in the morning and travel all day and make camp
and how he'd travel the next day and the day after and
keep traveling for a week to come and still not be out of
sight from this spot. It was like looking into time as well
as space, and it gave a person a feeling of not amounting
to much, when all was said and done, no more than a grain
of dust amounted to anything in relation to the whole wide
world.

And what did a man amount to? He was born, lived a
brief while, died — and the world was still there, pretty
much as he'd found it, in spite of all the howling and
scratching and struggling he'd done. What was Bonneville
and what was Wyeth and what was all their scratching and
scheming worth, so far as having any effect on a country
as big as this was concerned? And how much good would
the Metcalfs do, for all their fine dreams, and what was
the point in helping them make a pin scratch that time's
first breeze would wipe off the face of the earth, when all
that mattered to a man such as himself was . . .

That was the point. What did matter to him?

The sun was gone. All the others had left the promontory, leaving only himself and Ellen still standing gazing
out over the darkening land. What her thoughts had been
this past half hour he could not guess but for a moment

there seemed to be an understanding between them, complete and as near to the way it used to be as it could ever be again. Her voice came to him with a gentleness and a softness that held neither regret nor hope.

"What was she like, Clint?"

"Who?"

"Daniel's mother."

"She was where I was when I wanted her to be there. She was what I wanted her to be." He was silent a long while. "That doesn't make any sense, does it?"

"She was all the things to you that I could not be. That's what you're saying."

"Is it?"

She turned to him. In the faint light he saw that her eyes were glistening. "She had only you to think of, Clint. I had others."

"I realized that — later."

Their hands had somehow met. They stood there, gazing at each other for a long moment, then she smiled, squeezed his hands and turned quickly away. "Thank you for that, Clint. I've been talking like a foolish young girl. It won't happen again, I promise you. Let's go back to camp."

# 28

BACK AT Fort Boise when McKay and his men had tried to talk Burn Rapp into quitting the party and going to work for the Hudson's Bay Company, he had laughed in

their faces. Any old time he earned his living by taking
orders from a Britisher it would only be because he'd gone
clean out of his senses, he declared. Hell, he knew how the
Company treated its men! Like soldiers in an army. Like
slaves. The Company claimed to own all the beaver in
the country, live or dead, skinned or unskinned, and any
man caught trapping without permission was treated like
a poacher — put in irons, flogged, even hung if the Company took the notion. Damned if he'd put up with that
sort of nonsense!

"*C'est vrai,*" a French-Canadian *engagé* answered, shrugging indifferently, as if this were a fact of life to be accepted without protest. "What you say is true. But we
are fed, clothed and supplied. We are paid a yearly wage.
What more could you wish?"

"I got to be my own man."

"Ah, you desire freedom!"

"You're damned right I do!"

"Has it made you rich, this freedom you boast of?"

"I'm gettin' by."

"But you work now for the American bourgeois, *n'est-
ce pas?*"

"I'm givin' Doc Metcalf a hand. But only because I
want to. I'm still my own man."

The *engagé* laughed. "*Oui. Je comprends.* You are free.
But what is freedom? Only a word. Does it put powder in
the horn, food and drink in the belly? *Mais non!* Our way
is better."

Rapp didn't agree and he made no effort to conceal his
contempt for men who would trade their personal freedom
for a pinch of powder and the promise of a square meal.
Sure, he'd worked for wages last year. Would again if the
right offer came along. But there was a difference between
working for an American and a Britisher. A big difference.
In the one case you sold your employer your time and labor;

in the other you sold him your soul. The one treated you like a man; the other like a dog. If you didn't like the way your American boss held his mouth when he gave you orders, you could tell him to go to hell, quit and go to work for somebody else. But Hudson's Bay had a monopoly on the country out here — so it was take what their head men gave you or get out. He wanted no part of that.

It took the party fifteen days to cross the Blues. Because of the smoke haze, he saw little of the mountains until the day after the midnight windstorm cleared the air but that one day of sparkling sunshine and blue sky stirred a restlessness in him. It was getting on into September. He didn't have to look at a calendar to realize that. September signs were all around him — streams at their lowest level of the year, aspen, sumach and vine maple looking withered and dust-dry, ready to flame gold and crimson with the first touch of frost, which in these heights could come any night now that the air had cleared. Beaver pelts would be thickening under the coarse outer guard-hairs, turning glossy and fine and smooth. Soon be time for him and Fram to strike out for whatever trapping grounds they figured to work this year.

He did some brooding on that. The Three Forks region was too far to the east to be considered now but there were other nearer trapping grounds. When they reached Fort Walla Walla, they would be out of the Blues, he knew, and would swing east across open, rolling plains for a hundred miles or so to the Clearwater valley. That would be the end of the trail for the Metcalfs, and the chores he and Fram had undertaken to do would be finished. Northeast, east, southeast, most any direction a man wanted to go from the lower Clearwater except directly west lay sizable mountain ranges. He didn't know that country too well, but where there were mountains there were streams, where there were streams there was beaver, and the habit of long years was impatiently nagging him to get at the work he liked best to do.

The party reached Fort Walla Walla on the ninth day of September and rested there for three days, much to his disgust. Save for occasional headaches which still bothered him now and then, he had completely recovered his strength and considered the time spent at the fort as wasted, though he realized that the Metcalfs were exhausted and needed it. The post did not impress him at all favorably; he had the mountain man's ingrained dislike of flat, treeless country.

The fort sat on a sandy, wind-whipped tongue of land where the sluggish, narrow Walla Walla River joined the Columbia. All around it the country was bleak and arid-looking, with sagebrush-covered desert stretching off to the north, immense yellow hills rising to the east and south and the wide river making its final bend westward toward the sea through a gap between two black lava buttes which rose steep and tall from either shore.

Pierre Pambrun, factor in charge of the post, made them welcome, just as McKay had done, giving the Metcalfs rooms within the fort and seeing to it that the mountain men were given fresh vegetables, meat and an occasional cup of rum. The day after the party arrived a band of fifty Nez Perces rode in and made camp. They had come from the Clearwater country, they said, because one of their old men had had a dream. The dream told him that the Sent Ones were waiting at Fort Walla Walla. So they had come.

"When the Sent Ones are rested, we will guide them to our home."

Prowling restlessly about the post, Rapp was aware that a polite tug-of-war was going on between Pambrun and Two Bears. Pambrun had any number of sound, logical reasons why the Metcalfs should go downriver to Fort Vancouver. Two Bears was equally insistent that the Metcalfs go up-country now.

There was news of Wyeth and Bonneville. The brig

Wyeth had been counting on had never appeared in the lower Columbia and was now presumed lost at sea. He was finished, some said, all his fine schemes exploded in his face like pricked bubbles, and likely would be heading east shortly. Bonneville was still somewhere downriver, making his last desperate try, with the Company fighting him at every turn. If the word of François LeRoux, one of the post *engagés*, could be believed, the Company was winning.

"I 'ave met thees Captain Bonneville and he is wan fine fellow, *oui*. His *père*, he is my countryman. I drink weeth the captain and we laugh and talk and I lak him very much. But he is an American. The Company does not want him here. So the Company she squeeze him — " LeRoux smiled and gestured with thumb and finger, as if pinching the life out of a flea. "Lak so, the Company she squeeze him. He can get no beaver from the Indians. He can get no food. What can he do? Notheeng! So presently he go back where he belong."

"S'posin' he won't take that kind of treatment? S'posin' he tells the Company to go plumb to hell?"

"Words do not hurt the Company. She smile polite, she squeeze some more. It is all the same in the end. He go back where he belong."

"I hear him an' Pambrun had some trouble."

"Ah, *oui!* And for a leetle moment we think maybe M'sieu Pambrun lose his head and there will be fighting. But M'sieu Pambrun is no fool. If there is fighting, then perhaps there will come war, big war. So M'sieu Pambrun swallow his pride, smile polite and act very nice. Presently Captain Bonneville go away."

They were lounging in the dusk outside the fort walls, nursing cups of rum which LeRoux had hospitably provided, with a small fire flickering between them for company and light. Earlier the pleasant-mannered, plump little *engagé* had adroitly tried to pry out of Rapp what Clint and his men planned to do after they'd seen the Metcalfs through to the Clearwater valley, but Rapp had given him little satisfaction. In the first place he didn't know, except in a vague way, what Clint's plans were. In the second place he wouldn't have told if he had known, for there was something smug and complacent about the man's attitude that irritated him. Draining his cup, he put it down and poked scowlingly at the fire.

"Your boss is scared of Americans, ain't he?"

"*C'est possible.* They are not always easy to get along with."

"They don't like bein' shoved around, I'll vouch for that."

LeRoux laughed genially and refilled Rapp's cup. "What is the quarrel between M'sieu Pambrun and Captain Bonneville to us, *mon ami?* We are only employees, *n'est-ce pas?* As long as the belly is full and the heart light, what are the quarrels of others to us? No more than that!" He snapped his fingers. Taking a swallow of rum, he was silent a moment, then he slanted a look at Rapp and said, "You go trapping with the American *bourgeois* this season, *oui?*"

"No. I'm my own man."

"You work at the mission then?"

"What d'ye take me for, a damn hymn singer? No sir, I'll likely take off trappin' on my own."

The *engagé's* eyebrows lifted. "Alone?"

"Jest my partner an' me."

"Ah, that is a fool's game! Listen, *mon ami*, I will tell you a secret which is for your ears alone. M'sieu Pambrun has heard rumors which disturb him. The tales come from the country of the Kootenays. Soon he plans to lead a party of men there to find out what is truth and what are lies. If you and your friend wish employment —" LeRoux shrugged his chubby shoulders. "Ah, but of course you do not. You wish to trap alone."

Nothing more was said on the matter that evening, but Rapp was not so dense as to fail to see which way the ground sloped. It troubled him. Pambrun no doubt intended to try to put the same kind of squeeze on Clint and his men in the upriver country later this fall that was being put on Bonneville downriver right now. Likely the factor would do his damndest to stir up all the interior tribes against Americans. Which would make trapping there a risky business for a pair of men on their lonesome. Next morning, he sought out Oswald Fram and told him about it. Fram stared out at the river bottom where the cows were grazing and shook his head.

"Let him stir up trouble. It's nothin' to me."

"But, damn it, don't you see — we'll be caught in the same bind!"

"Not me, Burn. 'Cause I won't be goin' trappin' with you. I'm stickin' with Metcalf."

Rapp stared at him. "Doin' what?"

"Whatever he's got fer me to do. There'll be the cows to tend to. Couple of 'em are ready to drop calves most any day. There'll be timber to be felled an' cabins to be built an' land to be broke an' farmed when spring comes. He's got a heap of work to do and needs help bad. I figure to work fer him."

"What kind of wages has he offered you?"

"None to start with 'cause he's got no money. But he's writin' to the mission board back east an' askin' them to put me on the rolls at two hundred a year. He thinks maybe they'll do it."

"Hell, Oswald, you'd turn flunky fer a fool missionary fer two hundred a year? You'd leave me flat an' hire out to a milksop preacher an' a whinin' woman when you know I'm so deep in debt to Sublette fer traps an' fixin's I'll likely have to work my butt off all season to break even? You'd do that to me?"

Fram turned and looked at him, stubbornness in his face. "Doc Metcalf's no fool. You know he ain't, jest as well as I do. He's a good man. An' his sister's a good woman that's never done a minute's whinin'. Far as leavin' you flat an' in debt to Sublette is concerned — well, I've give that a lot of thought. You don't give a damn fer Sublette an' neither do I. Let him sing fer what we owe him. I'll never see him again — 'cause I'm done with beaver. An' it's high time you was done with beaver too."

"Damned if I recall givin' you leave to tell me what I was an' wasn't done with."

"All right, do what you like. But I'm done."

Try as he would, Rapp could not argue Fram out of it. Giving up in disgust, he was turning to walk away when Stanley Metcalf strode up and smiled at him. "Oh, Burn, I've been wanting to talk to you. Got a minute?"

"Reckon so," Rapp said sullenly. "What's on your mind?"

"We're starting for the Clearwater tomorrow morning. I'm writing the mission board today outlining my plans for the coming year. I've made a place for Oswald in those plans. I'd like to do the same for you."

"At the mission, you mean?"

"Yes."

"I ain't no farmer, Doc. Ner no cowherder neither."

Metcalf laughed good-naturedly. "Perhaps not. But you've got a strong back and a willing pair of hands. You've proved that to me time and again. There will be plenty of work you can do."

"I ain't sure I'm cut out fer that kind of work."

Metcalf glanced at Fram, then looked back at Rapp with a frown. "I had hoped you two would want to stay together. What are your plans?"

"Guess I'll stick to beaver, long as there's any left."

"Has Clint offered to take you on?"

"No," Rapp said harshly. "An' I wouldn't work fer him if he did. Not after what he done to me."

Metcalf's voice softened. "You'd better forget that, Burn. You can't nurse a grudge forever. It will do you more harm than it does the one you hold it against."

"I'm obliged fer yore doctorin'. But I won't hold still fer

no preachin'. What's between Clint an' me is our business an' nobody else's. I'll thank you to leave it that way."

"I'm afraid I can't," Metcalf said sharply. "Not when I feel that your grudge against Clint is keeping you from doing something that deep in your heart you would really like to do. Do you feel that Clint will look down on you if you go to work for me? Is that it?"

Rapp scowled down at the ground and did not answer. He would not admit it, not even to himself, but the fact was Doc Metcalf was probing around pretty close to the truth, and the probing hurt. How they'd talk, come rendezvous next summer, should he be done with beaver and turn to being a flunky for the Metcalfs! It was a thing he was of no mind to take.

"Well, think it over," Metcalf said, turning away. "If you change your mind between now and tomorrow morning, let me know."

That evening, Rapp looked up François LeRoux, who managed to wrangle another quart of rum out of Pambrun, and they did some more drinking and talking together. Rapp got a little drunk. Not blind drunk, for there was not that much rum. But drunk enough to say some things and swallow some things that up until now had always managed to get stuck in his craw. Drunk enough to bring on another one of his headaches next morning so that as he stood staring out across the flat, watching the Nez Perces, the Metcalfs, Fram, Clint and the other men in the party ride off toward the east at an early hour, the sun slanting in over the yellow hills glared painfully in his eyes. Yet he kept staring, even though drums were pounding in his head, until the party disappeared beyond a curve of hill. Then he turned, blinking angrily, and let his eyes run over the bleak, dust-whipped flat where the Hudson's Bay Company post sat.

LeRoux was standing beside him, chuckling complacently, "Ah, eet is a great pity that they would not listen to M'sieu Pambrun's most wise advice to go downriver. But they weel learn. *Oui*, they weel learn. For the Company she weel squeeze them, lak so — "

Rapp raised his eyes and stared at the twin flags fluttering above the fort, paying no mind to the *engagé's* chatter for a moment, then suddenly becoming aware of it and chopping it off with a bluntness that made the man's mouth drop slack and his eyes widen with a sudden start of fear.

"Shut yore mouth, you goddamn Britisher! You keep on squeezin' Americans, you bastards are goin' to learn somethin' too."

# 29

TEN DAYS after the party left Fort Walla Walla it made camp on the west bank of the Snake, directly opposite the mouth of the Clearwater. The last camp, Clint mused. Tomorrow they would cross the last river. And then there would be one last day's travel and the thing would end.

Evening quiet lay over the valley and the cooling air held the campfire smokes low to the ground. A sure sign of autumn, that, when smoke failed to rise. The canyon of the Snake yonder to the south was filled with a blue haze, and the treeless, bunch-grass covered hills rising from the river glowed a dreary yellow-brown, stark-looking, dead-looking, splotched here and there by dark outcroppings of lava. Big hills by a big river in a bigger land. And he was just six feet tall.

He sat smoking, brooding on the tall hills and the dull green surface of the swirling river below him while day faded. Zack Parkins strolled over and squatted beside him.

"Seem to of mislaid my tobacco. Got any to spare?"

"Help yourself," Clint said, tossing him his half-filled pouch.

Zack loaded and lighted his pipe, eying him quizzically. "Sour-bug bit you? Er did you eat some tainted fish fer supper?"

"Do I look that bad?"

"Wal, not bad exactly. Jest broody."

Clint smiled. "I've been thinking. Guess the strain shows."

"Thinkin'll do that to a man. What, f'r instance, have you thunk?"

Clint lounged on an elbow, watching the stars pop out as the sky paled. "What ever happened to the old days, Zack, when all we had to worry about was beaver, keeping our scalps and staying alive till next year's rendezvous?"

"You think they're mislaid?"

"I know they are."

"Wal, now, I will admit thet the past year er two things have changed a sight. Forts springin' up all over the country. People clawin' an' scratchin' an' squabblin' every way you look. But them curiosities are jest happen-so's. Only thing that counts in the long run out hyar is beaver. Always was that way. Always will be."

"Cows don't count? Nor plows? Nor missionaries?"

"Hell, Clint, what's a few cows er plows er missionaries in a country as big as this 'un? Nothin'! Not nothin' a-tall!"

Clint pursued the subject no further, though he knew Zack was wrong. They were both silent for a time, then Zack said, "What happens after tomorrow?"

"That depends."

"On what?"

"Metcalf, for one thing. Maybe he'll like the spot I've picked for him. Maybe he won't. If he doesn't like it we'll have to take him someplace else. If he does, we'll hang around for a week or so and help him get set for the winter. Maybe we'll hear from Judd by then. Or Bonny. If we don't, we'll try to gather up a few Nez Perce head men and see how they feel toward peace talks with the Blackfeet. Things go right, we might take a little jaunt up to the Kootenay country."

"I heerd talk back at Fort Walla Walla that Pambrun was plannin' a trip thataway himself. What do you reckon he's up to?"

"The same thing we are, likely."

"Don't recall you've ever told me jest what that is. Fact, thar's a hell of a lot about the things we're doin' er fixin' to do which I don't savvy in the slightest. Bonny wants beaver, don't he?"

"Among other things."

"Wal, the way to trap beaver is to head fer the mountains with a sack full of traps, go to work an' trap beaver! Least that's the way it looks to me. But Bonny goes traipsin' off down the Columbia, Judd wanders up to the buffler country, an' we ride herd on a pair of missionaries. Whar's the sense to it all, that's what I want to know!"

"Maybe there isn't any. But Bonny thinks so. And he's paying our wages."

"Jest 'tween you an' me," Zack muttered. "What do *you* think?"

"I don't know," Clint murmured, shaking his head. "I just don't know. But we'll do what we're paid to do."

They crossed the river next morning and traveled east up the right bank of the Clearwater. A gray overcast hung low over the bare hills, one of the few such days they had known since leaving rendezvous, and the air had a moist feel to it. Shortly after noon it began to rain, a fine, light rain falling in a windless hush, barely dampening their clothes. The river, which here was a hundred or so yards wide, was running very low, the high-water marks in its rock-strewn channel showing a good six feet above the present surface of the water.

For the past several days the number of Nez Perces traveling with them had constantly grown and though Two Bears rode wrapped in dignity his dark eyes glowed with the inner pride he was feeling in leading the Sent Ones to their new home. Fram, fussy as a mother hen, was having increasing difficulty keeping the curious Indians away from his cows. Both Stanley and Ellen were showing signs of strain, their eyes anxiously reaching ahead through the gray day to each far curve of the river valley, looking for they knew not what.

Tepees were scattered along the valley now, and Ellen, coming forward to ride alongside Clint, asked, "Do we have much farther to go?"

"Only a few miles. Are you tired?"

"A little."

Her face was pale and taut, her smile wan, and something in the flat deadness of her voice gave him an inkling of what she must be feeling. Way back in February the journey had begun for her, a continent away, and since then she had had no rest, no peace, no relief from the uncertainty of looking forward to a new home in a strange land among a people so different from those she had known all her life. Presently she would see the chosen spot. He hoped she was not expecting too much.

It was midafternoon when they struck a valley opening up to the south. A creek fringed with trees and carrying a narrow trickle of water joined the Clearwater here. The party turned to the right, past the Indian tepees strung along the

creek, past the horse herds scattered out across the valley
floor, and moved up the stream. Now the valley widened to
a breadth of several miles, with the creek flowing near the
base of bare hills to one side and more bare hills rising into
the gray gloom of midafternoon to the other.

And here Clint stopped.

"This is it."

Neither Ellen nor Stanley spoke. They sat on their horses,
looking out over the flat valley floor, looking at the yellow
hills which rose bleak and bare and cheerless on all sides,
looking at the sprinkling of tepees. Stanley's face was expressionless, save for a faint tightening of the jaw muscles.
In Ellen's eyes there was such a numbed, stricken look that
Clint could no longer bear to watch her.

Swinging down to the ground, he let them be, busying
himself giving camping orders to the mountain men in the
party and then lending them a hand as they stripped saddles
and packs off the horses. He was irritated to note that Fram
and one of the cows had dropped behind, the other animals
having been brought along by Beartracks Weaver, who was
grumbling about the chore that had been thrust upon him.

"What'll I do with the fool things?" Beartracks muttered.

"Let them graze. They can't go anyplace. Just make sure
the Indian kids leave them alone."

"Fool cows! A plumb nuisance, thet's all they'll be!"

"What happened to Fram?"

"Damned if I know! Come ridin' up to me a few miles
back, actin' crazy as a loon, an' said one of his cows was
down. Asked me to bring these hyar critters on. Said he'd
bring 'tother 'un along shortly."

Stanley had helped Ellen get down. Knowing how she
must feel, Clint had had her tent put up and he went to
them now, intending to suggest that she lie down and rest
for a while. But before he could speak Stanley said, "You
think this is the best location for the mission?"

Clint nodded, repeating what he had said before: that the location was central to all the Nez Perce tribes, that the soil was good, timber for building near, plenty of grass available, the climate mild because of its low elevation, and the valley well sheltered from winter's snows by the surrounding hills. He felt no need to explain to Metcalf such obvious things as the fact that at this time of year the hills looked their bleakest, that in spring they were green and beautiful, that in early summer they were covered with wildflowers, that later this fall after the frosts had come the ravines would flame with sumach. But for Ellen's sake he felt he must say something.

"It isn't as bad as it looks, Ellen. Not near. Take my word for that."

She smiled, but the stunned, hopeless look was still in her eyes. "I'm sure you know what's best for us, Clint."

Stanley's eyes were roaming about him, a restlessness in them now, a practical-minded thoughtfulness, as if he were trying to see the exact shape of the reality which faced him and was fitting into it the images of things to come. Turning to Clint, he said, "Call the men together, please. The Indians too. It's only fitting that we thank God for seeing us safely to this spot."

It took a few minutes to get the mountain men and Indians all assembled. They stood then, bareheaded and eyes on the ground, while Stanley Metcalf went down on his knees. In the hushed and waiting silence that fell as he was about to begin his prayer, the sound of a horse's hoofs was suddenly heard. Metcalf looked up in irritation. Oswald Fram, beside himself with excitement, rode up, carrying a squirming tawny body on the saddle before him, while behind his horse lumbered a clumsy, outraged cow, bawling at the top of her lungs. Oblivious to the solemnity of the moment, Fram tumbled to the ground, ran toward Metcalf and deposited a newborn calf on the ground before him.

"Look, Doc Metcalf — look what I got hyar!"

Metcalf stared. Blood and afterbirth slime stained Fram's hands. The calf, which could barely stand, toppled ludicrously to the ground as its indignant mother crowded in to lick its still-damp body. Fram was chuckling like a madman.

"It's a bull calf, Doc! Honest to God it is! A bull calf, you hear me?"

Metcalf smiled and murmured, "The Lord be praised! We have much to thank Him for."

Again they bowed their heads and fell silent. Clint caught a glimpse of Ellen's face. As the prayer began she was gazing at the calf, the taut bleakness gone, the numbed look gone, her eyes warm and smiling and bright.

Presently the prayer was finished. Stanley Metcalf rose, gazed out across the valley through the gray afternoon and murmured, "There is much to do. Tomorrow we'll go to work."

PART THREE

# a stone
# in the garden

## 30

TWO BEARS was not happy over the fact that the Sent Ones had decided to settle in this valley rather than in the mountains of his own Salmon River country but he soon became reconciled to it. He would not be selfish, he said. It was best that the Sent Ones live in a spot where they could minister to and teach all the Nez Perce people. This was a good place to live when the snows fell, though only a foolish man would stay in such an oven when the hot moons came. His own band would be returning to the Salmon River mountains from the buffalo country soon. He would go to them now and tell them what the Sent Ones had decided to do. Those who wished could return with him and his family and spend the winter here.

There was news from the buffalo country, for already Nez Perces from the Wallowa and lower Clearwater bands were passing through the valley, laden with dried meat and hides, eager to see the Big Medicine which they had heard was coming to their land. Sitting in Two Bears' tepee the second evening, Clint listened to their stories, prodding them with questions.

"See any Blackfoot?"

Yes, most all had had the usual brushes with Blackfeet, though so far as he could tell the scrapes had been mostly shoot-and-run affairs with little damage done to either side.

"Did you see Eagle-With-One-Wing, Small Crow and the white men with them?"

No, but they had seen other Indians who had and they had heard tales of a big fight with much shooting and many horses stolen, though where it had happened and what the details were no one seemed to know for sure.

"Hear any peace talk?"

Oddly enough, they had, though only in a twisted sort of way. It was Red Elk, a subchief of the Wallowa band, who told the story, and a most curious tale it was. He and half a dozen of his warrior friends had been hunting one day when, upon topping a ridge, they had suddenly come upon three naked Blackfoot braves bathing in a bush-fringed creek. The surprise was complete on both sides.

Save for the lone smooth-bored musket which Red Elk himself carried, none of the Indians had guns. Grabbing up bows, arrow quivers and breechclouts, the Blackfeet scrambled for cover. Two of Red Elk's companions managed to wing a few arrows at the Blackfeet, and he, had his musket not misfired, would most certainly have killed one and taken his scalp. But the three Blackfeet had safely reached shelter in the thick bushes, where it was impossible to see them.

Red Elk then gave Clint a long and detailed account of a typical Indian scrap. With the Blackfeet well hidden in the bushes, none of the Nez Perces was foolish enough to crawl in after them, and with the Nez Perces mounted and surrounding the bushes, the Blackfeet wisely stayed where they were. Neither side had any intention of wasting powder or arrows on targets which they could not see, so for the next few hours before darkness ended the battle it resolved itself into a contest of words, with the cornered Blackfeet trying to anger the Nez Perces by taunts and insults so that they

would rashly crawl into the thicket and the Nez Perces reply-
ing in kind, trying to goad the Blackfeet into crawling out.
Neither event took place, but the thing that interested Clint
in Red Elk's tale was the taunt which he reported a Blackfoot had called out to him.

"Where are the fine long rifles the Bald White Chief has
given you? Let them speak so that I may hear their voice!
Let them speak and I will swallow the bullets and spit them
out like pebbles! Where is the Big Medicine Talker and
She-Who-Rides-Sideways, who your chiefs claim bring you
such great magic? Show them to me so that I may tremble
with fear! Where are the white men who claim to be your
friends and pretend to be so brave yet who are so weak and
timid that they shiver in fear when they see the Gros Ventres
and bribe them with gifts of long rifles because they are
afraid to fight? Send your white friends to me so that I may
strip them and see if they own that which makes a man a
man or are only squaws dressed in men's clothes!"

Red Elk had been puzzled at the taunts then, though
since talking to Two Bears he had learned what they meant.
*News spreads fast,* Clint brooded. *It gets twisted, sure, but
it gets around. Now the question is, what effect will it have?*

Two Bears and his family left for Salmon River next day,
taking Daniel with them. The cub wanted bad to stay, Clint
knew, for he'd become something of a pet of the mountain
men and was having the time of his life lording it over the
other Nez Perce youngsters during the excitement of cabin-
building and getting the Metcalfs settled. Going to be
spoiled rotten if he didn't watch out, Clint admitted ruefully to himself, what with all the attention Daniel was getting from his indulgent grandfather, Ellen and the mountain
men, yet he had to confess it gave a man a nice warm feeling
to see his own youngster being made so much over. But
there was work to be done right now. Better to get the cub
out from underfoot for a spell.

Judd Smith and his four men showed up a week later, ragged and lean from the forced marches they'd made lately. They had parted with the Salmon River band on the other side of the Bitter Roots, Judd said, the Indians heading south and west toward home while he and his party had cut directly west across the mountains by way of the rugged Lolo Pass country and the old Nez Perce trail down the Clearwater. Considering the odds he was up against in the buffalo country, he'd done as good a job as any man could have been expected to do.

"You had it figgered about right," he told Clint. "The only time Eagle-With-One-Wing was willin' to talk about makin' peace with the Blackfoot was when he was sittin' safe in his lodge with no Blackfoot anywheres near him. He'd promise most anything then. But the minute the old coot laid eyes on one of the jiggers, he was all fer fightin'. I held him down, much as I could. But I got to admit he had his way a time er two."

"Any serious trouble come up?"

"Wal, now, outside of some hoss-stealin' an' piddlin' raids back an' forth thar was only one real bad fuss. It come on sudden an' accidental, like them things usually do. Guess they was fifty er sixty Injuns on both sides mixed into it, 'fore it was over, an' thar was some hair lost. Five Blackfoot was made meat of, by my tally, an' a couple of Nez Perce bucks went under."

"Did you get into it?"

"Didn't happen to be thar myself, no. But Luke Young an' Sam Jackson was. Way they tell it, the blame fight started an' ended so quick that thar wasn't no time fer talk, even if anybody concerned had been interested in talkin'. Seemed only natural fer 'em to jine in the tussle, so they flung a shot or two at the Blackfoot, jest to let 'em know they was thar." Judd chuckled. "It was real comical, Luke said, to see the way them Blackfoot cut an' run when they heerd them long rifles startin' to speak their piece."

"You got no chance to parley with any of the Blackfeet, then?"

Judd rubbed his jaw. "Matter of fact, we did manage one session. Me an' Small Crow an' a dozen er so of his bucks was up in the Hellgate country one day when we happened to see some Injuns watchin' us from a ridge a couple of miles away. Country was purty flat an' open, our hosses was fresh an' our main village wasn't more'n six, eight miles away. Didn't look like thar was more'n a dozen Injuns on the ridge, but the way the land lay we wasn't about to go ridin' hell-bent fer them an' a fight, 'cause thar was no tellin' what we might be gettin' into, an' they seemed mighty leery of tacklin' us. So we done some signalin' back an' forth. Purty soon they come easin' out on the flat an' met us whar we each had a good show to run er fight, should the need come to us. Turned out to be a band of Piegans. Managed to swap talk a while with 'em."

"Make any impression on them?"

Judd shrugged his bony shoulders. "Who's to say? Hell, best I could make out the things I was tellin' 'em weren't news a-tall. They'd heerd of Bonny. They knowed all about the Gros Ventres bein' at rendezvous. They'd heerd about the Metcalfs, too, an' seemed mighty curious." Judd chuckled. "I gave 'em an invite to come to the mission some afternoon fer tea. They said they'd think it over. Then they asked me a queer thing."

"What was that?"

"They asked me if they could buy long rifles from the Metcalfs cheaper than they could from the American trader in their country."

Clint frowned. "There aren't any American traders in Blackfoot country closer than Fort Union — and that's clear down at the mouth of the Yellowstone."

"They claim thar's one now. Built hisself a fort on the Missoury. Near the mouth of the Marias, best I could make out. An' thar's a steamboat come up the Missoury last spring bringin' him supplies. A mean bastard, from the way they talked — which he'd have t'be to keep his scalp in that neck of the woods — an' nothin'd suit 'em better than to peel his hide off his ornery carcass an inch at a time. But they seem t' think they got to put up with him, else the Crows'll wipe 'em out."

Clint was silent for a time, his eyes moving across the valley, which now was beginning to look like a settlement of some permanence, for the walls of the cabin had been raised, a shed and corral were being built for the cows, the second of which had dropped a female calf just yesterday, firewood was stacked in cords outside the cabin, and most of the Indians in the near vicinity had brought their tepees into the valley and set them up. Horses were dragging newly cut logs toward cabin sites, the sound of axes biting into wood could be heard, and the cheerful voices of men at work struck him as a civilized sound where always before the setting up of winter camp seemed no more than a temporay clatter in the wilderness, which, when spring came and the trapping party moved on, would once again lapse into its age-old silence.

Maybe Bonneville had been right all along. Maybe his ambitious, far-flung scheme to nudge here, poke there and whittle away a bit someplace else wasn't as foolish and hopeless as it had appeared to be at first glance. A man couldn't level a mountain with a toothpick, which on the face of it was what Bonny appeared to be trying to do. But water running downhill could level mountains aplenty. And the toothpick, if used right, could channel the streams the way a man wanted them to go.

Judd filled his pipe. "Any word from Bonny?"

"Not since we left Fort Walla Walla," Clint said, shaking his head. "Last I heard he was in the downriver country, throwing rocks at the Hudson's Bay Company."

"You ditched Burn Rapp, I hear."

"He ditched us. Went to work for the Company."

"The hell he did! Now what kind of man is that, to ditch his own kind an' go to work fer a Britisher? Wal, it's good riddance, I say. He had a knack fer stirrin' up trouble. Matter of fact, that was a bad day's work I done when I kept you from gun-whippin' him to death that time he went fer White Shield. It's give me some uneasy nights, knowin' he was with you, wonderin' what he might do, should he git the chance."

"He behaved himself well enough."

"Queer he'd split with Fram."

"Fram's a born farmer. But Burn had other notions."

"He must of had," Judd muttered, shaking his head with unconcealed disgust. "Any man that'd leave his own kind an' go to work fer a Britisher . . . "

# 31

EVER SINCE Oswald Fram had learned that the six cows had been bred in midwinter, he'd been worried about them. It was against nature, breeding a cow at such a time. Any farmer knew that. Summer was your best breeding period, for then your cows wouldn't drop their calves till the next spring when the grass had turned green again and they could find plenty of feed to supply milk for their sucking calves. But let a cow drop her calf in the fall and you had a real problem on your hands, particularly if you lived in a region of severe winters, because some way or other you had to make sure there was shelter and hay enough to carry her through the winter with an ample supply of milk.

Metcalf knew that too, of course. He told Fram that the reason he'd bought winter-bred cows in Independence last spring was that he wanted to make sure that they would calve in Oregon, just in case anything happened to his two bulls on the way out. Seemed he'd done a smart thing there, for he had lost the bulls. But Fram had been worried sick for fear the heat, the poor grass and the tough months of traveling would make the cows abort on the trail. Not a one had. And so far as he could tell the two calves they had dropped so far were as sound and healthy as could be. But winter was at hand.

The Nez Perces claimed that winters hereabouts were most always open. They said that they never gave their horses a thought, just turning them loose and letting them forage for themselves on the rich dry bunch-grass of the valley and its surrounding hills, finding them just as fat in the spring as they'd been when winter began. That might be so, but Fram knew a cow with a sucking calf wasn't near the forager a horse was. He would feel one whole hell of a lot easier in mind if he could lay in at least a few weeks' supply of hay against a spell of bad weather when snow might lay so deep on the ground that his cows would go hungry.

There was wild grass aplenty in the bottoms, some of it shoulder high, and he spent long days cutting it down with a scythe, pitchforking it onto a crude sled he'd made of poles and cross timbers, dragging it to the shed and storing it under cover. He paid no mind to the way the Indians made fun of him. Let the fools laugh. He meant to take care of his cattle.

He had just finished unloading the sled one afternoon when he turned to find a young Indian boy standing silently staring at him. Used to such onlookers, he started to brush past the boy, then stopped as the youngster said, "A *suyapo* comes from the north. He wants to make talk with you."

Fram scowled. "Who is he?"

"He says he is your friend." The boy made a sign indicating a place where trees stood thick by the creek. "He waits for you there. He asks me to tell you he waits to make talk with you."

The thing had a queer sound to it but before Fram could question the Indian boy further the youngster turned and fled. Fram glanced around. Metcalf, Clint and the mountain men were working near the cabin, so it could not be one of them. The place which the boy had indicated was a quarter of a mile down the creek. Why any white man should be so secretive about talking to him was more than he could fathom, but his curiosity had been stirred so he left the shed and, deeply puzzled, walked along the footpath which paralleled the creek to the spot where the boy had said the man would be waiting.

The man was there, all right. He was sitting with his back against a tree, his rifle in his lap, his knees raised, his hands folded around them and his head resting on his forearms. At the sound of Fram's step, he lifted his head and said in a voice heavy with weariness, "Howdy, Oswald."

Fram stared. "Burn! Fer God's sake, what's happened to you?"

"Been travelin' hard, that's all."

"You sick?"

Burn Rapp sat staring dully at the ground, not answering for a moment, not even appearing to hear. Two weeks' beard stubble covered his face, which looked haggard, thin and drawn. His eyes were glazed and bloodshot, filmed by a dullness such as Fram had never seen in them before. His hand, as he raised it to rub his temples, trembled visibly.

" 'Feard I am. Thar's somethin' wrong . . . somethin' in my head — "

"Lemme help you up. I'll take you to Doc Metcalf."

"No, not yet."

"Hell, Burn, if you're sick — "

"Not yet, I said!" Rapp growled. Again he was silent, his breathing harsh and labored. "Clint still here?"

"Yeah."

"I got to talk to him."

"Shore, Burn, soon as I take you to Doc Metcalf. C'mon now, I'll help you up."

"Alone. I got to talk to him alone — " Rapp rubbed fiercely at his temples. "Somethin's happened. I got to tell him."

Scowling, Fram recalled the way they had argued back at Fort Walla Walla when Rapp had tried to get him to quit Metcalf and head into the mountains trapping, recalled the angry words with which Rapp had replied to Metcalf's urging that he forget his pride and go to work at the mission, recalled Rapp's sullen desertion of his own kind to hire out to the Hudson's Bay Company. Likely he was still having trouble swallowing that damn fool pride.

"You quit the Company?"

"What does it look like I done?" Rapp grunted.

"Where did you leave 'em?"

"Yonder," Rapp muttered, gesturing vaguely to the north. "Talkin' sweet to the Injuns up in the Kootenay country, tellin' packs of lies. Got my belly full of 'em, I did, told 'em to go to hell an' quit. Now I got to see Clint. Alone."

"Why?"

"What's that to you? I got to see him, I tell you. You expect me to crawl to him on my belly with his whole crowd standin' around laughin' at me? But I got to see him."

"All right. What do you want me to do?"

"Jest tell him I'm here, waitin', wantin', to talk to him. Jest tell him, that's all."

After Fram had gone, Burn Rapp sat gazing bleakly down at the ground. He was vaguely aware that he was alone again, though the drums pounding inside his head made it hard for him to be sure of anything. The afternoon sunlight slanting down into the valley hurt his eyes. He felt weak and shaky. Ought to get up on his feet, he thought. Sitting down this way was no style to greet a man like Clint. But it would take Fram a spell to find Clint and send him back. He'd rest a while longer. Then when he heard Clint coming, he'd get up and greet him the way he should.

His mind was fuzzy. He pressed his eyelids together tight, trying to make his thoughts come straight. Had to get them straight if he was going to do what he wanted to do. But he was tired, so damned tired. Been a long pull from the Kootenay country and he'd walked most of it, best he could recall. Seemed to have lost a horse somewhere along the way. Always seemed to be losing horses. A sorrel? No, a paint horse, it was. Not lost. Stole. Stole from him by a Gros Ventre bastard. Same jigger that had made off with all the beaver plews him and Fram had gathered. And that's what he'd come here to fix.

Come to make the jigger pay fer what he'd done. Goin' to put it up to Doc Metcalf, because the Doc was a fair man and he'd see to it the jigger forked over. Right's right, Doc, and wrong's wrong. You know, don't you, Doc, what the Bible says about stealin'. . .

Wait a minute. Somebody tryin' to horn into the game. Git back, Clint. Git back. No call fer you to stick yore nose into this. Because right's right and wrong's wrong and Doc Metcalf says . . .

He laughed aloud. Fool Frenchman! Go to work for a Britisher? Hell, you can keep your rum for all I care, because any old time Burn Rapp goes to work for a Britisher it'll only be because . . .

No, he was getting off the track. What he'd come for was to make it clear to Oswald that he wasn't no farmer. Think how it'll be up in the high country long about now, Oswald, with snow dusting the peaks and the streams cold and clear and beaver fur turning thick and silky. And you remember, Clint, how I pulled you out of the river, out Humboldt way.

Saved your life, I did. Fine way to thank me, beating me half to death with a pistol. But I don't hold it agin you. Come to shake hands. Come to say let bygones be bygones. Come to warn you about the lies the Company's tellin' up in the Kootenay country. Come to crawl on my belly to you in front of your whole damn crowd because there's something wrong in my head and I'm sick, sick . . .

And you're to blame for it, damn you! All I want, all I been living for is a chance to get you lined up in front of my rifle's sights as you come walking up to me . . .

Clint was coming. He could see him dimly yonder, walking along the footpath with sunlight and shadow alternately on him as he passed among the trees. Time to get up. He struggled to his feet. The drums were pounding louder inside his head now and his hands were shaking so badly he could hardly lift the rifle. Moving back so that the tree hid his body, he steadied the rifle against it. Slowly he swung its long barrel around until its sights lined up on a spot slightly to one side of Clint's breastbone. Clumsily he thumbed the hammer back.

The target blurred and danced before his eyes. Going to crawl to Clint on my belly 'cause I'm sick, sick. Got to kill him first, though. Time to pull . . .

His world went suddenly black.

Puzzled by Fram's message that Rapp was here, sick and wanting to tell him something about what was happening up in the Kootenay country, Clint had come unarmed, no thought of danger in his mind. Man and gun had been half hidden in the shadows. But he heard the click as the hammer came back. And quite suddenly he saw both the rifle barrel centered on his chest and the crazed man holding it. For a timeless moment he knew that he was staring into eternity, with not the slightest ghost of a chance to save himself.

But even as he realized that, Burn Rapp's knees buckled, the rifle fell from his nerveless fingers and his body pitched silently forward to the ground.

An involuntary shudder ran over Clint. Then he shook himself, hurried forward and stooped down over the unconscious man. He turned Rapp over on his back. The tracework of scars showed clearly on the man's forehead and as Clint stared down he knew a moment's sickness of soul. How Rapp must have hated him, these long months past, nursing his hatred like a deep, gnawing disease for which there was no cure. Anger was one thing; it came and went, making a man willing to maim and kill while the raging fire was in him, but it soon burned out. Now, staring down at the scar-rippled forehead, Clint felt no anger, no hate, not even dislike. All he felt was a deep sense of pity and of shame.

He picked up a limp wrist. The pulse still beat. Retrieving the cocked rifle, he let the hammer down carefully, leaned the gun against the tree without so much as a thought that it might be dangerous to leave it here where Rapp could put it to use should he regain consciousness before he returned, and went to the cabin where the other men were working.

"Got a doctoring job for you, Stanley," he told Metcalf.

Metcalf went to the cabin for his medical bag, then returned with Clint and Fram to the spot where Rapp still lay. Fram lifted Rapp's head. Taking a small vial out of his bag, Metcalf uncorked it and waved it under Rapp's nose. Presently the man stirred, giving a low moan. Clint saw Metcalf peer closely at the big trapper's face, saw him move a hand slowly back and forth in front of Rapp's eyes, saw him turn back the eyelids and study the pupils intently. Slowly shaking his head, Metcalf looked at Clint and said quietly, "He's blind. Stone blind."

Clint stared down at the ground, unable to speak. Fram

muttered, "He said he had somethin' to tell you. Did he git a chance to tell it?"

Clint shook his head. "No."

"I think he wanted to let you know he had nothin' agin you. But he was too proud to come crawlin' to you in front of the others."

Clint remained silent.

His plain, homely face softened by an unaccustomed tenderness, Fram looked bleakly at Metcalf, "He was my friend, Doc. I'll take care of him. He can live with me."

"We'll all take care of him," Metcalf said softly. "This will be his home."

Clint raised his eyes and stared up the valley. Home. Queer to hear that word again after the long drifting years, sleeping where night found a man, camping for a week or a month or a winter with no more shelter than the bare minimum needed to keep dry and warm and no caring for the place he lived in and the place left and forgotten when the time came to move on. And it wasn't only the place a man left and forgot; he was continually putting behind him all the things he'd done there, good or bad, wise or foolish, for it was easy to forget when there were no tangible reminders around him to call them to mind. Like kids he'd fathered. Or buildings he'd throwed together. Or men he'd beat so bad with a pistol that they walked in blindness for the rest of their days.

No, he'd not been one to use that word much. But there'd be no moving on for the Metcalfs, for Fram, or Rapp. So the word was a natural one for them to use. Home. And a man was bound to wonder . . .

He helped Rapp to his feet, lifting him easy and gentle. He pulled a weak, unresisting arm over his shoulders, Fram took the other arm, and half carrying, half dragging the blind man, they led him toward the cabin.

Metcalf picked up the unfired rifle and brought it along.

# 32

STANLEY METCALF told Clint next morning that the blindness probably would be permanent but that he felt sure Rapp would recover his other physical faculties. He had slept well and had wakened quite sane and normal, though he remembered nothing he had done for the past week. The throbbing headache which he had been suffering for some time now was gone, so apparently whatever pressure had been bearing upon his brain had been relieved.

"What brought it on?" Clint asked.

"It could have been any of a number of things. A tumor. A fever of the brain from some obscure disease. A bursted blood vessel. An old head injury."

"From a pistol-whipping?"

Metcalf shot him a sharp look. "It's possible. But the blunt truth is I know next to nothing about the functions of the brain. No doctor does. You can't examine the inside of man's head while he's still alive. So it's pointless to speculate on what caused the blindness."

"You're being real easy on me, Stanley."

"You did what you felt you had to do. No one can blame you for that."

"I lost my head and tried to beat him to death when there was no need to carry it that far. That's what I blame myself for."

"That's between you and your own conscience. But don't brood on it. Who is to say whether it was your first or last blow that did the damage?"

"That's a queer way for a preacher to talk. Isn't it your job to lay blame where it belongs?"

"Judge not . . ."

"Seems you're bound to give me a way to squirm out of it."

Metcalf shook his head. "No. I know you've already accepted all the blame. But don't be too harsh on yourself. No man is able to foresee the results of his acts. Yours was in a good cause. Perhaps the Lord willed it this way."

While they talked they had been walking without purpose, and now they stopped on the bank of the creek. Turning, Clint let his eyes run over the valley, which was splashed with bright sunlight after a crisp, clear night that had brought them their first touch of frost. The Metcalf cabin had been finished, save for a bit of weatherproofing. It contained one large room to be used as a school for the Indian children until more suitable quarters could be built in the spring, a kitchen, and two small bedrooms for Ellen and Stanley. Shed and corral were done. Fram's cabin was far enough along so that he could finish it himself. It troubled Clint that he had as yet had no word from Bonneville, but he was worried even more over what Pambrun and his men might be stirring up in the Kootenay country to the north. He looked at Stanley.

"Feel like you're pretty well set for the winter?"

"I think so, yes. Why do you ask?"

"Seems high time the boys and I took a jaunt up into the Kootenay country."

"Have you given up the idea of having peace talks with the Blackfeet?"

Clint shrugged. "Way things look, they're in no mood to talk right now. Can't say I'm surprised. They're not going to change their ways overnight. But maybe next spring —"

A faint cry in the distance up-valley made him break off. A straggling band of Indians had appeared there and was moving toward them now, gathering followers from the lodges strung along the flat as they passed. They were Nez

Perces; there was no doubt of that from the way they were being greeted. Long ago Clint had learned to judge the mood of an approaching party of Indians almost as far away as he could see or hear it, for their movements and voices invariably proclaimed the state of their feelings. These Indians, he sensed, were riding in deep sorrow and mourning.

"Who are they?" Metcalf asked.

"Part of Two Bears' band, looks like. And they've had some trouble."

"How can you tell?"

"Listen."

The wails of grief were unmistakable now. One of the Indian men riding near the head of the party saw them and turned his horse in their direction, riding slowly, his head down, his eyes on the ground. As he drew nearer Clint recognized him as Spotted Wolf. Clint raised his hand in greeting and made the sign which meant brother. Spotted Wolf's horse came to a stop and the square-shouldered, usually cheerful Nez Perce sat staring down at the ground in abject silence for some time. Clint waited. At last the Indian raised his head, his eyes black pools of sorrow, and began to speak.

"My brother, my heart is in the dust. My father Two Bears has gone to the Spirit Land. And your son Daniel will soon follow him. We have brought him back to you that you may see him before he dies."

The world was full of death, full of pain. A man learned that, came to accept that. A man steeled his belly and mind against it because a sick belly and a numb mind were of no use to him in a brutal, violent world where any moment he might be forced to run or fight. But it was somehow different when the blood was your own blood. The day suddenly swam before Clint's eyes.

"Daniel?" he muttered. "Daniel?"

He felt Metcalf's hand on his elbow, heard Metcalf's voice as if from a long way off. "Clint, what's the matter? What's happened?"

"Two Bears is dead. And Daniel's been hurt."

"Good heavens! How did it happen?"

Feeling as if he'd just been kicked in the pit of the stomach, Clint questioned Spotted Wolf, who sadly told his story.

"My father Two Bears came to our village on Salmon River. He said that the Sent Ones had decided to live here and that all of us who wished to spend the winter near them must return with him at once, before the snows came. Many did wish to come, as you see. Others did not, for Eagle-With-One-Wing warned them that many Blackfeet were near, living on the fringes of our country as they do each winter, and that the Blackfeet would fall upon them and kill them on the trail.

"Two Bears laughed at Eagle-With-One-Wing. He said that he was not afraid of the Blackfeet, for the white men were his friends. He said that the Sent Ones had a great medicine that would protect all Indians who were in their care. He said that the talk of war and of killing was foolish, for you were going to hold a great peace parley soon which would make all Indians brothers.

"We set out. There was sign of Blackfeet. We saw it, but Two Bears was not afraid. He said that the Blackfeet had come to our country because they were curious to learn if the things they had heard were true. When they saw that they were true, that we did want peace, that the Sent Ones and the white men had really come to live among us and protect us, they would show themselves and make peace.

"Two days ago a Blackfoot chief rode out alone into the trail ahead of us, made the sign for friend and said he wished to talk. Some of us were suspicious and wanted to kill him. Two Bears would not let us. He talked with the chief and they parted in peace, agreeing to meet at another place farther along the trail, when the Blackfoot chief would bring in all the members of his band and we would smoke and talk as brothers.

"The Blackfeet were there, waiting where the chief had told us they would be. But it was a trap. Many more Blackfeet were hidden in the bushes and among the trees and behind the rocks all around us. Even as Two Bears walked forward to greet him as a brother, the Blackfoot chief clubbed him to death and sounded the war cry.

"We fought. Some of us were killed, many were wounded. My wife was killed, fighting beside me as bravely as any man. Daniel picked up a stick and ran about screaming and beating at the legs of the Blackfeet until he was struck in the head with a war ax. I would let no Blackfoot come near my father's body to take his scalp, even if it meant my death to stay there. I killed three braves, one with my gun, two with my knife.

"We fought until we had driven the Blackfeet away. Then we put our wounded and dead on horses and brought them here." Spotted Wolf bowed his head. "I have no more words."

"Where is Daniel?"

"The women are looking after him. I told them to take him to the cabin."

"He's bad hurt, you say?"

"He breathes and his heart still beats. But the fire of life in him burns low. The old ones who have seen many wounds and know about such things say he cannot live to see another sun rise."

There was little that Metcalf could do for the child save to cleanse the wound, stitch up the broken skin and then make Daniel as comfortable as possible on a bed of skins and blankets laid on the dirt floor. There were other wounded to care for, young men, old men, women, children, and the floor of the room soon became littered with their pallets. The room was quiet, for none but the most seriously injured made any outcry, and Metcalf and Ellen spoke but rarely as they went about their work.

Sitting cross-legged on the floor beside the pallet on which Daniel lay, Clint heard nothing but the boy's shallow, labored breathing, saw nothing but the still face and the closed eyes. Wait, Metcalf had said. Wait and pray. That was all a man could do, and neither was a thing Clint could do well.

How long he sat there he did not know. Once Ellen came over, got down on her knees, turned back the blankets and checked Daniel's pulse. Covering the boy up again, she gave Clint a wan smile. "There's no change. We can still hope."

He did not speak.

She put a hand on his shoulder and said gently, "We must have faith, Clint. God won't let him die."

"I let him get hurt. That's all I can think of."

"You mustn't blame yourself for that."

"Who else is to blame for the peace-talk nonsense I stuffed Two Bears with?"

"It wasn't nonsense. It was the Christian thing to do."

He shook his head and did not reply. She moved away. Restlessness grew in him presently and he got up and went outside. The sun was moving into the western section of sky and the hour was well past noon. There was no hunger for food in him. But another kind of hunger was stirring, a need as basic and elemental as life itself. Seeing Judd Smith and Zack Parkins squatting smoking in the shade by the shed, he walked to them. They looked up, their eyes questioning him silently.

"Get the men together. I'll talk to Spotted Wolf and see

how many fighting bucks he can round up. Pack for fast traveling. We'll light out soon as we can get ready to go."

They got to their feet, their faces cold. Judd said, "Is it more damn fool talk we're after this time? Er blood?"

"It's blood," Clint said, his bitter eyes on the hills to the south and east. "What else does a Blackfoot understand?"

# 33

NIGHT WAS almost gone. There was no lifting of its blackness yet down in the meadow below, no brightning of the timbered slopes which rose steeply from either side of the meadow, but yonder over the mountains, eastward, a glow of luminosity edged the dark skyline and the fainter stars had disappeared. A stillness lay over the land. Night-prowling animals had ceased to move about; the breeze was dead; the frosty air seemed to slumber.

Clint's right leg had gone numb, for he had sat here unmoving for more than an hour now, his rifle covered to keep out the dampness, his legs crossed under him, his body huddled under a blanket to ward off the biting chill of the night. Carefully he shifted his position, wriggling his numbed toes. Needles of pain pierced his foot and leg as feeling returned. Pulling the blanket more closely around his shoulders, he resumed his patient, silent waiting.

It would not be long. He could feel his heart beating slow and steady against his ribs, feel his belly expanding and contracting as he breathed. Other than that there was no feeling at all in him. He was a purpose without a body. He was a mind waiting for a moment in time, with all time behind that moment and all time beyond it meaningless and without reality. Without his willing them into being, memory pictures flashed across his mind.

He recalled Ellen's face, frightened and pale, as she at last realized why the tone of the wailing and keening in the Nez Perce village had changed, why the Indians were dressing up and painting their faces. She had never seen Indians make up for war before; never seen white men prepare for a hunt whose quarry was to be men rather than animals. Yet she had recognized the preparations for what they were, finally, and, being a woman, had protested strongly. *There must be some other way. There has to be some other way.*

He recalled Stanley's face, the bleak, harsh look of it, as Stanley shook his head and said, "No, Ellen. No. Clint knows what he has to do. Leave him alone."

Queer to hear Stanley say a thing like that. But Stanley had known it had to be. He wouldn't say it was the only way, wouldn't say it was the right way, but he'd seen the dead, doctored the wounded, heard the women wailing in the lodges. And a look had come into his eyes when he had first bent over Daniel and seen what a war ax could do to a child's skull — a look that had still been there when the war party was ready to ride out.

"Let him go, Ellen. Let him go. And may God give strength to his arm."

He remembered Spotted Wolf's face. *A face that used to know how to laugh. But it will be a while before Spotted Wolf laughs again. Quite a while, for it's no small thing to see your father murdered before your eyes. Three Blackfoot lives aren't enough to pay for that. Not near enough.*

"I want the lead, my brother. I want the place of first

danger. Let me be the bait for the trap. Let me lead the Blackfeet into the trap, that I may turn upon them when the trap is sprung and kill, kill, kill. My brother, I must have the lead."

And he remembered the faces of the white men. The hard, weathered, keen-eyed faces of men who had grown calloused to danger and to death, who had killed in their time because they had to kill — never with hate, but learning to hate now. Judd, Zack, Beartracks, Luke, Hugh . . .

"Never hunted an Injun afore jest fer the sake of killin' him. Ready to larn the game now, though. They'll be afoot, Clint, like they always are when they come skulkin' around after hosses an' hair. Up in the high country, likely, this side of the Salmon . . ."

"Got to git 'em spotted first, Clint. Be best fer most of us t' keep out of sight till we're ready t' spring the trap. Gimme one Nez Perce that knows the lay of the land . . ."

"You got to keep a tight holt on Spotted Wolf an' his Nez Perce hellions, Clint. Don't want 'em flushin' our birds till we're set fer 'em. Sam an' me'll find 'em, never you fear. Jest you keep a tight holt on Spotted Wolf . . ."

It had been no easy thing, keeping the impatient Indians in check this past week while the quarry was being located and the details of setting the trap were painstakingly worked out, for the only strategy they understood was finding the enemy, striking fast and hard, then breaking off the fight until they could again have the advantage of surprise on their side. From time immemorial Nez Perce and Blackfoot had fought in that fashion, with only rare battles in which either side suffered serious casualties. But a new day had dawned. The white man had come, bringing talk of peace. Because Two Bears had listened to the talk and had believed peace could be brought about, the Blackfeet had been given a fine opportunity for treachery. And Two Bears had died. Very well, if the Blackfeet did not want the white man's peace, let them have a taste of the white man's kind of war.

It was ironic, Clint brooded, that he should hear from Captain Bonneville at a time such as this. Only yesterday afternoon a Cayuse Indian messenger had brought him a note from Bonny, a brief, cryptic note that said nothing beyond the fact that the captain and his party were crossing the Blues, eastbound, and that he would await Clint and his men on Snake River, directly to the south of the Salmon River country. He said nothing about how he had fared on the lower Columbia. There was no need to say anything. The very fact that he and his men were heading east at this time of year could mean but one thing: he had failed. And when this day's work was over, Clint and his men would travel southward to the appointed meeting place on Snake River to report yet another failure. But first they had one last chore to do.

Daylight grew in the east, burning out the stars. Black shaded to purple, to deep red, to flame-pink, and down in the meadow there was now a grayness in which objects could be made out. Frost rime silvered the grass. The floor of the valley was from one to three hundred yards wide, winding northeastward between timbered slopes, open and clear for the most part. There was no sign of life anywhere.

Time ticked on, while the full light of day spilled into the valley. An easterly breeze began to stir. Peering into the sun, whose orange bulk was just now edging above the timbered ridge above the valley's northward curve, Clint made out a faint but unmistakable curl of smoke. The Blackfoot camp was waking; the very fact that the Indians were building fires even in this early morning hour when the smoke could be seen and smelled a long distance away indicated the safety they felt and the contempt they held for their old enemies, on the borders of whose country they were camped. *But they'll learn, damn 'em. They'll learn.*

Below him and to his left he heard a horse's hoof clink against a stone. Moments later a dozen Nez Perce braves, led by Spotted Wolf, appeared in the meadow below. Riding at a walk, they moved single file up the valley, looking neither to the right nor left. Spotted Wolf carried a rifle balanced across his saddle before him, a bow and arrow quiver were slung across his back, and his bronze, square face was as if carved of stone. Slowly the party of Indians rode on, seemingly unaware of the hundreds of pairs of watching eyes that followed them, and presently disappeared around a bend up the valley.

Clint got to his feet, letting the blanket fall to the ground. Taking the cover off his rifle, he checked its priming. All around him in the timber he heard small sounds as other white men and Indians moved restlessly, making their final preparations. Then there was no more sound.

He was not aware of measuring distance and time, but within him a clock was ticking, ticking. In his mind's eye he could see the Blackfoot camp stirring in the chill gray of dawn. He could hear the grunts of the Indians, see their cold-numbed figures stooping to stir the ashes of their nearly dead fires; he could see their cheeks distend as they bent low, feeding crumbled bark and dry punk and twigs to the glowing embers, could hear the crackling as the twigs caught. Likely the horses they had captured and staked out would be snorting, their breaths white wreaths in the frosty air. Then some quick-eared brave would hear it: a hoofbeat, a stick snapping, a captured horse nickering a greeting to another of its kind down-valley. And the camp would come alive.

The Blackfeet would grab up their arms, taking no chances, even though their first guess might be that the approaching horses were riderless and merely seeking company. Then they would see the dozen Nez Perces riding around a spur of hill. What pleasure that would give them! Here were a dozen scalps dropped plop into their laps. Here were a dozen unwary enemies out hunting horses or meat, blundering smack into a Blackfoot war party which outnumbered them five to one. And then . . .

Clint heard the sound of a distant rifle shot as it shattered the waiting quiet. On its heels came a wild cry, blurred and distorted as the steep hills reflected its echo. There come the low thunder of hoofs, followed by more cries, more shots, and the brightening day was suddenly full of sound. He cocked his rifle. The metallic click as the hammer came back was like the brittle snap of the jaws of a trap closing.

*Now let it begin. Now. Now.*

He stared into the sun, waiting. The dozen Nez Perces came loping around the bend up-valley, doing just what any blundering hunting party would do, running away because they were outnumbered. But they were not running very fast. Behind them came a swarm of Blackfeet, a few riding bareback on the horses they had hastily mounted, but most of them on foot, yipping with the kill-hungry eagerness of hounds on the trail of a limping, wounded deer.

There was no need to give orders. The mountain men and Indians hidden on the slopes knew what to do. He saw a Nez Perce brave fall from his horse as an arrow caught him in the back. Another Nez Perce buck quickly stooped and gave him a hand up. Spotted Wolf, who had discarded his rifle after the first shot, for he would have no time to reload, wheeled around and drove three arrows in rapid succession at the trailing Blackfeet. One of the arrows caught a mounted Blackfoot squarely in the throat and he went reeling to the ground. Calmly, unhurriedly, Spotted Wolf turned his horse about and rode slowly on.

Now the dozen Nez Perces were passing directly below, with the Blackfeet close behind. Too close, Clint thought, and he cursed Spotted Wolf for his insolent courage. Lifting his rifle, Clint laid its sights on a Blackfoot buck mounted on a tall bay horse. He squeezed the trigger and the Blackfoot toppled headlong to the ground. Then from the slopes on either side a cloudburst of bullets and arrows rained down death into the narrow valley.

The eager cries of the Blackfeet changed to howls of panic and terror. Wheeling about, they tried to take flight back up the valley, only to find themselves cut off there by fifty Nez Perce warriors who had risen from their places of concealment to pour down and cut off any possibility of retreat. They tried to go down-valley, but Spotted Wolf and his braves had turned back and, reinforced by another horde of blood-crazed fighting men, were charging upon them with gun, war ax, bow and arrow and knife. Cut off in both directions, the Blackfeet scuttled for the shelter of the timbered slopes, only to find the mountain men and more Nez Perces hidden and waiting there.

If the Nez Perces had been less eager to close with the Blackfeet and battle them hand to hand, there was not the slightest doubt in Clint's mind that no Blackfoot buck would ever have gotten out of the trap alive. But after his first shot with his rifle and two shots with his pistol he hardly dared fire again, for there was no longer any way to make sure that a bullet would not strike a friend rather than a foe. War axes and knives were rising and falling. Indians were tumbling over and over in individual hand-to-hand combat. He saw a Blackfoot club a Nez Perce to the ground, whirl and come racing up the slope. He swung his pistol toward the Indian but before he could fire a rifle barrel was thrust out, the Blackfoot tripped and fell, then, with a whoop as wild as any Indian's, Zack leaped upon the Blackfoot's back and was driving his knife down.

Spotted Wolf had been pulled from his horse and now stood swinging his war ax like a scythe. Two Blackfeet went down before him, their skulls crushed. Another leaped on his back, his left arm around Spotted Wolf's throat, his right lifting a knife. Clint shot the Indian through the head before the knife could fall.

All the trappers were in the melee now, rifles forgotten, pistols used more often as clubs than as guns. Clint, though he had not intended it to turn out this way, found himself in the midst of it too. A panic-stricken Blackfoot swung a short-barreled trade gun at his head. Clint ducked under it, seized the brave about the waist and threw him to the ground. He got his hands on the Indian's throat, lifted his head and beat it against the ground until the brave went limp. As he started to rise a numbing blow suddenly struck him on the back and sent him sprawling on his face. He rolled over and stared directly up into the eyes of a Blackfoot standing above him with a war ax in his hand. The weapon lifted, poised to strike.

A huge muscular arm shot forward out of nowhere and circled the Blackfoot's neck, while at the same time a hand closed on the wrist of the arm which held the war ax. Clint saw the Blackfoot's body being bent backwards, heard a shrill scream; there was a sound like a dead limb snapping, then the Blackfoot dropped limply to the ground while Beartracks Weaver's howl of victory went thundering up into the morning sky.

Clint got to his feet and stared around him. He saw Spotted Wolf bending over a fallen Blackfoot, wielding his knife as he lifted a scalp. He saw two Blackfeet disappearing into the timber to the left, already wounded from the way they limped along, with a dozen howling Nez Perces hot on their heels. He saw another Blackfoot on a gray horse break through the milling Indians around him and gallop out of sight up-valley. He saw Hugh Marlow sitting with his back against a tree, white-faced and sick-looking as he clutched as his right shoulder with bloodstained fingers. But save for the wounded Blackfeet strewn along the valley — which the Nez Perces were quickly dispatching — the battle was over.

"Hell!" Judd Smith muttered at his elbow, staring after the Blackfoot rider who had managed to get away. "Thar's one fish slipped through our fingers! Ain't that a shame? I was hopin' fer a clean sweep of the whole kit an' kaboodle of the jiggers!"

"We can spare one," Clint said. "In fact I'm glad he did get away."

"Glad?" Judd grunted, staring at him blankly. "When we could of made meat of him easy if the Nez Perces hadn't got so blamed overanxious? What's there to be glad about?"

Not answering for a moment, Clint gazed up-valley. There were two kinds of peace, he realized now. One stemmed from weakness and a craven fear to fight. The other stemmed from strength, which made your enemy so respect you he left you alone. That had been the root of the trouble here. The Blackfeet had misunderstood. But they would misunderstand no longer.

"He's taking a message from us to his people, Judd. A message it's high time they heard."

# 34

CAPTAIN BONNEVILLE'S shot at the moon had fallen somewhat shy of its mark. He admitted that to Clint as they sat smoking and talking by their after-supper fire with the late October dusk deepening around them. But bleak as his disappointment had been on hearing the news Clint had brought him he had no reproaches.

"You did the only thing you could have done under the

circumstances. At least you taught the Blackfeet a healthy
respect for Americans. I wish I could say I had accomplished
as much with the people who bedeviled me. You've no idea
what I had to endure."

"Did the Indians pester you much?"

"Pester me? Good God, no! Not once did they raise a
finger against me. I wish they had. They'd have been easy
enough to deal with then. They simply wouldn't trade
with me, no matter what inducements I offered. They would
sell me no furs, no food — nothing."

"I heard you had some trouble with Pambrun."

Bonneville's eyes smoldered. "I tried to have. But he
wouldn't meet me halfway, I'm sorry to say." Raising his
head, the captain stared broodingly out across the darkening
Snake River plain. "The Company won't fight openly, Clint.
They're afraid to, for they know they would lose. What do
they have to fight with? Pasty-faced clerks not old enough
to shave yet, spoiled dandies and fops sent out from London
because their fathers own stock in the Company, a few hundred spineless French-Canadian *engagés* who would turn
and run when the first bullet whined. Oh, there are a few
men like McKay and Ogden and McLoughlin who could
give you a tussle if they were of a mind to, but I'll take oath
that if the army would give me one company of well-trained
soldiers I could take all Oregon." He smiled wryly at
Clint. "Assuming there was provocation, of course. Which
there isn't at the moment."

"You're headed east now?"

"Yes. My time is up."

"What happens to the men?"

"I'll split them up, sending some to the party wintering
on Bear River, others to the Wind River crew. They can
bring what furs they gather to next summer's rendezvous.
I won't be there, I'm afraid, but I'm hoping they'll bring in
enough pelts to pay off some of the debts I've contracted."

"Speaking of debts," Clint said, gazing into the fire, "I don't mean to press you, but I could use some money."

"I'm badly pinched but I'll do what I can for you. I'd like you and your men to join up with the party working the Bear River country. Before we part company, I'll give you my personal note for what I owe you. I'm sure Bill Sublette will honor it and you can draw against it at rendezvous next summer."

Clint's face was frozen. "Your note will be fine, Captain. But I'd like it now."

Bonneville gave him a sharp, puzzled look. "If you insist. But why do you want it now?"

"Because I'm not going to Bear River. I'm heading back to the Clearwater first thing in the morning."

"Alone?"

"Yeah."

"You can't trap alone in that country."

"Wasn't particularly thinking of trapping."

"What will you do?"

Clint shook his head. "I can't say. But I got to go back there, seems like."

Bonneville fell silent, his dark eyes thoughtfully staring into the fire. It was hard to tell just what he was thinking. Brooding maybe, brooding over the four years he'd spent wandering over the wide empty deserts and high tumbled mountains of the West while he chased big dreams that now were turning to dust. Wondering maybe, wondering if a bit more effort here, a bit better luck there, a bit smarter move somewhere else might not have tipped the scales in his favor.

"Tell me something, Clint, just for my own personal satisfaction — do you think the Metcalfs have come to stay?"

"Looks that way. They're dug in for the winter, anyhow."

"But after that — next year and the years to come — do you feel that they're really here to stay?"

Clint's mind spanned the miles of autumn-bleak desert and mountains which lay between this spot and the valley where the newly built mission buildings set. He recalled them as he had last seen them: the shed, the corral, Fram's cabin, the Metcalf cabin, the smoke curling skyward faint and blue from the chimneys. They had looked as if they had been there for a long while and would be there for a longer while to come.

But it took something more than buildings to make a permanent settlement. It took will and courage and heart. It took a willingness to work and build toward a dream. It took a burning desire to serve the God you believed in and to teach His ways to a people less enlightened than yourself. Most important of all, it took a wanting to make a new land your home. And the only way you could be sure if people had those qualities was to know what they had inside them.

He nodded. "They'll stay. They're that kind."

"Metcalf told me that if prospects looked favorable he intended to ask the mission board for reinforcements next year. Do you know if he's done so?"

"He sent the letter from Fort Walla Walla. He asked the board to send out farmers, a blacksmith, plows, a printing press and somebody to run it, women to teach in the school, oxen, wagons — "

"Wagons? But I understood you were forced to leave the wagon at Fort Boise. McKay said you decided it was impossible to take a wagon across the Blues."

"When did a Company man ever tell the truth? With oxen there's no reason why wagons can't get through. No reason at all."

Beyond the circle of light the wide and empty land lay silent and dark. Watching Captain Bonneville, Clint suddenly got the notion that Bonny was no longer thinking of the four wasted years, no longer brooding on the way one

bitter defeat had piled upon another until they added up to
as complete a sum of failure as any man had ever faced.
Instead, his eyes had grown bright and warm and dreaming.
Like last summer, when he'd been making plans at rendez-
vous. And the summer before, when he'd been talking about
California. And the summer before that . . .

Captain Bonneville lifted his head and gazed out into the
night.

"By Heaven, that will be a stone rolled into their garden
that they'll never move!" he murmured softly. "And who's
to say we didn't help put it there, Clint? Who's to say?"

Shortly after dawn next morning Clint rode north alone.
His goodbyes to Judd and Zack had been casual. Trails often
parted out here. Maybe they'd come together again some
day, maybe not. It had been a long while since he'd win-
tered in low country; been a longer while since he'd stood
still long enough in one spot to give his roots a chance to
sprout. Maybe this stirring in him, this feeling in the soles
of his feet that he was done with wandering, wasn't roots
reaching down at all but only a new kind of restlessness
brought on by growing older. There was no way to know.
Still, the stirring was there . . .

Days later, he rode around a low spur of hill and saw the
valley spread out before him. He was cold and weary. Rain
slanted down through the gray of late afternoon. There
were tepees just ahead, and beyond them the shed, the corral, the small cabin and the larger one. Smoke was spilling
into the slate-gray sky, speaking of food and fire and warmth
and friends waiting to greet him. Sadly, maybe, for there
was little hope in him that the news would be anything but
bad, but they would be there and that would help ease the
sting.

A Nez Perce woman came out of one of the lodges, saw
him and turned and called to those within. And suddenly

there were Indians all around him, calling out cheerful greetings. The cries went ahead of him, spreading like ripples on a pool. He did not stop, would not stop, for he had eyes now for nothing but the cabin at the far end of the valley, but his throat was swelling with a gladness greater than any he had ever known.

His horse came to a stop in the yard before the cabin. He swung to the ground. Long before he reached the cabin door, it swung open, Daniel came tottering out and ran toward him with a wordless cry. Stooping, Clint caught the boy up in his arms and held him, murmuring, "Daniel! Daniel!"

Over by the shed, Fram appeared in the corral and stood with one foot on the fence, grinning at him and lifting a hand in greeting. The door of Fram's cabin opened and Rapp stood there, holding onto the door jamb, his head cocked to one side as he listened and tried to make out what was happening. Stanley Metcalf appeared from behind the larger cabin with a load of firewood in his arms, stopped and stood smiling, saying nothing as he gazed at Clint and the boy in his arms. And Ellen was there now in the doorway, wiping her hands on her apron, her eyes holding a welcome that needed no words.

He knew then. He knew.

He had come home.